She drove him mad had to struggle to resist it

Even if Shauna was interested in him, nothing could ever come of it.

She was human.

He was a wolven, and an alpha at that. That was a vast chasm to overcome. Danyon knew that those differences would never allow her to fully understand the depth of his true nature, even if she was his Keeper.

Still holding on to her arms, he suddenly became aware of the feel of her skin beneath his palms. Soft…silky…warm. Very warm.

Danyon felt his pulse quicken and his nostrils flare.

At that moment, he should have felt guilty. Two of his werewolves were dead. He'd just wiped their blood from his hands.

But Danyon felt no guilt.

There was no room for it. At that moment, every one of his senses was on high alert. Each excruciatingly aware of *her*.

And it left him ravenous.

Books by Deborah LeBlanc

Harlequin Nocturne

The Wolven #101

DEBORAH LEBLANC

Award-winning and bestselling author Deborah LeBlanc is a business owner, a licensed death-scene investigator and an active member of two national paranormal investigation teams. She's the president of the Horror Writers Association, Mystery Writers of America's Southwest chapter and the Writers' Guild of Acadiana. Deborah is also the creator of the LeBlanc Literacy Challenge, an annual national campaign designed to encourage more people to read, and Literacy, Inc., a nonprofit organization with a mission to fight illiteracy in America's teens. For more information go to www.deborahleblanc.com and www.literacyinc.com.

DEBORAH LeBLANC

THE WOLVEN

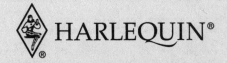

HARLEQUIN®

TORONTO • NEW YORK • LONDON
AMSTERDAM • PARIS • SYDNEY • HAMBURG
STOCKHOLM • ATHENS • TOKYO • MILAN • MADRID
PRAGUE • WARSAW • BUDAPEST • AUCKLAND

Recycling programs
for this product may
not exist in your area.

ISBN-13: 978-0-373-61848-4

THE WOLVEN

Dear Reader,

Of all the books I've written over the years, this one had to be the most fun and adventurous. I had a blast diving into the world of vamps, shifters and werewolves, a world where anything and everything is possible—including great sex! That the story took place in New Orleans, a city whose heartbeat is part of my own, was a lagniappe, a gift, of the highest order. The crème de la crème of the entire project, however, was working with Heather Graham and Alexandra Sokoloff. Both are brilliant, hardworking and funny ladies. It's impossible not to have fun writing with those two. I'm truly grateful to have had the opportunity to work with them.

And I'm grateful to you, dear reader, and honored that you chose to spend a little time with me here. Life is short and minutes are precious. The fact that you shared a few with me does not go unnoticed. And I'm equally honored that you chose this book over the thousands available to you. Because of you, I'm able to continue a tradition I've loved for a lifetime—storytelling. Thank you for that gift.

Best,

Deborah

For Dad—I miss you terribly.

Chapter 1

A thin pink line across light brown flesh.

She'd cut herself...again.

Shauna MacDonald looked up from the palm she'd been reading and into the wide, bright eyes of its owner, Lurnell Franklin. Lurnell was a large Creole woman in her mid-thirties with an affinity for spandex and a rock-solid determination to be married before she hit forty. She visited A Little Bit of Magic, the mystic shop Shauna owned with her sisters, Fiona and Caitlin, at least twice a week for a palm reading. For some reason Shauna still didn't understand, Lurnell had zeroed in on her. Fiona was very gifted at reading tea leaves, and Caitlin was exceptionally intuitive when it came to Tarot cards, but Lurnell would have nothing to do with either of them. She always sought out Shauna for a reading, then would argue adamantly that the marriage line, which didn't exist on the side of her palm, just below the pinky of her right hand, was certain to appear any day. Even if she had to produce it herself.

"Didn't I tell you?" Lurnell said, tapping a three-inch, hot-pink fingernail on the reading table. "It's like I been sayin', right? I know you was thinkin' I was crazy, but this big girl here, she knows what she's talkin' about. You feelin' me? You hearin' what I'm sayin'?"

Shauna eyed her.

Lurnell waggled her head. "Oh, uh-uh. Don't you be givin' me eyes." She kissed the palm of her left hand and held it up. "Look here. I swear, hand to God. All I did was wake up this mornin', and there that line was, all pretty and pink."

Shauna took hold of Lurnell's right hand and turned it pinky side up. "That's a cut, and you know it. And you know it because you put it there. You can't *make* a marriage line, Lurnell. It's either there or it's not."

Lurnell cocked her head, narrowed her eyes. "You sayin' I'm lyin' about it being for real?"

"Yep."

Shauna let go of Lurnell's hand, sat back and folded her arms across her chest.

Lurnell mimicked the pose. "And what makes you so sure, Ms. Big Drawers? You don't have no second sight. You just a reader, and look at you actin' like you all that, tellin' me I'm lyin'."

"Because you are. Just like you did the last two times you tried pulling this stunt. Look, just because you don't have a marriage line doesn't mean it's the end of the world. Time changes things, and palms change with it, so if you've gotta cut something, cut yourself some slack, will you? If you keep cutting your hand like that, you're going to wind up with a bad infection."

Lurnell tsked loudly and unfolded her arms. "Who taught you palm readin' anyways, girl? You don't know nothin'."

Shauna grinned. She couldn't help it. Lurnell always brought the same banter to the table, and she enjoyed swatting it back. "Well, if I don't know anything, how come you keep asking me for a reading?"

Pursing her lips, Lurnell turned sideways in her chair. Shauna knew from experience that this was her way of regrouping, thinking of a good comeback. Normally she would have pounced on the opportunity and thrown out a one-liner just to fluster Lurnell, but a sudden uneasiness settled over her.

An intuitive whisper.

She sat silent, keeping her facial expression neutral while she listened for her inner voice, waiting for it to identify the source of the unrest.

The only thing that came to her was the scent of cinnamon wafting through the air.

King cake.

Her oldest sister, Fiona, was a firm believer in lagniappe, giving their customers a little extra treat with their purchases. It was usually something to eat, like pastry samples, homemade cookies, or pralines. With Mardi Gras only three weeks away, it didn't surprise her that Fiona had chosen to share the holiday's traditional cake.

Evidently catching wind of the scent, as well, Lurnell jumped to her feet before Shauna had a chance to push away from the reading table. "Whoa, that be smellin' good. It's okay if I go get some, right?"

"Of course." Shauna got up, and the uneasiness rose with her. Since she couldn't find a rationale for it, she mentally pushed the feeling aside. Whatever was meant to be revealed by the intuitive whisper would come in due course, that much she knew. She simply had to wait it out.

Lurnell patted her stomach, her eyes sparkling with delight. "Girl, I do love king cake. Hey, you got some of that lemon drink? You know, like the kind y'all had last week?"

"You mean lemon-snap tea?"

"Yeah, there you go." Lurnell slapped her hands together. "I think I'm gonna have some of that, too. That'd be good with king, right?"

"We're out of the lemon-snap, but I can hook you up with a cup of green tea if you'd like."

Lurnell frowned. "Ain't green tea the one's got all them anti-oxidations in it? You know, that stuff that cleans out all your potty pipes."

"Yep, it has antioxidants, but that's a good thing. Keeps you healthy." Shauna grinned. "Don't worry about your pipes."

"Girl, you bes' be right." Lurnell flapped a hand, signaling Shauna to lead the way out of the room and be quick about it. She evidently feared a rush on the king cake and didn't want to miss out. "You know there ain't nobody in Sistah's but me. What I'm gonna do if a customer needs somethin'? I can't just s'cuse myself and go to the commode, not with the crazy people they got today. Uh-uh. I'd be back in the bathroom and they'd be out front, helpin' themselves to all my stuff, robbin' me blind."

Lurnell was the sole proprietor of Sistah's, a mystic shop located on the corner of St. Ann and Rampart, which bordered the north end of the French Quarter. Like most of the tourist shops in the Quarter, it was tightly sandwiched between other shops that sold various baubles, beads, and T-shirts. Sistah's carried similar items to those in A Little Bit of Magic—crystals, scented candles, herbs, and oils—but it served a different clientele, primarily those who dabbled in voodoo. Although Lurnell didn't claim to practice voodoo, her specialty items easily led people to believe otherwise. Seven-day spell candles that promised to reverse a curse, remove a hex, or bring wealth and love in abundance. And incense oils that supposedly cured everything from toothaches to temper tantrums, headaches to hemorrhoids. The shop did relatively well considering the neighborhood that surrounded it and the fact that a major competitor—Papa Gris Gris' Voodoo Shop—was located only three doors down. It was no secret that Lurnell and Papa Gris Gris didn't play well together. In fact, they'd been enemies for years.

Shauna led Lurnell into the heart of the store, where

she spotted Fiona placing slices of king cake onto a platter near the register. Caitlin was at the opposite end of the shop, talking to an elderly woman who had an exceptionally long, hooked nose. Quite a few customers were wandering about, each stopping occasionally to examine a wall display, an item on a shelf, or something showcased in a curio cabinet.

Business had been brisk all day, which came as no surprise, given that Mardi Gras was just around the corner. The parades and balls weren't scheduled to start for another two weeks, but that didn't matter to the diehard partiers who made their annual pilgrimage to New Orleans. Most of them came early so they wouldn't miss one of the main local events known as Nuit du Dommage. Literally translated, it meant Night of Damage, and the parties associated with it certainly lived up to its name. It was a pre-Mardi Gras free-for-all, and it was only three days away.

Dommage and Mardi Gras were always great for business, but both drove Shauna crazy. The streets and sidewalks stayed jammed with so many people it was hard to walk and breathe at the same time. Even worse was the noise. Drunken voices shouting, singing, laughing, talking, and all of them tumbling over hawking, squawking strip-joint barkers and a melange of blaring music—jazz, blues, rock 'n' roll—that poured out of the bars in the Quarter. Because Shauna's hearing was so acute, all that noise at such a high volume pained her considerably. It felt like an endless number of needles jabbing into her eardrums.

Still carrying a sense of uneasiness, Shauna mingled with a few customers, making herself available in case anyone needed help.

Lurnell had already shoved her way to the front counter and was hovering over the platter of cake. Fiona stood not far away, ringing up another customer at the register. Lurnell must have viewed Fiona's preoccupation as a grand opportunity because she slipped two pieces of king cake into her oversized purse. She was reaching for a third when Shauna saw Fiona turn toward her. Judging from the small smile dancing on her sister's lips, Fiona had not been oblivious to the heist. Still, she smiled more broadly, walked over to Lurnell and offered her another piece of cake. Always the gracious hostess.

Not for the first time, Shauna wished she was more like her sister.

Being the caboose on a train of three sisters wasn't always easy. More often than not, Shauna felt like the odd woman out. Fiona was tall and slender, with long, thick hair the color of gold, her eyes a perfect cornflower blue. Caitlin had the same slender build but stood five-nine, a bit taller than Fiona. Her long hair was a darker shade of blonde, which matched beautifully with her magnificent silver-gray eyes. At five-eight, Shauna had height, like her sisters. She also had the same build. Her hair, which she kept pulled up in a ponytail most of the time, was more auburn than blonde, however, and she thought her eyes were a boring shade of green.

To Shauna, Fiona and Caitlin were the epitome of femininity. The way they walked, talked. Even their closets held proof of it. Both were filled with silky dresses, pastel skirts, and elegant blouses. Shauna's, on the other hand, held mostly jeans and T-shirts. She did own a couple of skirts, but she kept them tucked away for dress-up emergencies.

Besides height and build, Shauna shared another similarity with her sisters. She was a Keeper, responsible for maintaining harmony and balance between the humans and the three main underworld subcultures—vampires, shape-shifters, and werewolves—that lived in and around the city. Shauna watched over the werewolves, Fiona the vampires, and Caitlin the shape-shifters.

Their parents, Jen and Ewan MacDonald, had been unique Keepers, each born with the power to maintain all three subcultures. When they combined their powers, it had created a seemingly indestructible wall of protection around the city.

Or so Shauna had thought.

She had been fifteen when they died. A savage war had broken out between the subcultures, and the power her parents had to call upon to block the warring parties had cost them their lives. No Keeper, no matter how strong, could release that much power and survive. That had been ten years ago.

Shauna and her sisters didn't possess tri-power the way their parents had. Instead, each of them possessed the power of the clan they were responsible for. Shauna couldn't imagine what it would be like to have all three. The weight of responsibility associated with that much power must have been monstrous. Although she was still young and learning, always learning how to be a better Keeper, the load she carried felt heavy enough.

"Hey, you okay?"

Shauna started, surprised to hear Caitlin's voice behind her. She turned, offered her sister a small smile. "Yeah, fine."

Caitlin studied her face for a moment, as if assessing the truth of the response. "You were pretty zoned out there for a while."

"Daydreaming, that's all."

Before Caitlin had a chance to respond, a heavyset man wearing Bermuda shorts appeared seemingly out of nowhere and pushed his way into her personal space. "Are you her?"

"Excuse me?" Caitlin said.

"Are you the one who reads Tarot cards? The lady working the register over there said her sister, Caitlin, read cards, then she pointed this way. I wasn't sure which one of you she meant, though."

"She meant me," Caitlin said, then directed him to the reading room. "If you'll wait for me in there, I'll only be a minute." She waited until the man waddled away, then turned to Shauna. "See the couple standing over by the herbs?"

Shauna glanced in that direction, saw a young man and woman, both with spiked, multi-colored hair. They swayed slightly on their feet as they pointed to different bags of herbs and giggled. "They look wasted."

"Wouldn't surprise me. They were asking for help a minute ago. Tend to them while I do that guy's reading, will you?" With that, Caitlin headed for the reading room before Shauna could protest.

Shauna let out a heavy sigh. She had a sneaking suspicion that the help the couple wanted wouldn't involve questions about the healing properties of certain herbs. More than likely they would want to know if the store carried pulverized bats' wings or hogs' hooves, or some other nonsensical item that someone had told them they needed to cast a certain spell. Normally, no matter how spaced out they were, Shauna would have taken the time to give them the 411 on herbs and try steering them away from the stupid cliff. But she wasn't up for it today.

The unrest that had swooped down on her earlier was turning into a case of the jitters. She felt agitated, on edge. Maybe it had something to do with the mingling energies from all the people in the store. All those energies swirling right alongside her intuitive whisper might have tilted her off-center. Whatever the case, she was in no shape to steer anyone in any direction right now. If the couple wanted bat wings, she would simply send them to Sistah's. Lurnell would be more than happy to sell the couple a half ounce of ground up seaweed or Spanish Moss, all the while swearing it was pulverized bats' wings that had been harvested back in the eighteenth century in Transylvania.

As Shauna headed toward the couple she tried tuning into the center of her mind, to the only truly quiet place she knew. She had discovered that place as a child, when her keen sense of hearing wound up collecting too much data from too many directions and over-stimulated her.

Fiona had been the one to teach her how to find that special place. How to close her eyes and focus on the small dot of light that always appeared behind her eyelids. Her sister had told her that the light was her center, and that if she concentrated hard enough, that light would always lead her back to a balanced, peaceful place.

For the most part, Fiona had been right. Over time, Shauna even figured out that she didn't have to close her eyes to find that light. All she had to do was let her mind's eye find it, focus on it, and bring her back to center. That certainly made things easier when she was walking through a crowded mall or heading toward a stoned, spike-haired couple.

Shauna's mind had just latched on to that dot of light when a strange sound caught her attention and stopped her dead in her tracks.

It was an odd, low sound. So low that even with her sensitive ears she wondered how she'd heard it at all, with so many people talking in the shop, Lurnell's voice booming above them all, noise pouring in from the street.

She closed her eyes for a moment, concentrated on the sound. It grew louder and made the hair on the back of her neck stand on end. She'd never heard anything quite like it before.

Not quite a moan…

A distant wail…

No. More like an elongated…*howl*.

The moment Shauna thought "howl," her intuitive whisper became a shouting banshee. What she heard was keening. Someone in the throes of such grief, their physical body couldn't contain it.

It was the wail of death.

A plea to the universe.

A howl of mourning.

And it was coming from one of her weres…

Chapter 2

So much blood.

Facial features distorted. Almost unrecognizable.

And the eyes—dull with death, yet imprinted with a final, indescribable emotion. A concoction of panic, fear, surprise, horror. The kind of look that might haunt a living man who'd seen it forever.

Danyon Stone was no stranger to death. Being alpha of the Wolven pack that lived along the East Bank in New Orleans, he'd witnessed the fallout from territorial battles that occasionally took place between his weres and those from other packs in surrounding parishes. When weres fought to the death over territory, or over a mate, the evidence from those fights generally looked the same. Clothing ripped to shreds, gouged flesh, puncture wounds, and blood. Sometimes a lot of it. But this death was far from common.

The victim was Simon Filk, a young were from Danyon's pack. Simon had been bright and loyal, eager to learn anything his leader was willing to teach him. Although Simon hadn't known it, Danyon had been training him for a leadership position. He'd had big plans for him. Now, seeing the young were lying dead at the foot of the levee, Danyon wished he had told Simon.

In fact, he wished a lot of things right now. He wished he had someone around to explain what the hell he was looking at.

Heavy cable had been wound about Simon's chest and feet, binding his arms to his sides and his ankles together. Another cable had been wrapped around his neck. His clothes were only tatters of cloth strewn about his body, and he was soaked in blood. What left Danyon gaping and boggled, however, was that Simon remained in were-state—except for his claws and fangs, all of which had been ripped from his body.

How in the hell is this possible?

Different breeds of werewolves carried certain traits, particularly when it came to the triggers that caused their transformation from human to werewolf and vice versa. Some breeds mutated at will, others only in the face of a full moon. The wolven were different in that their transformation usually occurred when they reached an intense emotional state, be it anger, fear, even sexual arousal. As a wolven matured and learned to control the range of his or her emotions, the mutation trigger became more controllable, the transformation more a matter of will. The same controlling factors existed when it came to reverting back to human form, only reversed, the transformation occurring when the heightened emotion was abated, satiated, or controlled. The only time this didn't apply was at the time of death. Without any exception that Danyon was aware of, the moment a wolven's heart stopped beating, no matter the manner of death, he assumed human form. The fact that Simon was dead but remained in were-state was incomprehensible to him.

"Who would do such a horrible thing to Simon?" Andrea Doucet cried.

"Ain't no way it was a *who,* girl," Paul Mire, who was standing beside her, said. "It had to be a *what* to mess him up that bad. Look how that poor boy's tore up. Thing I can't figure, though, is how come he ain't changed? Why's that, Danyon, huh? Why's Simon stuck like that? How come he didn't change back?"

Wondering the same in spades, Danyon glanced over at his two weres. He had been so taken aback by Simon's condition that he'd forgotten Andrea and Paul were even there. The two of them had stumbled across the body while walking home from Roosters, a small bar and grill where they both worked, waiting tables.

Danyon shook his head, indicating he had no answer. The truth was he feared if he opened his mouth right then, the anger roiling inside him would take charge and force a transformation that would demand vengeance. He had to keep a clear head. He might not have answers now, but he was determined to find them or die trying. Right now, his weres were frightened, and, as their leader, he had to take charge and keep his emotions in check. If he didn't, his entire pack might get skittish, and then he'd have an even bigger problem on his hands.

He turned to Andrea. Her eyes were swollen from crying, her square, chubby face blotchy. "I need you to go to the Quarter and find Andy Saville. You know who I'm talking about, right?"

"Man, anybody's ever gone to Jumani's Bar knows Andy," Paul said, unfolding his arms. "That bugger's gotta be the biggest bouncer in the state of Louisiana. All he's gotta do is look sideways at a drunk, and they pee their pants they're so scared."

Sniffling, Andrea gave an adamant nod of agreement.

This wasn't the first time Danyon had heard Andy's reputation preceding him. He was indeed the largest were in the East Bank pack, and the only one Danyon trusted implicitly. No matter the situation, he could count on Andy to watch his back, keep his mouth shut, not ask questions, and follow orders to the letter. If ever those attributes were needed, it was now.

"Go to Jumani's first," Danyon said. "I don't think Andy's on shift until later, but he usually goes in early. If he isn't there, Joe, the owner, will know where to find him. Tell Andy I need his SUV. Let him know where I am, but don't say a word about Simon still being in were-state. Got that?"

"Y-Yes, but wh-what do I say if he asks me why you need his SUV?"

"He won't, not if you say I'm the one asking for it. Tell him to bring a couple tarps, a hacksaw, a pair of wirecut—"

"No…wait…I can't remember all of that." Andrea wrung her hands. "I'm gonna forget something, I just know it!"

Danyon patted her arm gently. "Okay, never mind, it's okay. Think you can remember just the tarp?"

"Y-Yeah."

"Perfect. All you have to do is tell Andy to bring two big tarps. Then tell—"

"B-But what a-about the other stuff? All the other things you wanted?" she asked.

"Just tell him I said that the job is messy, it'll be dark, and metal is involved. If you can remember to tell him that, Andy will know what to bring. Can you do that?"

"Wait, you mean we're gonna leave him here 'til dark?" Paul asked. He was pacing now, a short tight path between two trees. "We just gonna let the flies start collectin' on his eyes and stuff?"

Andrea let out a loud sob and covered her face with her hands.

Danyon shot Paul a look.

"What? What'd I say?"

"Do you have to be so graphic?" Danyon aimed his chin at Andrea, hoping Paul caught the message. *She's upset, numb-nuts, so cool it.*

Evidently catching the gist of Danyon's meaning, Paul looked down at his feet. "I was only askin' is all," he mumbled.

"No, we're not going to leave him here until dark." Danyon walked to the opposite side of the road, then pushed his way through the thicket until he found a patch heavy with bramble and foliage. "We're going to leave him here, where no one can see his body."

Andrea slowly slid her hands away from her face, peered in Danyon's direction. "Is…will…are you sure Simon's going to be okay in there?"

"Really," Paul said. "Like there's no snakes or rats or stuff like that in there, huh?"

"S-Snakes?" Andrea's face drained of color.

"Shut up, Paul!" Danyon warned.

Paul's mouth fell open in surprise. Then he snapped it shut, pouted, and folded his arms across his chest.

Ignoring him, Danyon walked back over to Andrea. "Don't worry, honey, Simon will be fine here. I promise. Do you remember what you have to tell Andy?"

"Tarp—messy—dark—metal," Andrea said, ticking the items off her fingers.

"Good girl." Danyon gave her a reassuring smile.

"What about me?" Paul asked. "I can remember to tell Andy stuff."

"You're staying with me. I need help moving the body."

"Whoa, no way!" Paul took two quick steps backward. "Andy'll help you. W-Wait for Andy."

Having already positioned himself at the head of the body, Danyon glared at him. "Simon's been out here too long as it is. Somebody might drive or walk by here any minute. He has to be moved now, so suck it up. Come over here and take hold of his feet."

"You mean, like actually touch him? No *effin'* way!"

A low growl rumbled at the back of Danyon's throat. He allowed it to rise in volume to make sure Paul heard it. "I said, take hold of his feet."

Paul ran a shaking hand through his shoulder-length hair. "Yeah, o-okay, but…I—I don't know if I can touch him. I—I mean, look at all that blood. What if…what if I, like, throw up or something? Maybe we—"

The sound of moving brush grabbed Danyon's attention, and he held up a hand to silence Paul. He cocked an ear to the sound.

Someone…something…running toward them.

Danyon lifted his head, sniffed, caught the scent of panic—fury—a male were. Instantly, the muscles in his body began to ripple, burn—preparing for the change, instinctively engineered for fight or flight. For Danyon, though, it always meant fight. Flight simply wasn't in an alpha's DNA. No way anyone or anything was going to take them by surprise.

Andrea must have picked up on the sound, as well, because she let out a loud gasp, then cried out, "They're coming!" She suddenly dropped into a squat and covered her head with her arms. "We're going to die just like Simon! They're coming to kill us, too!"

"Who? Where—what?" Paul spun about. First left, then right, then left again, trying to look everywhere at once. "Someone's…coming? Where?"

Danyon sniffed the air again, wanting to get a handle on how quickly the runner was closing in.

"We'd better go then, right?" Paul said. He hurried over to Andrea and grabbed her by the arm. "Danyon, let's go, okay? I don't wanna…I mean, Simon was a good guy and everything, but I…I don't wanna wind up like him. Let's just go, okay?"

"Wait," Danyon commanded. The runner was closing in fast, his scent stronger…much stronger now.

It was one of his weres.

No sooner did the realization strike Danyon than Ian Sykes thundered out of the brush. He was in mid-transformation from were to human, panting, gasping, until he pulled up short on two legs right in front of Danyon.

"She's dead!" Ian cried, frantically searching Danyon's face as if all the answers to life hid there. "They killed her—somebody killed her!"

Danyon felt a burning sensation in the center of his chest. It was the fire. The key to every wolven. Their light…their life force…their core. Just as the earth fed upon the fiery core that gave it life, they drank from the lava pool within each of them. It was sustenance that strengthened body, mind and spirit, and heightened all five senses. It bubbled higher and higher in Danyon's chest.

Another death.

Another life snuffed out on his watch.

"Who?" Danyon asked, then immediately regretted asking the question. He already knew the answer. There was only one person whose death would affect Ian this way.

"Nicole," Ian said, his voice sharp with incredulity.

Andrea gasped. "Oh, no, not Nicky! Please…it can't be her, Ian. She can't be dead!" She put a hand to her mouth, sobbing uncontrollably now.

Ian nodded slowly, his eyes lost to a scene that belonged to another time and place. When he spoke again, his voice was barely above a whisper. "They…they found her body between two pilings off Barataria. Sh-she was a-all messed up…bad. Lotta blood." His focus reconnected with Danyon. "She's dead. She's really dead."

Ian Sykes and Nicole Bergeron had been a couple since they were pups. You never saw one without the other. They'd been inseparable.

"Why?" Ian asked. "Wh-Why would anyone want to hurt her? She was…" As Ian struggled to find the words to express his horror and the magnitude of his disbelief, he suddenly did a double-take and gawked. He'd spotted Simon.

Ian looked up at Danyon, back down at Simon, back to Danyon. "Just like N-Nicky…just l-like that. They killed her…just like that, Danyon."

"Did she change back?" Paul asked quietly. As though fearing the answer, he crossed his arms and tucked a hand under each armpit. He rocked nervously from side to side. "Did she? Or…or did she, uh…stay stuck, like Simon?"

Ian covered his face with his hands, dropped to his knees. "She…she's still were. I—I don't understand it.

My girl's still—" Sobbing, he dropped his hands, then threw his head back and let out a wail, then a mournful howl so loud and long, Danyon felt it in his soul.

At that moment it would have been easier for Danyon to climb Mount Everest with only one leg than to control the fury growing inside him. Two of his weres were dead. Both stripped of their claws and fangs, the two things that protected them, fed them.

His fury was certainly justifiable. But Danyon knew if he allowed it to manifest, he would be under its control. Raw vengeance would consume him. Even now, struggling to keep himself together, he wanted to rip through something, anything. If he allowed the fury to take over, he would lose clarity, the ability to wisely discern. For Simon and Nicole's sake, for the safety of the entire pack, he couldn't let that happen. Justice would never be served that way. In fact, it wasn't being served now. Not by him standing here, getting angrier by the minute. He needed answers to questions that seemed too improbable to pose.

Who or what was powerful enough to hold down a were, restrain it, then tear out its claws and fangs?

Why on earth had the murderer chosen Nicole and Simon? Neither would have purposely harmed a soul.

There was only one person Danyon knew who might have some answers or at least be able to lead him in the right direction to find answers. August Gaudin.

August was the master elder of all the were packs in the South. Every alpha reported to August and was responsible to him. He was a wise, fair leader, and everyone respected him immensely.

This situation was so out of the ordinary, though, that even August might not have answers. Whatever the case, Danyon had to find the elder right away and let him know about the deaths—and not only because it was his duty. He had to report and make himself accountable to August, before the rage took over.

Before he wound up being a murderer instead of finding one.

Chapter 3

Trying to act normal with all her senses on high alert, was like trying to shove an elephant into a linen closet.

Hopeless.

Shauna felt certain a were was in trouble, but she wasn't sure what to do about it. She had no idea who the were might be or what kind of trouble he or she might be in. Intuition was usually a given for a Keeper, but she hated when it didn't provide enough details for follow through.

She had to do something besides pace, though. For her own sanity and to reassure Fiona, who kept looking over at her every couple of minutes from behind the register.

Fortunately, Caitlin had been too busy to notice how fidgety she'd gotten. Unfortunately, her sister's heavy workload came from picking up Shauna's slack. She had managed to help the spike-haired couple Caitlin had directed her to earlier. Thankfully they hadn't asked about pulverized bats' wings or hogs' hooves, as Shauna had suspected. They'd wanted gum mastic and dried anise, the first to snort, the second to smoke. All because a friend swore both gave quite the buzz. She'd been slightly abrupt with a response, stating that if they considered death a buzz, then they should go for it. That had certainly sobered them up.

Once she was rid of them, Shauna had tried helping another customer or two, but she'd been unable to concentrate on their questions long enough to answer them. She felt useless.

That horrible, mournful keening sound haunted her. It wasn't as loud as it was earlier, but it was still there. No less distressing, so painful to hear. Stabbing her repeatedly in the heart. It seemed to call to her. Beg for her...

She considered talking to Fiona about it. Since she was the oldest and the most experienced Keeper, Fiona might be able to tell her what she should do, if anything, about what she heard. Then Shauna reconsidered. The wolvens were her responsibility, and if she was so certain it was a wolven's cry, she wanted—needed—to handle it on her own. Just because she was the youngest didn't mean she always had to run to her big sister for help. If she was ever to fully understand and trust her instincts, *she* had to work through them. Right now, though, instinct was telling her to get the hell off her butt and do *something.* She just wasn't quite sure what that 'something' should be.

As if hearing her thoughts, and it wouldn't have surprised Shauna if she had, Fiona signaled her over. Shauna reluctantly headed her way. If her sister asked her what was wrong, she couldn't lie to her, no matter how badly she wanted to work things out on her own.

Just before she reached the counter, two middle-aged women dressed in expensive linen suits walked up to the register, wanting to check out. Shauna offered a silent thank-you to the universe for the reprieve.

"Hey, where the baby at?" Lurnell asked, while chewing on yet another piece of king cake. She hadn't moved from her spot at the counter, the one nearest the cake platter. The baby she referred to was the pink, plastic, one-inch doll always hidden in a king cake. Tradition had it that a year's worth of good luck and fortune belonged to whoever found the doll in their piece of cake. To keep that luck rolling, that person had to buy another king cake and share it with friends and family.

"If you didn't find it," Shauna said, "there must not have been one."

"Girl, you crazy. You know they all got babies."

"Well, if it did, you would have found it, since you ate most of the cake."

"Huh?" Lurnell glanced down at the platter…of crumbs. "Uhh…" She dusted the crumbs off her hands. "Yeah, guess you right. Probably had a machine broke down to the cake fact'ry or somethin'. They bes' hurry up and fix that. People gettin' kings with no babies like that, they ain't gonna know what to do. It could get nasty."

"Excuse me…" One of the women Shauna had seen standing near the register a moment ago now stood beside her. She held up a hand, pinky and forefinger slightly extended as if preparing for high tea. "I could not help overhearing your conversation, and my curiosity simply got the best of me. Would you please explain what a baby has to do with a cake?"

Lurnell snorted. "You ain't from here, huh?"

High tea became a small, dismissive wave. "Heavens, no. I'm from the Valley."

"Where that's at, the Valley? Out by Shreveport?"

The woman rolled her eyes. "It's in California, dear. San Fernando, to be exact."

Lurnell's educational background might not have been extensive, but she didn't need a Harvard degree to know she'd been talked down to. Her nostrils flared, the first sign that Mount Lurnell was about to blow.

Fiona must have realized the same thing because she suddenly appeared, holding a small, pink, plastic doll. "Look what I found," she said. "Probably fell out of the cake when I was slicing it." She smiled, then handed it to Lurnell. "You're the one standing closest to the platter, so I think you should have it."

"For real? Me?" Lurnell said, eyes wide as she took the doll. Her notion to teach Ms. High Tea a few manners had obviously taken a backseat to more important matters.

Lurnell held the plastic luck charm up for everyone to see. "Look here, y'all. I got me the baby!"

A handful of customers applauded, and Lurnell did a little jig and a booty-bump.

As Lurnell carried on about the luck coming her way, which, of course, included getting the man of her dreams, Fiona tapped Shauna on the shoulder. "You okay?" she whispered.

Relieved her sister hadn't asked what was wrong, Shauna said truthfully, "Just antsy."

"Too much noise?"

Shauna nodded. That was the truth, as well. That constant keening rising and falling in volume *was* upsetting her. She knew Fiona meant the noise in the shop, but who was she to split hairs?

"I know we're busy," Shauna said, "and I feel like a heel for asking, but would you mind if I went out for a while?"

"Not at all." Fiona gave Shauna's shoulders a little rub.

"You don't think Caitlin will care?"

"Why would she?"

"Because she'd be stuck doing work I should be doing."

"Don't worry, we'll be fine. I planned on closing early anyway."

"Early? Why, when we're so busy?"

"Keeno's, you know, the place in Lake Charles where we get our herbs, essential oils, specialty soaps, stuff like that? They can't get a delivery here until next week, and we can't wait that long. I was thinking maybe we'd take a ride out there and pick up the order ourselves. The way I see it, we either lose a partial day's business today or lose a lot of it the rest of the week because we're out of stock. Besides, we can use the breather before all hell breaks loose this weekend anyway."

Really feeling guilty now, Shauna said, "I can just go out for a short walk, then come back and watch the shop, if you and Caitlin want to drive out there."

Fiona smiled. "I said *we* could use the breather. All of us. That doesn't mean you have to come with us to Lake Charles, though."

Shauna held back a sigh of relief. "Won't you need help when you get out there? You know, loading—"

"Will you stop worrying? Go, take a walk. Better yet, go for a run. I know how much you love running. It might help burn off—"

"My word! What is that?"

Shauna and Fiona turned in unison.

High Tea was pointing at the large display window at the front of the shop, her expression sour, as if she'd just bitten into a persimmon. Shauna didn't see what was so appalling until she looked through the window with the eyes of a tourist. Then it became obvious.

An extremely thin woman, wearing faded red Daisy Dukes, a dirty, pink T-shirt and black stilettos, was pacing the sidewalk in front of the shop. Her stringy brown hair had been corralled into a crooked ponytail, and she held two lit cigarettes, one in each hand. She puffed on one then the other in rapid succession, all the while talking to herself.

"You allow homeless people to stand in front of your store that way?" High Tea asked. "Don't the police do anything to keep them off the street?"

Now Shauna wanted to teach the woman a few manners herself. "And where do you suggest the police take them? Their high-rise on the back forty?"

Fiona tugged on the back of Shauna's T-shirt, her signal to back off.

Shauna caught the message but couldn't help adding, "For all we know, that woman might not even be homeless. Maybe she's—"

"Nah, that ain't homeless," Lurnell said, making her way to the window. "That's trash."

"Don't say that," Shauna said. "Maybe she's just down on her luck. That doesn't make her trash."

Lurnell batted a hand at her. "Girl, they trash if they out runnin' a line of blow while they babies at home alone with no food and in stinky diapers. Oh, yeah, that's trash. That be a whole damn trash truck if you ask me."

"You know her?" Shauna asked.

"She ain't like my friend or nothin', but, yeah, I know her. She works in one of them bars over at the casino. They call her Mattress Mattie, 'cause she always spreadin' them skinny legs so she can make that green. She got two babies—two, you hearin' me? And what you think she be doin' with that little extra somethin' she makin' on the side?"

"Buying drugs," High Tea said, her tone definitive.

"See that?" Lurnell said. "Even Miss Thing got the set up, and she ain't even from around here."

High Tea beamed as if she'd just won a prize.

Lurnell tapped on the window, apparently to get Mattie's attention. The woman kept pacing, smoking, talking to herself.

"Yeah, she hurtin' right now. Needin' some blow. Bet she out there waitin' for her dealer."

High Tea gasped. "You allow them to deal drugs out there?"

"Of course not," Fiona said sharply. "We can't control what people do on the street, though. Did you see a drug deal take place in front of this shop? If you did, please tell me because I obviously missed it."

With a haughty lift of her chin, High Tea tsked. "Well, if I owned this establishment, I would—"

"Now what you think that piece of shrimp bait's doin' out there?" Lurnell said, planting a fist on a hip. "That boy is trouble all by his ownself."

Mattie had company now. She was talking to Banjo Marks, a young vampire who came from an old bayou family. Shauna knew he *was* homeless *and* a junkie. The guy eagerly swallowed, snorted, or injected, anything and everything he got his hands on. His weekly regimen consisted of LSD, pot, crystal-meth and cocaine. Whatever he scored in between those primers, Banjo considered lagniappe. He was tall and lanky, and had thin, scraggly blond hair that hung in greasy strands down to the middle of his back. Most of the time he smelled like wet, soured towels.

As if life hadn't piled enough on Banjo's plate, he didn't fit the standard vampire profile, even for this area. He ate and drank like a human. Shauna didn't know if the years of drug use had caused him to mutate, which in turn allowed him to digest food, or if he was the by-product of an accidental cross-breeding. Either way, it was strange to see. He came to the shop often, always looking for a handout. And Fiona, being the Keeper of the vampires and the kind-hearted mother hen that she was, never failed to give him food and something warm or cool to drink, whichever the weather dictated.

As for Shauna, she never liked being around Banjo, and it had nothing to do with his drug use or smell. He had a high-pitched voice and an odd, twittering laugh that sounded like a hyena mating with a screeching macaw. It sawed on her last nerve.

Mattie and Banjo were yelling now, standing almost nose to nose. Although Shauna could easily hear their conversation, both were so hyped up that most of it came across as gibberish.

"—today, asshole, you said today!" Mattie jabbed Banjo's shoulder with a finger. "You said—I been waitin'… Where's at? Where?"

As Mattie poked at Banjo, he shuffled left a few steps, then turned about and moved up one step in the other direction, as if he were square-dancing alone. Then came that horrid, twittering laugh.

"Swear, swear to Gawd, gonna be here," he gibbered.

"Little problem, gonna be here, though. Yeah, you gonna see—fresh, fresh, fresh. Gonna come, swear to Gawd."

Mattie shoved him, and Banjo stumbled backwards, his arms pin-wheeling for balance. She trapped him against a nearby light pole, jabbing a finger at his chest this time. "You—shit…sonofawhore! You promised, you motherf—"

The twittering laugh—that God-awful twittering laugh…

Their fight grew so intense people crossed the street to avoid them.

"Enough's enough," Shauna said, and headed for the door. She really didn't care if they pulled each other's hair out. What she'd had enough of was Banjo's laughter.

"Shauna wait," Fiona said. "I'll call—"

"Yeah, you best hold up, girl," Lurnell called after her.

Shauna glanced back at her, then returned her attention to the street in time to see Mattie throw a punch at Banjo's face. To her surprise, he ducked in time to avoid getting hit. Instead of his face, Mattie's fist connected with the light pole—and dented it.

Shauna gaped. Every light pole in the city was constructed of heavy metal due to the narrow streets, heavy traffic and drivers with little to no peripheral vision. No way a skinny woman with bad aim would be able to do that much damage.

"Whoa! You see that?" Lurnell said.

Just then the keening sound that had kept Shauna on edge for the last couple of hours grew in volume. Within seconds, it was all she heard. She saw Lurnell's mouth moving but heard no words.

Only that pained, mournful cry…loud and long.

It sank deep into Shauna's chest—threatened to yank out her heart.

She had to find the source.

No doubt in her mind…something was happening… had happened…would happen. No doubt in her mind, it was bad.

All of it very, *very* bad.

He ran.

Hard, fast…

Breathless…

Mindless.

It was all Danyon knew to do.

Act on instinct.

After Andrea left to find Andy, he and Paul had moved Simon's body into the thicket. He'd ordered Paul to stay put and keep watch. If anyone came into the area, he was to steer them away from the thicket, by any means necessary. Paul, who'd puked his guts out the entire time they moved Simon, had all but burst into tears, not wanting to be left alone with a dead body.

With no other choice but to leave him in a sniveling heap, Danyon had followed Ian to a set of pilings off Barataria Boulevard, where he'd found Nicole's body.

Ian had been right. She was in the same condition as Simon. Clothes tattered and strewn about, lying in a pool of her own blood, bound about the chest and ankles, and in full were-state, claws and fangs ripped away. There was one difference between the deaths, however. Unlike Simon, heavy cable hadn't been used to restrain Nicole. Only thin, silver wire.

The pain from the silver alone would have been excruciating. It had burned through Nicole's fur and flesh, then lodged itself in bone. Definitely enough to keep her restrained all by itself.

Danyon hadn't had the opportunity to examine Simon fully yet, but he suspected that, initially, the same silver wire had been used to incapacitate him. Since he was bigger and stronger than Nicole, the cable would have been necessary to keep him securely restrained while they removed his claws and fangs. Nicole, on the other hand, was petite. Even when fully transformed into were-state, she had been no bigger than a six-month-old German Shepherd pup.

Seeing the young female were stuffed between two pilings had been bad enough, but what really got to Danyon was her fur. She was double-coated, covered with beautiful light brown fur streaked with different shades of gold and white. She literally sparkled when she ran through the sunlight. Seeing that beautiful coat covered with blood, the deep-set eyes once filled with innocence and ease now frozen in terror, had been his undoing. Rage overtook him, and he transformed almost instantaneously.

Fortunately, part of his brain had remained rational, reminding him that he had to tell August Gaudin, the leader of all the were packs in the South, about the deaths. That human thought battled with his feral nature as he ran toward the city, toward the French Quarter, where he would find August. That thought was the only thing that kept Danyon from hunting anything breathing just so he could slaughter it.

Running helped him push past the pain of what he'd witnessed.

By the time he reached Orleans Avenue, which was six blocks north of the Quarter, he had calmed enough to return to human form. His clothes were nearly non-existent, since he all but doubled in size as a wolf, so he'd had to dodge in and out of alleyways and behind buildings to avoid being seen.

He'd gone straight home, which was the entire fifth floor of La Maison Pierre, a five-storey hotel he owned on the south side of Ursulines. Once there, he'd slipped through the back entrance, took a private elevator to the top floor then quickly changed into slacks and a button-down shirt.

Now he headed for Canal Street and August's office complex. He kept his walk brisk, his head down, watching his shoes as a maelstrom of questions blew through his mind.

Why would anyone want to kill Simon and Nicole? Neither one would ever have harmed a soul.

Is someone targeting my pack, or were Simon and Nicole simply in the wrong place at the wrong time?

The biggest question that plagued him, though, was who or what had been able to capture them. It would certainly have taken more than one human to keep Simon under control once he transformed into were-form, even if they had subdued him with silver before wrapping him in cable. In human form, Simon had been six foot one and weighed at least a hundred-seventy-five pounds. As a wolf, he towered over seven feet, and just the additional flesh and muscle mass added another seventy-five pounds or more to his weight. No, it would have taken more than an entire army of men to hold Simon down.

Another thought crossed Danyon's mind, and it nearly stopped him cold. Both death scenes had been covered with blood, but aside from Simon and Nicole being declawed and defanged, he hadn't noticed any other major injuries. No gunshot wounds to the body or head. No blunt force trauma. He hadn't examined either close enough to check for stab wounds, which he planned to do when he met up with Andy later, but aside from that possibility, what had actually killed his two weres?

Danyon was still deep in thought when a woman suddenly appeared in his line of sight, only inches away from his face. Instinctively, he reached out and took hold of her upper arms to minimize the collision.

"Excuse me," he said. "I…" The sight of her fiery green eyes sent a jolt of recognition through him. It was Shauna MacDonald.

He'd met her a few times at the bi-annual council meetings, when the underworld subcultures in New Orleans and the surrounding area met to discuss communal issues. He knew Shauna owned A Little Bit of Magic, the mystic shop on Royal, along with her sisters, Fiona and Caitlin. And he knew all three were Keepers.

Every time he saw Shauna, her beauty captured his attention to the point of distraction. She was tall and slender, her long, strawberry blonde hair usually up in a ponytail. Her skin, although fair, had a healthy glow. Only a dead man wouldn't take notice of her.

Even more problematic for Danyon was Shauna's scent. It was a pheromonal tidal wave of passion, femininity and latent sexuality. It drove him mad with desire, and he had to struggle to resist it.

Shauna, on the other hand, appeared to have little or no interest in him at all. Whenever they were in the same room, she refused to make eye contact with him and usually kept her end of the conversation brief, clipped, as though being around him irritated her, and she couldn't wait to get away.

It was just as well.

Even if Shauna were interested in him, nothing could ever come of it.

She was human.

He was a wolven, and an alpha at that. That was a vast chasm to overcome. Danyon knew those differences would always keep her from fully understanding the depth of his true nature, even if she was his Keeper.

Still holding on to her arms, Danyon suddenly became keenly aware of the feel of her skin under his palms. Soft…silky…warm. Very warm.

He felt his pulse quicken, his nostrils flare.

He should have felt guilty right then. Two of his weres were dead. He'd just wiped their blood from his hands.

But he felt no guilt.

There was no room for it. Not now. For every one of Danyon's senses was on high alert. Each one excruciatingly aware of *her.*

And the effect left him ravenous.

Chapter 4

Shauna pulled out of Danyon's grasp more abruptly than she'd intended. She'd been lost in thought, not paying attention to where she was going and had nearly collided into him. It had taken a couple of seconds for her to blink all six foot four of him into focus, but once she did, recognition was instantaneous. That didn't surprise her. Danyon was not a man easily forgotten. That exceptionally broad chest, sharp facial features and strong chin…his eyes, the color of honey still on the comb. His thick black hair, a little longer than shoulder-length, was combed back, away from his face. He smelled of soap and testosterone at full throttle. Shauna had never allowed herself to get this close to him before, and had it not been for this accidental encounter, probably never would have.

And all for good reason.

Her mind turned into a puddle of goo every time she was around Danyon. Her tongue stuck to the roof of her mouth, and she would start fidgeting, like a nervous school girl, something she never did. His extraordinary good looks, sharp intellect and wit, and the smoldering sexuality that seemed to ooze out of him when he moved, made her heart beat too fast. She kept her distance to maintain control of her mind and her body, something she would never admit to another soul.

As a Keeper, Shauna had a lot of expectations to live up to. Being the youngest Keeper made things even tougher, because it came with its own set of challenges. She always felt she had to prove her competency twice as much as her two sisters. And in order to do that, she had to keep her mind and body strong and focused. She couldn't afford to appear vulnerable. Especially to a wolven. Even one as breathtaking as Danyon.

"Something's happened," Shauna said, hearing her words come out as a statement rather than the question she'd intended.

Danyon nodded, his eyes wary, quickly scanning both sides of the street. In profile, his hair glistened with a blue-black sheen.

Shauna's heart quickened. She had to force herself not to take a step back.

"What did you hear?" he asked.

Shauna looked up at him questioningly.

"I mean who told you? What did they tell you?"

She glanced away from the intensity of his stare. "No one told me anything."

"Then how did you know?"

"That there was trouble?"

He tilted his head, and his gaze intensified.

How was she supposed to explain what she'd heard in the shop? That weird keening she'd instinctively known was a cry for help? Or that she'd heard it over a shop filled with tourists, city noise pouring in from the street and Mattie and Banjo's fight? How was she to explain that without sounding like a kook?

Shauna opted for the direct route. "I heard it," she said.

"Heard what?" He frowned, evidently confused.

She chewed her bottom lip a moment. "I'm not really sure. It felt…it sounded like a wolven in trouble. I was going to August's to find out if he knew anything."

"I'm headed there myself." Danyon didn't appear surprised in the least by what she'd said.

"What do you know? Anything?"

His face hardened. "Unfortunately, yes. Two of my weres are dead."

Stunned, this time Shauna did take a step back. "Who? When?"

"Simon Filk and Nicole Bergeron. Not sure when they were killed, but both were found a couple of hours—"

"Wait. They were killed? As in murdered?" Shauna's head reeled. The name Simon Filk rang a bell, but she couldn't place a face with the name. Nicole, on the other hand, she knew. Nicole and her boyfriend, Ian, came to

A Little Bit of Magic often, especially the tea and coffee kiosk. She even remembered their usual order: bayberry tea and pecan scones.

"It appears so, yes. Two other weres from my pack were headed home from work when they found Simon at the foot of the levee near River Road. Ian found Nicole. She'd been shoved between two pilings off Barataria."

"God…poor Ian. The guy must be—"

"Devastated. And even that's an understatement."

Shauna shook her head in disbelief. "But murdered? How…? You're sure?"

Danyon gave her what sounded like a condensed version of what he knew so far and what he'd seen. As she listened, Shauna felt her stomach roll over, her knees weaken. By the time he finished, though, she was so angry, she could have tortured and killed the murderer bare-handed. She was also furious with Danyon.

"I can't believe you moved the bodies," she said.

"What do you mean you can't believe it?"

"You should have alerted someone first," Shauna fumed. "The police, August, me. You might have destroyed vital evidence."

Danyon's eyes darkened. "And what do you think would have happened if a human, or anyone else for that matter, had come across them the way Andrea and Paul did? They were in were-state, Shauna. What did you want me to do, just leave them there? Maybe throw a tarp over the bodies?"

"Don't be crass." Shauna shoved a hand in the back

pocket of her jeans. "When did you plan on telling me about this? Next week? Next month?"

"When did you suddenly become my mother?"

"I'm the Keeper of the wolvens! I have every right to know what's going on at all times."

Danyon stood tall, jabbed a thumb to his chest. "And I'm the alpha of the East Bank pack. Those were my weres! I'm responsible for them, and I can take care of my own."

Shauna leaned toward him. "But I'm their Keeper. And, in case you've forgotten, yours, as well."

"What does that have to do with anything? Simon and Nicole are dead. Just what is there to keep…Keeper?"

She snapped her head back as though slapped.

Regret flickered in his eyes, but it went away as quickly as it arrived.

"May I remind you, Mr. Stone," Shauna said through gritted teeth, "it's my responsibility to keep peace between the wolven, the other races, and the humans in this city. By not telling me, you put everyone in danger. When word of this gets out, too much or too little information can end up open to interpretation. Have you forgotten about the cemetery murders six months ago, or what happened when the walk-ins tried taking over the city three months after that? In both cases, vampires suspected the shape-shifters, shifters pointed at the weres, everybody pointed at everybody else. If Fiona hadn't taken charge of her vampires during the cemetery murders and Caitlin her shifters in the walk-in disaster, we might have had another war on our hands. The same kind of war that killed our parents."

By that time, Shauna's anger had grown to such a fever pitch, she stepped closer, pushed against him. "Look, you might be the big dog on campus when it comes to the East Bank pack, but—"

"Big dog? Now who's being crass?"

"But I *am* the Keeper of the wolven in this city. Moving those bodies was poor judgment on your part. The police should have been notified immediately."

Danyon's expression went cold. "How many times do I have to tell you? Simon and Nicole were in *were-state*. What sense would it have made to involve humans when we spend half our time hiding our true identities from them so they don't destroy us? None, period. I was *not* going to take the chance that Simon or Nicole would be seen in that condition."

"You didn't have to involve a human," Shauna said. "You could have called Jagger DeFarge. You know perfectly well he's a homicide detective."

"A homicide detective *and* a vampire."

"Which only means he'd be more sensitive to the situation. He's part of the underworld. He knows what has to be protected."

Danyon looked away for a second, and Shauna could have sworn she heard a low growl rumble from his throat. "We are wolven!" he declared. "We don't want a vampire involved in our business. I don't need DeFarge's help, nor do I need you questioning my actions. Nicole and Simon were my responsibility. I *will* find their murderers. And believe me, there *will* be justice."

"And as their Keeper, I *will* be involved, whether you like it or not!" Realizing her voice had gotten a little too loud, Shauna glanced about, making sure their conversation was still private.

This time there was no mistaking the low growl emanating from Danyon. Without another word, he whipped around and headed down the street, his long legs quickly widening the distance between them.

Furious that he'd so abruptly dismissed her, Shauna hurriedly back-tracked a block. She planned to detour to a side street that led to the rear of August's office complex and beat Danyon there.

She walked fast, talking herself out of breaking into a full run. This was starting to feel ridiculous, as if she were one of the last two children left in a game of musical chairs, and only one chair remained. She'd always hated that game.

Okay, so she might she have gotten a little exuberant— upset, even—because she hadn't been contacted when Simon and Nicole were discovered. Still, that was no excuse for Danyon to get so huffy. She probably could have handled things more diplomatically, but he didn't have to go storming off as if she'd peed in his Cheerios, for heaven's sake.

If she really wanted to be honest with herself, though, the buck stopped with her. She had a temper and knew it. It's what made it too easy for her to run off at the mouth. Along with that, Danyon gave her mush-brain.

Not the man's fault, but she was living proof that temper and mush-brain made for a bad combination. Any man, wolven or not, would have gotten upset by the way she'd handled the situation. Her responsibility as a Keeper was to help keep peace between the subcultures and humans in New Orleans. The way she'd confronted Danyon had been anything but peaceful.

Shauna slowed her pace.

This wasn't a game of musical chairs. And it wasn't about her or Danyon or her attraction to him.

It was about Simon and Nicole, about finding their murderer.

It was about justice.

Chapter 5

When Shauna finally reached the main lobby of August's office complex, Danyon had already arrived. He was standing alongside Rita Quinn, August's executive assistant, near the entrance to the hallway that led to August's maze of offices. As always, the middle-aged were looked immaculate. She wore a lavender pencil skirt and a white silk blouse, and her light brown hair had been rolled into a perfect French twist. Elegant and tasteful, just like everything in August's life.

When Rita spotted Shauna, she smiled warmly.

Danyon barely looked her way.

"How wonderful to see you, Ms. MacDonald," Rita said. "Your timing is perfect, as always. I was about to lead Mr. Stone to the conference room. Mr. Gaudin is expecting both of you."

"He is?" Puzzled, Shauna glanced over at Danyon, wondering if he'd somehow managed to call ahead and let August know they were coming.

As if reading her thoughts, he shrugged, indicating he had no idea how August knew.

"Of course," Rita said, then motioned for them to follow her. "Mr. Gaudin is already in the conference room. He's on a call at the moment, but he insisted I bring both of you to him the moment you arrived."

They followed Rita down a long, wide hallway, a runner of plush beige carpet stretching along the oak-wood floor.

Shauna felt a little awkward walking beside Danyon. She'd acted like a child earlier and was embarrassed about it. Figuring the adult thing to do was probably apologize, she sneaked a peek at him out of the corner of her eye to get a handle on his mood. He was stern-faced, eyes locked forward. As far as he was concerned, she might as well have been in another parish.

Maybe later for that apology.

Maybe.

Rita led them to a set of heavy double doors, then opened one and motioned them inside. The room held a mahogany conference table, massive and oval and sur-rounded by twelve leather wing-back chairs. In the south corner of the room, near the back, stood a standard-size mahogany desk. August stood beside it, phone to his ear. He nodded an acknowledgment when he saw them.

"Make certain it is taken care of immediately," he

said to whoever was on the other end of the line, then he turned slightly, listening intently.

Even in profile, the elder was a formidable figure. He was shorter than Danyon, although not by much. His silvery-white, shoulder-length hair was a testament to his age, but his stature, the breadth and depth of his chest and shoulders, and his large strong hands appeared to be in direct opposition, for they were appropriate to a much younger man. August's presence radiated a quiet confidence and wisdom, but when called for, he elicited fear just as easily. He was an attorney by trade and had been elected to the city commission, and also worked with the tourism board. Shauna had always been impressed by his accomplishments, but that wasn't what bonded her to him.

August was the leader of all the werewolves throughout the South, and certainly the fact that she was Keeper of the werewolves in this city had something to do with the kinship they shared. But the connection between them ran much deeper than that.

August had fought alongside her parents in their struggle to avert the great war between the races, and when they died, he immediately took Fiona, Caitlin and Shauna under his wing. He'd raised them as his own. Taught them what it meant to be Keepers. Made sure they were well educated, well fed, loved and protected. He was like a grandfather to Shauna, and each time he looked at her with those gentle, powder blue eyes she felt unconditionally loved. They might not have been biologically connected, but sharing DNA never assured anyone of love.

As soon as August hung up the phone, Shauna walked over and gave him a hug. He returned it warmly.

"Would anyone care for something to drink?" Rita asked, still standing at the threshold of the room.

"No, thank you," Shauna said.

Danyon, who was standing at the far end of the conference table, shook his head. "Nothing for me, thanks."

"That will be all, Rita," August said.

Rita nodded and quietly backed out of the room, shutting the door behind her.

August put an arm around Shauna's shoulder and led her to the table. After pulling out a chair for her, he motioned to Danyon. "Please, make yourself comfortable."

When everyone was seated, Shauna asked, "Rita said you were expecting us, August. How did you know we were coming?"

"Simple logic," August said, "I heard about the deaths half an hour ago."

"From whom?" Danyon asked.

"Rayo Black, one of the bartenders at Jumani's. Apparently he was working when Andrea went into the bar looking for Andy Saville. Rayo saw how upset she was and offered her a drink to calm her nerves. He claimed after Andrea downed a couple, she began to cry and told him about the dead weres. He called me immediately. Since the weres were from Danyon's pack, and since you,

Shauna, are their Keeper, it was only logical that the two of you would come to me."

August sighed deeply, propped his elbows on the table and steepled his fingers. "Details, please," he said to Danyon. "Tell me."

For the next forty minutes Danyon relayed the details of how Simon and Nicole were discovered, who had found them, and the condition of their bodies when found. He also told August about his decision to hide the bodies so passersby wouldn't stumble on them, and that he'd summoned Andy Saville to help with the transfer after dark.

Hearing it all again, Shauna's anger sparked anew. She still couldn't believe someone had actually killed the young weres. The emotions hammering her must have been minuscule in comparison to August's, though. As he listened to Danyon, the elder's eyes went from powder blue to cobalt. His lips drew into a thin, tight line. Shauna noticed his neck muscles ripple; then, like a wave in motion, that ripple traveled across his chin and up to his cheeks. He was fighting transformation.

Ever since Shauna was a child, she'd known August to be master over his human form and his werewolf identity. Not once had she ever seen his emotions overtake him and the transformation occur spontaneously. He had always been in control. It was understandable that August would be upset about the were deaths, but for the news to have this great an effect on him, there had to be more going on in his head than processing what he'd just heard.

Danyon leaned across the table. "I plan on examining the bodies more closely before they're returned to their families. Something—"

"Have them taken to my lake house in LaPlace," August said sharply. "I want to see them for myself. Do you remember how to get there?"

"Of course."

"Wasn't that house damaged during Hurricane Katrina?" Shauna asked.

"Yes, but it's been renovated, and I had a large workshop built beside it. Forty by forty, plenty of fluorescent lighting. Andy can bring Nicole and Simon there. I'll take care of notifying the families, as well. Although I'd be surprised if news hasn't already reached them by now." August turned to Danyon. "You were about to say more before I interrupted. Please continue."

"Just that something occurred to me when I was on my way here."

"Yes?"

"Well, Nicole and Simon had obvious wounds from being declawed and defanged, but I didn't notice anything that specifically pointed to the cause of death. No gunshot wound or blunt force trauma. There was a lot of blood, but I don't believe either of them bled out. The silver wire used on Nicole—and I suspect on Simon, as well—definitely did some damage. Burned right through fur, flesh and muscle. But as torturous as that sounds, I don't believe that's what caused Nicole's death. Simon's either. They may have been stabbed, but I won't know that for sure until I examine the bodies. But, August, the bigger question is how is it possible that both remained in were-state after they died? I've never witnessed that before. Never even heard it was possible. Have you?"

August bowed his head, pushed away from the table and slowly got to his feet. He walked over to an occasional table that stood against a far wall beneath a six-foot painting of St. Louis Cathedral. On the table sat a crystal pitcher filled with ice water and surrounded by six crystal tumblers. August filled one of the tumblers with water, lifted it to his lips and drank slowly until it was drained.

Shauna had never seen August act this way, and it frightened her.

After setting the empty glass back on the occasional table, August turned toward them. His face had gone from grave to gray. "Yes, I have witnessed the phenomenon before."

He walked back to the head of the conference table, but instead of sitting, he paced slowly back and forth, like a lecturer preparing to give a speech. When August finally spoke, his voice was low and distant, the voice of a man pulling up a memory that he would prefer not to disinter. "I witnessed the kind of death you mentioned nearly six decades ago. I was in Romania at the time. A group of local weres had captured a rogue were—a wolven, as it happened—who'd been responsible for the mutilation and deaths of three human children. He was brought before the were-council, and it didn't take long for them to pronouce him guilty and sentence him to death. I concurred with the council's decision, of course, as did the magistrate who was serving at the time. But the magistrate wanted the rogue's execution to be as severe as his crime."

August took a deep breath, stopped pacing, and faced them. "He had the rogue bound in silver and steel, then beaten relentlessly while the silver burned through his flesh. Of course that intense pain created the emotional state that was needed to force his transformation. As soon as the transformation was complete, he was stripped of his claws and fangs."

"I don't understand," Shauna said. "How did that serve as an execution? Did he bleed to death?"

"No. The manner of death was far worse. You see, there is a metaphysical power inherent to a werewolf's claws and fangs. That power is so potent that when they are torn abruptly from the body, the were undergoes a molecular restructuring."

"How so?" Danyon asked.

"The cells of the body begin to pressurize, which automatically seals the body in were-state," August explained. "The cells continue to pressurize until the body mimics a pressure cooker, except without a release valve. Eventually the pressure becomes so great that the were's heart literally bursts."

Shauna slumped in her chair, overwhelmed by the thought of such a horrible death. She glanced over at Danyon. He was sitting ramrod straight, hands on the table, his fingers laced together and white-knuckled. The expression on his face looked treacherous, hard and cold.

"Believe me," August continued, "even back then, I was no innocent regarding death. I had seen far too many die in battle. But I will never forget the sounds of agony that came from that rogue. It was, and still is, indescribable. It affected everyone who was there, every council member. Even the magistrate." August looked over at the portrait of the cathedral, kept his gaze there. "That wolven screamed…pleaded. He cried for mercy so loudly…I didn't think any being had the vocal capacity to produce such volume. And it would change from howls to human screams to…something…"

August turned to them, his eyes dull with sadness and regret. "The look of terror on that rogue's face…if ever a being looked death square in the face, he did. That look remained on his face even after his heart burst, as though even death itself gave him no relief."

Shauna leaned forward, put a fist to her mouth and slowly shook her head. She couldn't imagine Nicole and Simon suffering that way.

August returned to his chair. He looked utterly drained.

They sat in silence, everyone seemingly at a loss for words.

Shauna's mind played reruns of Nicole and Ian at the shop. The two laughing—talking—holding hands. Nicole's smile, how it flashed in her eyes and lit up her face.

"Why them, August?" Shauna asked quietly. "I didn't know Simon very well, but Nicole…she wasn't a threat to anyone. Why them?"

The elder shook his head. "Chances are it had little or nothing to do with whether or not they were threats. My guess is that Simon and Nicole were simply in the wrong place at the wrong time."

"Random killings? In that manner? Then it would have to be someone who knew about the molecular restructuring. Still, why would they choose that manner of death? There are easier ways to kill a were. Are we dealing with a lunatic? Somebody who gets his kicks from seeing others suffer?"

"I don't think it's a lunatic or someone killing for recreation," August said. "The metaphysical power in the claws and fangs can affect others, as well. Not just the victim. Because of its potency, it only has to be ingested by another being, and he or she becomes empowered with the same traits as a werewolf. Not transformation, but strength, speed, agility, heightened senses, even sexual prowess."

Shauna spotted Danyon throwing a glance her way.

Then he cleared his throat and asked, "How would someone ingest claws and fangs?"

"By pulverizing them to fine powder," August said. "The killer may be doing this simply for profit."

"A drug dealer?" Shauna asked.

"In essence, yes," August said. "The one advantage we have is that the metaphysical power is not common knowledge. It's usually kept within the council. So it is possible that the killer may only be someone hunting trinkets, the way a trapper collects bear claws and alligator teeth, then sells them as jewelry. We can only hope that is the case. If not, if we are dealing with someone who understands the power involved, then the death count will grow astronomically. Once this person, this…being, realizes the financial potential, there will be no stopping him. Needless to say, it is crucial that the information I have shared with you not leave this room."

"It won't." Danyon got to his feet, his hands curling into fists at his sides. "I'll find whoever's responsible for Nicole and Simon's death. The reason for the killings doesn't matter. The murderer will be stopped, and if I have your permission, he'll be stopped by any means necessary."

August nodded. "You have my permission. But understand this, Danyon. If it is as I fear, more murders will follow so quickly, all the alphas in this territory combined may not be able to stop it."

A shiver ran up Shauna's spine, and she prayed it wasn't another intuitive whisper. But somewhere deep in her heart, she suspected her prayers would be futile.

For August's words rang far too true.

Chapter 6

"There's no need for you to come," Danyon said to Shauna, for what seemed like the fiftieth time since they'd left August's office.

"And I said I *am* coming," she said—again.

As if he'd expected anything different.

August had advised Shauna against going to the murder site, saying that there was no reason for her to subject herself to such gruesomeness. But she'd dug her heels in, refusing to be deterred. "I'm their Keeper," she'd said. "And if I'm to fully understand what's going on, I have to see it firsthand."

Unfortunately, August hadn't ordered Shauna to stay away as Danyon had hoped. And so far, every form of persuasion he'd tried to keep her from coming had failed.

Danyon had traveled to August's office on foot, and he'd planned to return to Simon and Nicole the same way, especially after he heard August's accounting of the rogue were's execution so many years ago. Danyon hadn't been able to shake the mental images that had formed, images of how Simon and Nicole must have suffered before they died. He needed to run to clear his head. As a human, running was therapeutic for him. As a were, it was his one saving grace when he was on emotional overload. The last thing he needed to deal with right now was a fainting female.

Regardless of how attractive she was.

Even if they took shortcuts through alleyways and cemeteries, it was still three miles from August's to River Road. Walking that distance would take too long, but Danyon refused to give the stubborn strawberry blonde the satisfaction of riding in a cab. Besides, he didn't want any cab driver, human or otherwise, even close to the sites. He had to make sure word about the deaths didn't get out until it was absolutely necessary.

Frustrated, but having no other option except to tolerate her tagging along, Danyon had started their journey off with a brisk walk, then quickly cranked it up to a jog. Finally, he warned Shauna that he had to move faster, and if she planned to follow, she had to either keep up or be left behind. With that, he'd sped off in a full run.

They were already two miles into the run, and Shauna had kept pace with him every step of the way. Danyon couldn't help but be impressed by her stamina. She wasn't even breathing hard. Her reflexes remained sharp. If he cut hard to the right, she was immediately at his side. If he veered left without notice, she matched the move instantly and without effort.

Three quarters of a mile from the levees, Shauna suddenly pulled up short. "I hear a motor. Sounds like a car engine idling."

As though her words sharpened his own hearing, Danyon's ears suddenly perked to the sound. He glanced over at her, curious as to how she'd heard anything. They were still a decent distance from River Road. Close enough to hear a revving engine, maybe, but an idling one? No way.

"I'm sure it's Saville," Danyon said. "I sent Andrea to find him and have him bring back supplies and his SUV, so we can move the bodies."

Under normal circumstances, Danyon would have contacted the coroner about the deaths, then the coroner would have dispatched one of his assistants to make the pickup. But normal meant Simon and Nicole would have been in human form. The fact that they remained in were-state called for a different strategy.

They reached River Road before Danyon had a chance to ask how she'd heard the idling engine, so he tucked the question away for later. As he'd suspected, Andy's black SUV was parked on the side of the road facing the levee.

Andy got out of the SUV as soon as he spotted them. He was taller than Danyon and twice his weight and bulk. His skin was the color of slate, and his thick black hair was braided in multiple rows, each braid hanging down to the middle of his back.

"What you got, boss?" Andy asked.

"A nasty clean up," Danyon said. "And I need you to keep quiet about it."

"Zipped lip, boss, you know me." Andy looked over at Shauna, and Danyon saw from his expression that he thought her being there was a huge mistake. Although Danyon agreed, he had to respect the fact that she was their Keeper.

Andy gave her a short nod. "Ms. MacDonald."

Shauna returned the greeting. "Andy."

"Where's Andrea?" Danyon asked him.

"The kid was bad off. Really upset. So I told her to stay put, have a drink to calm herself down."

"Good call. Did you bring the tarps?"

"You know it. Andrea told me you said messy, and metal, too, so I brought wire cutters, a hacksaw, gloves, stuff like that. Oh, yeah, and flashlights." Andy leaned into the open driver's window of the SUV and pulled out two Maglites.

"Perfect." Danyon grabbed both, turned one of them on and aimed it at the thicket about three hundred feet away. "Get one of the tarps and meet us over there."

Andy nodded and headed for the back of the SUV.

"Ready or not," Danyon said to Shauna, then signaled for her to follow.

"Where's Paul?" she asked.

"He's supposed to be keeping watch over there."

When they got halfway to the thicket, Paul came running out of the shadows. "Man, am I glad to see—" He did a double take when he saw Shauna, looked back at Danyon. "I thought you didn't want us to tell nobody?"

Shauna jumped in before he had a chance to answer. "You know I'm the wolvens' Keeper, Paul," she said. "It's important that I be involved in this."

"Uh…okay."

Grateful that they didn't have to explain further, Danyon asked Paul, "Any problems?"

"Just that you took too long. Other than that, nothin'."

"Good." Danyon held a flashlight out to Paul. "Hang on to this. When we get back there, I'll need you to aim the light where I tell you. I want to—"

"When we get back where?" Paul asked, frowning.

"To Simon. I want to take a closer look at his body, make sure we're not missing any—"

"Whoa!" Paul jumped back as if the flashlight was ready to strike out and bite. "Why…why you gotta do that? They're gonna do all the examin' over at the morgue, right?"

"Not with Simon in that condition they're not," Danyon said. "We can't let anyone see him that way."

"But somebody's gonna start asking where Simon's at anyway," Paul said, pacing a short, two-step path. "Somebody's gotta eventually see him."

"Word will get out to the wolven soon enough, but nobody else needs to know right now. We take care of our own, remember? I'll make sure Simon's well taken care of, don't worry."

Paul whimpered and paced faster, almost spinning in

place. "Danyon, I—I know…I know we need to take care of him. I know we gotta, but I can't do it. I'm—I'm—I been sittin' here like you said. I been doin' good, so don't make me, okay? D-Don't make me hold the light. P-Please, I can't—don't make me hold the light."

"I'll do it," Shauna said. She held a hand out to Danyon. "I'll help with the flashlight and whatever else you need help with. Looks like Paul's been through enough today. Maybe he should go home."

"Yeah, like she said." Paul gave an enthusiastic nod. "I should go home. Like now, okay?"

"You really don't want to see this," Danyon said to Shauna. "Trust me, it's far from pleasant."

"If I wanted pleasant, you think I'd be here?" Her hand still extended, she wiggled her fingers. "I'm doing it, so you might as well hand over the light."

The determination on her face told Danyon any further discussion would be futile. He sighed, then signaled to Paul that it was okay for him to leave. The young were didn't have to be told twice. He was gone in a nanosecond, obviously scared Danyon might change his mind.

"You sure about this?" Danyon held a flashlight out to Shauna.

She took it from him. "Positive. Now where's Simon?"

He aimed his flashlight to the right. There was no missing the small arc of blood near the edge of the thicket. "There."

"Got the tarp, boss," Andy said, coming up behind them. "Where you want it?"

Danyon redirected the beam of light. "Stretch it out

on that patch of grass. We'll lay the body on it once we get it out of the thicket."

Andy paused mid-step, and Danyon could almost hear his thoughts.

Body? Thicket?

To the man's credit, Andy snapped back into action and did as he was told without saying another word.

When the tarp was in place, Danyon handed Shauna his flashlight. "Can you manage both? I need two hands to help pull him out."

She nodded, looking a little green around the gills.

"You okay?"

"Yes…fine."

Suspecting she had chosen bravery over telling the absolute truth, Danyon headed for the thicket.

"The body's under heavy brush, so we won't be able to lift it," he said to Andy. "We'll have to each take a leg and pull him out."

"Got it," Andy said.

Danyon squatted beside the arc of blood. "Here. Just reach in and grab hold." He didn't have to instruct Shauna on lighting. She already had both flashlights aimed perfectly.

Andy hurried to Danyon's side, dropped to his knees and reached into the thick brush.

Finding Simon's right ankle, Danyon wrapped both hands around it, glanced over at Andy. "Ready. You?"

A frown had settled over Andy's face. "Uh…yeah, but something don't feel right, boss."

"I know. Just pull on the count of three, okay?"

Andy nodded, then bit down on his bottom lip.

"One, two...three."

The body slid out a lot more easily than it had gone in. Once it was in full view, a beam of light settled over Simon's face, and Danyon heard Shauna gasp.

"Sweet mother of pearl," Andy said, breathing hard, his voice a hoarse whisper. He dropped Simon's leg and quickly scrubbed his hands on his jeans.

Suddenly blinded by light, Danyon threw the back of a hand over his eyes. "Hey, Shauna, light!"

"S-Sorry," she said, and corrected her aim. "I—I... God, he—" Her mouth snapped shut, and Danyon understood. Sometimes, when faced with something horrible, it seemed a little ridiculous to state the obvious.

"Let's move him onto the tarp," Danyon said to Andy. "You take his feet. I'll grab under his arms. Then we lift on go."

Stationing himself at Simon's head, Danyon locked his hands under Simon's arms, then he nodded and waited for Andy to grab both ankles before counting down and saying, "Go."

In less than a minute, they had Simon settled on the tarp. Shauna stepped closer but stood over to one side, so the flashlight beams weren't obstructed by Andy's head. Her eyes were wide, and she, too, was breathing hard.

"I don't get it, boss...I don't get it," Andy said. "How come he's still...?" He glanced over at Shauna, then back at Danyon. He lowered his voice. "How come he's still were?"

"You don't have to whisper, Andy. She sees him, too. She knew about it before she even got here."

Andy nodded as if he understood completely, but the furrows in his brow said differently.

"The fact that he's still were is what has to stay quiet," Danyon said to him. "It stays on the QT until we have a chance to figure out what happened and who's involved. Got it?"

"Yeah."

No matter how hard he'd tried to steel himself, seeing Simon's body again had kicked up a cloud of emotions in Danyon. He saw the same thing happening to Andy, so he cleared his throat to get the man's attention.

"Get the hacksaw and wire cutters, will you, Andy? Gloves, too."

When Andy left to get the supplies, Danyon looked over at Shauna. She was standing ramrod straight, arms out, flashlights swaying.

"Why him?" she asked quietly. "Why do you think they chose Simon? I mean, look at him. There's so much blood. I don't understand how anyone could do this."

"None of it makes sense."

"Damn straight it doesn't," Andy said, returning with a large duffle bag. He set the bag on the ground, opened it and pulled out a hacksaw. Without saying another word, he took the saw and went to work on the cable wrapped around Simon's ankle.

The sound of metal shrieking against metal made Danyon cringe. He dug through the duffle, found a package of latex gloves and two pairs of work gloves. He chose the latex, opened the package and slipped on a pair. Then he walked over, positioned himself near Simon's head and started working his fingers through the blood dried fur, feeling for other wounds.

The shriek of metal seemed to go on forever as Andy cut through layer after layer of thick cable. When he finally cut all the way through, he breathed a choice expletive and sat back on his haunches.

"What?" Danyon asked, getting to his feet. So far, save for the missing fangs and claws, he'd found no other wounds.

Andy pointed to Simon's ankles. "Look at that. Like the kid didn't go through enough."

Danyon signaled for Shauna to bring him one of the flashlights, then he knelt at Simon's feet and aimed the light where Andy had indicated. As he'd suspected, a thin, silver wire had been wound about Simon's ankles beneath the cable. Not enough silver to kill him, but enough to burn through fur, flesh and muscle before lodging into bone.

As he studied the damage, Danyon heard a deep guttural sound, felt its vibration, heard it change quickly to a low growl. And he knew all too well what it meant.

Anger over the injustice of what was laid out before him was getting to Andy. Without intervention, it would soon take over and force his transformation to were. Once that happened, the anger would turn into full blown rage, causing Andy to lash out at anything within clawing distance. Including Shauna.

"Steady, Andy," Danyon warned.

"Steady as she blows, boss."

"Sounded like you were getting a little itchy on me."

"Not itchy one bit."

"Good. You've got to keep a handle on it. I need you. And I need you with a cool, clear head."

"Oh, it's clear, boss," Andy said, his voice now raspy. It was already changing tenor. "It's clear I'm gonna kill the sonofabitch that did this to him."

"Uh…Danyon…?"

Danyon heard Shauna, but didn't dare turn toward her. Not only had Andy's voice changed, his forehead had begun to protrude, and his neck muscles were bulging. If he lost Andy's attention now, he knew he would have a seriously pissed-off were on his hands. And given Andy's size, he would probably have to kill him to stop him.

Danyon quickly stripped off the latex gloves, tossed them to the ground, then grabbed Andy by the forearms, forcing him to look into his eyes. Andy growled and snapped at him, incisors already twice the length of a human's.

Squeezing hard, Danyon dug his fingers into Andy's arms. "I—need—you—to—focus," he enunciated, his own voice low and hard. "Hold it together. I *command* it! Do you understand?"

Andy snarled, snapping at him again.

Pressing his fingers deeper into Andy's arms, Danyon let out a deep guttural growl. A warning that his own transformation was imminent. "Do you *under-stand* me?"

Evidently recognizing the voice of his alpha, Andy's eyes suddenly cleared, and his incisors withdrew. He immediately lowered his head.

"I want you to go and sit in the SUV," Danyon commanded. "Wait for me there. When I'm finished looking over the body, I'll wrap it in the tarp, then you'll help me load it into the SUV. Until then, you're to stay in the driver's seat until I call for you. Is that clear?"

Andy gave one quick nod, then quietly hurried away as ordered.

Danyon breathed a silent sigh of relief. He hadn't feared Andy's transformation for himself. He'd feared it for Shauna. As angry as Andy had become, there might have been no controlling who or what he attacked. Chances were good that he would have taken on the feral madness of a vengeful wolven, its mind lost to understanding anything but destruction.

Danyon turned to Shauna, saw an expression on her face he couldn't quite define.

Fear? Awe? Possibly both.

"That's just another reason why you should have stayed away," he said. "You're lucky. No telling what might have happened if I hadn't stopped his transformation."

She looked at him steadily. "I'm his Keeper," she said calmly. "He wouldn't have harmed me."

He looked at her standing there—tall, slender, delicate wrists and arms, long, beautiful neck—and knew Andy would have snapped her like a twig. Danyon might have laughed at the absurdity of her statement had it not been for the way she said it. Not haughty, like someone acting too big for her britches. It sounded confident, like the voice of experience. That puzzled him. When had she ever been up against a raging were? He shook off the question. Now wasn't the time to contemplate the matter. He had more serious issues to contend with.

He headed back to Simon's body. "I'll need more light over here."

Shauna hurried over, directed the flashlights as he indicated. As light flooded over Simon's body, she let out another, smaller gasp.

Danyon chose to ignore it. No time for emotional females. It was already late, and they still had Nicole to see to. He scrounged through the duffle bag again, and grabbed wire cutters and a pair of pliers. He snipped the silver wire wrapped around Simon's ankles with the cutters, then, using the pliers, he carefully wiggled the wire free from the trench it had formed in the bone.

With that task complete, Danyon reached for the hacksaw and went to work on the remaining cables, the ones wrapped around Simon's neck and chest.

It was a long and tedious process, sawing at awkward angles, blade slipping again and again until he managed to cut a thin rut in the cable. Sweat ran into his eyes, soaked the back of his shirt.

By the time Danyon had removed the cables and the additional silver wire he'd found beneath them, two hours had vanished. It dawned on him, too, that throughout that entire time, Shauna had not said one word.

He looked up to check on her and was surprised to find her sitting back on her haunches beside him.

She handed him a pair of latex gloves. "Thought you might be ready for these."

He studied her face, saw no trace of fear. Only profound sadness.

"Thanks," he said, and took the gloves from her. After slipping them on, he sank his fingers into the fur on Simon's right leg, then worked them slowly upward, feeling for wounds.

"I don't think this was done by a human," Shauna said.

"I agree." He kept his fingers moving. "The minute that silver touched him, he would've mutated instantly from the pain, then slaughtered anyone in sight. And if by chance he was in were-state *before* they used the silver...they never would have gotten close enough to wrap it around any part of his body."

"What about a group of humans?"

Danyon shook his head. "Not even an army of three-hundred-pound men. Once a wolven is at full power, even a young one like Simon, all they have to do is backhand a man, and the strength of that blow would crush his face. One swipe from his claws, and the man's chest is ripped open, his heart pierced. And even if it had been a hundred men, all attacking at the same time, Simon wasn't stupid. At the first hint he was being overpowered, he would have fled, and a wolven's too fast and agile for any human to catch him."

"What about shifters, then?"

"I don't think so."

"But if shifters mentally paired with a wolven, then became wolven themselves, couldn't they have overpowered Simon? Or—"

"Not the shifters from here. They can transform into any being through molecular mapping, but only in appearance. They wouldn't possess the full power of a wolven. Maybe three quarters at best."

"What if they morphed into something bigger than a wolven? Wouldn't size alone give them power?"

"Maybe, but in order for them to transform into anything, they have to see it, mentally map it." Danyon arched a brow. "Have you ever seen anything in New Orleans—hell, in the entire state of Louisiana, that was bigger than a full grown wolven?"

Shauna pursed her lips and shook her head.

"Me either. That's why I think the scenerio's doubtful."

"Okay...vampires? I don't think one could've done it alone. But two or three might have, if they glamoured Simon before he turned were, then restrained him with silver and cable and lifted the glamour. You said Simon would have morphed from the pain caused by the silver, right? Well, once he turned were, all they had to do was... what was done to him."

Through with the examination, Danyon stripped off the gloves and tossed them onto the tarp. He'd found no other wounds that might have caused Simon's death. He could only assume it was as August had said—Simon's heart had burst. Unfortunately, an autopsy couldn't be performed to confirm it. Not with Simon still in were-state.

"What do you think?" Shauna asked.

Danyon got to his feet and began gathering tools. "It's possible, but I don't think it's probable. Nicole and Simon were found during the day and judging by the condition of their bodies, they'd probably only been dead about four or five hours. That means the murders took place during the day, as well. The local vampires can move about in daylight, but they're considerably weaker than they are at night." He shook his head slowly. "I don't know what the answer is, Shauna. I just don't know."

"Well, if it wasn't humans, shape-shifters or vampires, that leaves us with…other weres. Other wolven."

He looked away.

"Is that possible?" she pressed.

Danyon glanced over at Simon's body. He didn't want to entertain the idea that the murderer was a wolven. Of course wolven fought, sometimes to the death, but they didn't purposely torture their own.

"Danyon, I think we need to get the leaders from the other races involved in this—"

"No."

Shauna got to her feet. "Isn't it better to swallow a little pride than lose more weres?"

"It's not about pride," he said angrily. "We can't afford to have the three biggest subcultures in New Orleans pointing fingers at one another again. It's like you said earlier about the cemetery murders and the walk-ins. You were right. Every group blamed every other group. Even though both cases have been solved, that wire between all three groups is still taut. Getting the other leaders involved would mean their people would find out, and you know it. Fingers would start pointing again, only this time, that wire might very well snap."

"I don't think—"

Danyon held up a hand. "Look, I know two heads are better than one, three better than two, yada, yada, yada. But Simon and Nicole were my responsibility. They died on my watch. I *have* to find their murderer."

"And *all* the weres—including the wolven—are my responsibility. We have to do what's right for the entire community."

Danyon knew she was right, but there was something in him that simply refused to admit it at that moment. Call it pride, determination, the word didn't matter. Nicole and Simon shouldn't have died. He should have been there to protect them. He *needed* to find who—or what—had murdered them.

"Twelve hours," he said. "At least give me that. If I don't come up with something by then, we'll call in the others, okay?"

Shauna studied him for a long while, then said, "All right. Twelve hours." With that, she turned and headed toward the SUV.

Danyon watched her walk away, suspecting she feared

she'd made a mistake in allowing him the time he'd asked for.

He understood.

Because in that moment, he feared the exact same thing.

Chapter 7

Lightning ripped a jagged tear through the night sky, and the thunderclap that followed shook the ground beneath Shauna's feet. She felt the first few spatters of rain on her head, her shoulders. Fat, wet drops that promised many more.

Shauna glanced up at the sky, wishing for it to burst open and wash her, bath her in luxurious warmth and take away the spatters of blood on her clothes, the dirt on her hands, the emotional weight on her heart.

She'd never felt more exhausted in her life. It wasn't that she'd tackled anything physically laborious, but being so close to Simon and Nicole while Danyon examined them, watching as his fingers worked through bloody fur, had taken a greater toll on her than she'd thought.

The entire time she'd held the flashlight, Shauna wondered why both weres had to suffer such horrible deaths. She thought of their families and the pain and sorrow awaiting them. So many whys, too many questions. Who was she supposed to go to for answers? How could anyone explain the unfairness of the universe when it presented life this way?

Some questions in life simply had no answers; that much Shauna knew. But to her, not having answers to such grievous questions was almost as unbearable as the situation that prompted them in the first place.

Once Simon had been loaded into the SUV, she'd helped Danyon clear the area of bloody clothes, anything that might cause a passerby to take notice and call the police. Shauna had thought that after helping with Simon, she'd built up enough emotional stamina to handle Nicole.

She'd been wrong.

Although Nicole had died in the same manner as Simon and had also remained in were-state, there was something in her eyes that looked all too human. Shock—terror—innocence lost forever. That look had literally dropped Shauna to her knees. She'd openly wept while Danyon examined the young were. It was incomprehensible how anyone could kill something so fragile. To make matters worse, Nicole's body had been hidden away in an alley behind wooden crates, since there was no brush anywhere near the pilings. Seeing her slumped in a heap in that alley, like so much garbage, made the emotional stress ten times worse.

The only thing that had comforted Shauna that night was seeing how gently and respectfully Danyon had cared for both weres. His large, powerful hands had moved so gently over their bodies. Nicole had been small enough for him to lift on his own, so Danyon had carried her to the back of the SUV, cradling her in his arms like a child.

Danyon had Andy remain in the truck while they'd tended to Nicole, refusing to let Andy even see her. That had been a wise decision. As angry as Andy had gotten when he saw Simon, had he seen Nicole, Shauna feared he would have been beyond even Danyon's control. She was confident that August would know how to handle Andy once he arrived at the lake house and had to unload the bodies.

Now, the only evidence that remained to prove Nicole had even been in the alley or between the pilings were bloodstains. If the rain didn't wash them away, time would.

Another zipper of lightning raced across the sky.

"There's nothing more we can do here," Danyon said. "We should go before the storm really lets loose."

Shauna hadn't thought about how she'd get home once this was over. A cab made the most sense, but they were scarce in this area, even at midday, and non-existent in the wee hours of morning, which it now was. Barataria was a good distance from the Quarter, but walking there was not an option. Just the thought of trudging across a street right now made Shauna want to collapse. She could barely put one foot in front of the other as it was.

"My place isn't that far from here," Danyon said. "Much closer than yours. You're welcome to hang out there until the storm passes. Maybe grab a shower, have something to eat while you wait."

Although she'd give anything for a hot shower and a cheeseburger right now, Shauna didn't think it would be a good idea for her to go to Danyon's. Being alone with him sounded too tempting. She wanted to say no. The rain, her exhaustion, the distance between here and her home, the convenient closeness of his place—all of it felt like one big cliché. Like the guy whose car just happens to run out of gas on a deserted road on the first date.

Still, when he'd invited her, she'd felt something tug at her core, urging her to go. She *needed* to say no, had to resist—wanted to maintain control—but found herself nodding yes, instead. Albeit reluctantly.

Food and a shower, nothing wrong with that, right? She could do both, then head home as soon as the storm let up. Easy-peasy, chillin' cheesy.

Shauna repeated the name of those two food groups as she followed him home.

They walked for what felt like hours. Long enough for her mind to go numb and her body even more numb. Every once in a while, as they walked, Shauna found herself leaning against Danyon without meaning to. The moment their bodies touched, however, she'd quickly straighten, determined to keep a respectable distance between them.

It didn't take long for the sky to release its payload, drenching them in wet, warm sheets. Still, they walked, casually, purposely taking their time, as though the night were dry and cool.

Before Shauna knew it, they were at the corner of Burgundy and Ursulines and standing under an awning at the back entrance to La Maison Pierre. She was familiar with the old, five-storey hotel, having gone past it a few times on her morning runs.

Danyon tapped a code into the lock-pad near the door.

"You live in this hotel?" she asked.

"I own it." He pushed the door open.

Shauna arched a brow. *La Maison Pierre—The Stone House. Interesting...*

They took a private elevator up to the fifth floor. There, Danyon led her down a short hallway to a massive, ornate wooden door, where he tapped yet another code into another lock-pad.

He opened the door and motioned Shauna inside. "Make yourself at home."

Everything about the spacious, multi-room penthouse spoke of luxury. Twelve-foot ceilings with double crown molding, plush designer rugs over wide-planked wood floors, antiques from the Louis XIV era, a huge fireplace with a fluted mantel, and paintings that looked like works by Rembrandt and Van Gogh.

"You live here alone?" Shauna asked.

"Yes. Well, unless you count Raul. He checks in a few times a day to make sure I haven't turned the place into a total pigsty."

"Raul?"

"He's head of housekeeping here at the hotel."

Danyon led her down another hallway to a large bathroom with gray and white marble floors. It had a granite double-sink vanity and shower stall, and a whirlpool tub that was big enough for six. Plush, white towels hung from a wide, wooden towel rack.

"Feel free to freshen up, shower, whatever you need. There are a couple of clean bathrobes in the linen closet behind the door."

"Bathrobes, huh? You must do quite a bit of entertaining."

"You'd be surprised how little." He smiled. "If you decide to shower, you can toss your clothes out in the hall, and I'll make sure they're cleaned before you leave. When you're done, just head back the way we came, only turn right at the archway instead of left. That'll lead you to the kitchen. I'll whip up something for us to eat after I grab a quick shower."

At the mention of food, Shauna's stomach grumbled to life. She couldn't remember the last time she'd eaten. "Sounds good," she said, suddenly feeling self-conscious. She must have looked like a troll.

With a smile and a nod, Danyon backed out of the bathroom, closing the door behind him.

Shauna locked the door, then leaned against it for a few seconds and closed her eyes. Thunder rumbled in the distance. Despite the deluge they had walked through moments ago, it sounded like the storm was only getting started.

Gathering up what little energy she had, Shauna

opened her eyes, pushed away from the door and went to the vanity. She gasped when she saw her reflection in the mirror. She was beyond filthy. Her T-shirt, once blue, now looked like a bad Pollock imitation—wet, dirt smudged, and dotted with blood spatter. Her jeans were worse than her shirt. Her face, neck and arms were dirt and mud-smeared, and it looked like she'd been digging ditches with her fingernails. Seeing the filth made Nicole and Simon's faces zoom up close in her mind's eye.

She couldn't get into the shower fast enough.

Once under the hot spray, Shauna tried not to think of anything, just feel the warmth of the water flowing over her, listen to the hiss of the spray. She had no idea how long she stayed in the shower, but by the time she got out, her fingers and toes were pruned.

After drying off and combing her hair out with her fingers, she wrapped herself in one of the thick, terry cloth robes she found in the linen closet, then headed out of the bathroom in search of the kitchen.

Shauna felt a little weird trekking around Danyon's penthouse barefoot and naked beneath the robe. But better that, she figured, than stinking up the place with the dirt and grime that had covered her earlier.

She found the kitchen a few minutes later and saw Danyon standing over a stainless steel stove, stirring a pot of marinara sauce. He wore jeans, a white unbuttoned button-down and was barefoot, as well.

"Pasta and sauce okay?" he asked. When he turned toward her, his smile faltered. His eyes traveled quickly over her body, settled on her face—consumed her soul.

With her heart thundering in her chest, Shauna cleared her throat. "Uh, sounds good. Anything I can do to help?"

"You can grab a couple of plates for us if you don't mind." He aimed his chin at an upper cabinet to his left. "They're up there."

Shauna went over to the cabinet, opened it, and saw that the plates were on the uppermost shelf. She reached up and found herself inches short of the goal, which made her laugh. At five foot eight, people usually asked *her* to retrieve things from high shelves.

"Ah, sorry. I keep forgetting that the rest of the population isn't six-five." Grinning, Danyon turned the burners off on the stove and walked over to her. "Let me help you with that."

Standing behind her now, Danyon reached up and over her head and plucked two plates off the shelf. Then he froze, plates still in midair.

Shauna felt like those plates, locked and hovering in space. She couldn't have moved even if she'd wanted to. Although Danyon hadn't pressed against her, hadn't even touched her, she still felt heat from his body radiating through the bathrobe and onto her back. It soaked into her skin, vibrated, stole her breath. Whatever resonated between them was so strong, it blocked off the rest of the world. Shauna heard nothing but his breathing. She saw nothing—felt everything. Her body suddenly ached with a need that transcended the physical, a need that encompassed her entire being. She feared even twitching lest he misread it and back away.

Danyon slowly lowered the plates and placed them on the counter just below the cabinet. As he did, Shauna felt his breath on her right cheek, and her body reacted immediately, nipples hardening, arms trembling.

"Shauna…" His voice was huskier now, deeper.

She heard him, but more than his voice. All of him seemed to call to her—and it felt primal.

Shauna turned to face him, and in less than a second, her lips were pressed against his.

Danyon wrapped his arms around her, pulled her in close. Their kisses grew ravenous immediately, tongues probing, deeper, deeper, both craving more. His fingers traveled lightly along the nape of her neck, and Shauna moaned.

In response, Danyon's hand moved slowly down to her shoulder, his thumb latching on to the edge of the bathrobe near her collarbone and lowering it. Then his fingers trailed lower—lower still. By the time his fingertips reached the swell of her breast, the world had become a swirling kaleidoscope, and he was its fulcrum. He brushed the top of her left breast, then, keeping his touch feather-light, he moved toward her nipple. Stopping just short of the hardened nub, he circled it slowly with a finger, again and again, each time his fingers moving ever closer to her nipple, yet not…quite…touching it.

Shauna gasped with desire, wanting to scream, *Now! Now!* And just when the ache in her body became so excruciating she thought she could bear no more, Danyon suddenly lifted her up and sat her gently on the counter.

He looked into her eyes, looked into *her*—and she was lost.

Neither said a word.

None were needed.

Nothing spoke louder than this.

Danyon kissed her long and deep, then lowered his mouth to her breast. Shauna cried out, dug her fingers into his shoulders and pulled him closer. She felt frantic, alive, the need inside her mounting to the point of desperation. His hands moved deftly, slipping the bathrobe off her shoulders, then cupping both her breasts. Her nipples strained against his palms, and he moaned, lifted his head, kissed her lips, her neck.

Shauna gasped, wrapped her hands behind his head, tangled her fingers in his hair. Part of her wanted to push away, to stay in control. But the other part of her, the one wrapped in his arms and melting under his touch, refused to listen.

He stepped into her, parting her legs with his body. She opened her mouth to protest, to moan, and his tongue was inside her mouth, teasing, plunging. His hands slipped between her legs, and his thumb began to stroke her, circling the small mound that turned her body into liquid fire. She arched her back, and he groaned, breathed her name, then his fingers pressed into her hot wetness. Her breath came short and fast. She moved in rhythm with his fingers.

The heat she'd felt emanating from him only moments ago, now felt like a furnace at full power. Combined with the heat from her own desire, she felt as if she were burning from the inside out.

Then with one sure thrust of his fingers and swirl of his thumb, the orgasm that had been coiling inside her, taut, tight, like an over-wound spring, suddenly let go, and Shauna cried out from the force of it. She felt herself contract around his fingers, her wetness drenching them. He groaned her name, and she let out a guttural moan, sounds she'd never heard herself make before. Danyon growled with desire, and before Shauna knew it, he scooped her into his arms and carried her out of the kitchen.

As he walked, he kissed her lips, her eyes, her forehead. She wrapped her arms around his neck, clung to him. The only space and time and matter that existed were right here, right now, and him. She no longer had any desire to maintain control. In fact, she wanted to lose what little she had left. Lose it to him, fall into him with complete abandon.

Within minutes, Danyon was lowering her down on a royal blue comforter atop a huge four-poster bed. She sank into it, her mind and body still wrapped in heat and desire. His lips never left her as he removed his shirt. Then he stood and stripped off his pants.

He was huge, the length of him fully engorged. His abdomen was taut and cut, the muscles in his chest, his arms, and his thighs massive and highly defined. Shauna saw them ripple, noticed that his eyes had gone from honey-colored to intense brown. Something told her he was riding the edge of transformation. Instead of frightening her, it excited her all the more. It caused the heat and need inside her to explode into a roaring inferno.

He leaned over her, placing a hand on either side of her shoulders. He pushed her thighs apart with one knee. His eyes never left hers.

"You're so beautiful," he whispered. "So beautiful." His voice sounded nothing like Danyon. It was raw, almost feral—and it rang familiar to her ear.

The length of him brushed up against her sex, teased her swollen mound, stroked the cleft of her. She strained toward him, arching her back. "Yes, yesss." Then her words were replaced by sounds animalistic in nature, mirroring the power and fierceness of the need inside her. The need to control returned once more, only this time she wanted to control his movements, to grab him, force him deeper inside her.

He inched forward rubbing against her, steel against satin. The ridge of him entered her, drove her mad, to the point of incomprehension.

She moaned, urging him inside her, digging her fingernails into his shoulders, raking them across his back. She felt the muscles beneath her hands undulate all the more.

"Yesss," she growled.

And he thrust forward, plunging the length of him into her swollen well of heat. She cried out, pulled him in closer, bit into his shoulder. He thrust deeper, harder, in—out—in. She was filled to overflowing, consumed with the pleasure of the hugeness inside her, the weight of him on top of her.

This time her orgasm felt like a tsunami, and she screamed with its release. She heard him growl, then he plunged into her again, and his body became one undulating mass of taut muscle. She heard his howl of release, and her mind settled into a gentle, swirling fog.

The next thing she knew, Danyon was stretched out beside her, and she lay in the crook of his arm, naked flesh to naked flesh. He smoothed her hair with a hand and whispered her name.

Then he drew her in even closer and it felt like home.

Chapter 8

It was seven the next morning before Shauna reached home. Danyon hadn't wanted her to go, but she'd already begged off half a day's work the day before and didn't want to leave her sisters in a bind, especially with them bringing in a new load of inventory. If given her druthers, though, she would still be with Danyon, snuggled against him under a thick, down comforter. She'd be there now, tonight, tomorrow...

Shauna smiled to herself, remembering how Danyon had teased her this morning after she'd discovered her clothes on a small table in the hall near the bathroom. They had been cleaned, folded, and neatly stacked. Even her sneakers looked like new. She'd asked Danyon how they had gotten there, and when he told her that Raul had taken care of her clothes as he had asked him to, she'd hid under the comforter, embarrassed. What time had Raul dropped off her clothes? And what had he heard? Last night she'd experienced the best sex she'd ever had in her life, and she knew she'd not exactly been—quiet during that experience.

First the embarrassment of Raul possibly hearing more than he should have, and now having to face her sisters. She wasn't one to stay out all night, so she already knew Fiona would bombard her with questions, and Caitlin would probably tease her to no end.

Shauna sighed, preparing herself for the inevitable. She stood near the gate that led to the main entry of the center building they called home. It was surrounded by a ten-foot brick wall, and the gate opened up to a path that led past a small garden to the front door.

Inside, the foyer offered two hallways, one to the left, the second to the right. The grand staircase in the middle of those hallways extended to the second floor. From her perspective, the house was basically three large apartments joined together by a common living area. The commons had a huge dining room that also served as a ballroom, and a large kitchen in the center. As for the apartments, Fiona lived in the east wing, Caitlin in the west, and Shauna in the middle. Each had kitchenettes, bathrooms, bedrooms and a sitting area. Sometimes Shauna felt like she had to go through an entire subdivision just to get to her place. There was no sneaking in—ever. Whether she liked it or not, it was time to face the music.

As she suspected, Fiona and Caitlin were in the main

kitchen. Fiona was at the stove scrambling eggs in one skillet, while flipping ham slices in another. Caitlin stood at the island counter slicing kiwi and fresh strawberries. Both looked up when she walked in.

"Well, well," Caitlin said. "Our little night bird is back." Her silver eyes twinkled with mischief.

"I thought you were sleeping," Fiona said. "You've been out all night?"

"Can't you tell by her eyes?" Caitlin said, grinning. "They're redder than Dorothy's ruby slippers."

"They are not," Shauna said, marching past her. "Any coffee left?"

Fiona hitched a thumb toward a side counter. "I just filled the carafe."

As Shauna poured herself a cup of coffee, she felt her sisters' eyes boring into her back.

"So," Fiona finally said, "did you have a fun evening?"

Caitlin chuckled.

Shauna took a couple sips of coffee, then turned to them and leaned her back against the counter. "Okay, what's so funny?" she asked Caitlin.

Caitlin held up a hand, feigning innocence. "What?" The Cheshire cat grin on her face widened.

"I heard you snicker. I'm just curious as to what's so funny."

"Hey, I don't snicker," Caitlin said, then snickered.

"Come on, spill it already."

"Well, it's kind of obvious that you *did* have fun last night," Caitlin said.

"Huh?" Shauna quickly checked her shirt and jeans. Both were unwrinkled and clean; the same as when she had put them on earlier.

"Not your clothes, silly." Caitlin laughed. "Your face."

"Cait, stop picking on her," Fiona said. Her lips twitched as she struggled to hold back a grin.

"What's wrong with my face?" Shauna asked. She turned and leaned over to see her reflection in the toaster. Besides the dark rings under her eyes from too little sleep, she looked the same as she always did.

"Not *on* your face, *in* your face."

Shauna blew out an exasperated breath. "That makes no sense. What the heck are you talking about?"

"You've got the glow bug."

"All right, you two." Fiona carried a platter of scrambled eggs and pan-seared ham to the kitchen table. "Eat up. We need to get to the shop early today. Jagger and Ryder are already over there unloading the merchandise we picked up at Keeno's yesterday. Everything needs to be priced and shelved."

Still grinning, Caitlin carried the bowl of sliced fruit to the table.

Shauna followed, coffee cup in hand. "Okay, I know I'm going to be sorry for asking this but…what the heck is a glow bug?"

Fiona pointed to the table. "Sit—eat—both of you. Caitlin, stop teasing her or we'll never get through breakfast."

"But I want to know what she means by 'glow bug,'" Shauna said, taking her place at the table.

"What it means, little sister," Caitlin said, while spooning fruit onto her plate, "is that…" She paused, took a bite of strawberry and chewed it—slowly.

Shauna tsked. "Aw, c'mon!"

Caitlin took her time swallowing. "Come on, what?"

"Finish what you were saying."

Fiona shook her head. "For heaven's sake, you two, give it a rest."

"Okay, okay." Caitlin rested an elbow on the table and aimed her fork at Shauna. "It means you found a Mr. Wonderful. You know, a man who finally turned all your lights on, flipped all your switches, banged all your buttons."

Embarrassed, Shauna tsked again and quickly spooned eggs onto her own plate.

"So, did you?" Caitlin asked.

Shauna ignored her.

"Hey, it's nothing to be embarrassed about. Ryder definitely turns all my lights on, and there's no question that Jagger does it for Fiona. You've seen her when he's around. Especially after he spends the night."

"Caitlin!" Fiona said, blushing.

"Well, it's true."

Jagger DeFarge was a vampire and a homicide detective for NOPD's eighth precinct. He was also Fiona's fiancé. Ryder was Caitlin's groom-to-be. He was a shifter and a bounty hunter and had played a significant part in stopping the walk-ins before they destroyed the city and everyone in it. Shauna liked both men. They were strong, yet kind, good-looking, but not vain. What she liked most about them, though, was that Jagger and Ryder took good care of her sisters, and it was obvious that they truly loved them.

Caitlin might have been teasing, but she was right about Fiona. Every time Jagger came around, it looked as if someone had turned a thousand-watt bulb on inside her. Whenever he stayed the night, the following morning, Fiona would float into the kitchen either singing, humming, or whistling. A nuclear bomb could have gone off next door, and Fiona would have sworn on everything sacred that all was right with the world. When Caitlin and Ryder spent time together, Caitlin had the same case of happys, but her afterglow had a different attitude than Fiona's. It was mellower. More, *"Yeah, I know all isn't right with the world, but who cares?"*

Still embarrassed about how easily they'd fingered her, Shauna moved eggs around on her plate with a fork. "You two act like I've never had a boyfriend. I'm not a kid anymore you know."

"Oh, honey, we know that," Fiona said. "But you have to admit, it has been a while since you've…well, since you've kept company."

"A while?" Caitlin laughed. "Try like two years."

Shauna shot her a look. "It has *not* been two years." She quickly turned back to her eggs, suspecting Caitlin was right again. It *had* been a while. The last guy she dated had been Jay Beranger, a furniture store owner from Metairie. He had been nice enough, well spoken, decent looking, but just like the other guys she'd been with—and there had been painfully few—something was missing. When Jay had tried to push the relationship forward by proclaiming his undying love and proposing, Shauna broke up with him. She knew she would never marry him, so it didn't make sense to her to keep leading him on, letting him think the possibility of marriage existed.

By other women's standards, Shauna figured she'd probably be considered overly picky, and then reminded herself that the 'perfect' man only existed in romance novels. But she'd never looked for perfection. Just someone who *got* her. A man who knew where every switch inside her was located.

"What's his name?" Fiona asked.

Stalling, Shauna took another sip of coffee. Then another.

"Yes, who is this Mr. Wonderful?" Caitlin asked, her expression one of an eager sponge.

"His name is Danyon Stone."

"Oh, yes," Fiona said, her eyes brightening with recognition. "I've met Danyon a couple times at the council meetings. Very handsome. And if I remember correctly, he's alpha of the East Bank."

"You mean he's a were?" Caitlin asked.

Shauna frowned. "Yeah, he's wolven, so what?"

"Oh, I didn't mean that in a bad way," Caitlin said,

eyes twinkling. "It just makes you an official member of the taboo crew, that's all."

"Huh?"

Caitlin turned to Fiona. "You know, if we're not careful, the title Keeper is going to take on a whole new meaning in this city."

This time Fiona laughed.

"All right, you guys, stop already." Shauna dropped her fork onto her plate. "What am I missing here?"

"Don't get mad," Caitlin said. "I'm only teasing. See, Fiona is the Keeper of the vampires, and Jagger is a vampire. I'm Keeper of the shifters, and Ryder is a shifter. You're the Keeper of the weres, and this Danyon Stone, alpha wolven of the East Bank, is definitely were. We Keepers are certainly keeping our own, don't you think?"

Shauna shrugged, sipped more coffee. She wasn't sure how to respond.

Keeper of the weres? Yep, right here.

Keeper of Danyon, the man? She doubted any woman had ever kept him and doubted one ever could.

"A wolven, huh?" Caitlin said. "Sister, if those dark circles under your eyes are any indication, Mr. Stone must be packing—"

"Caitlin!" Fiona swatted a hand at her. "Don't be so uncouth."

"Okay, look." Shauna set her cup down on the table a little too hard, and coffee sloshed over the brim. "Y'all want it straight? Last night wasn't all about staying over at Danyon's. He's really great at…you know, that other part—"

"I knew it!" Caitlin clapped.

Fiona jabbed her lightly in the side with an elbow. "Stop. Let her talk." She turned to Shauna. "Go on, honey."

Shauna looked from Fiona to Caitlin. Breakfast had been forgotten. Both stared at her intently, obviously eager to hear what she had to say.

"So it wasn't all about sleeping with Danyon and…?" Caitlin said impatiently.

"Did you go dancing?" Fiona prompted. "To the movies? What—"

"We moved dead bodies," Shauna said abruptly.

Fiona's mouth fell open.

Caitlin's fork clattered to her plate. "What?"

"Did you say *dead* bodies?" Fiona's face turned ashen. She set her fork down beside her plate, nice and proper, as if preparing herself and everything around her for the worst.

"Uh…yeah."

Fiona and Caitlin glanced at each other, disbelief etched on their faces.

"Well…go on," Fiona said hesitantly.

Shauna told her sisters about Nicole and Simon, about how they had been found, and how she'd held the flashlights while Danyon examined the bodies.

"My God," Fiona said. "Why didn't you come home and tell us right away?"

"You weren't here," Shauna said. "You had taken off for Lake Charles, remember? Keeno's?"

"Does August know about this?" Caitlin asked.

"Of course he does. He wanted the bodies moved to his lake house in LaPlace so he could see Nicole and Simon for himself. He wanted them laid out somewhere decent when the families arrived. Not in the back of an SUV."

"Why didn't Danyon call the police?" Fiona asked. "I know how the clans feel about taking care of their own, but two murders? He should have called someone."

"I agree," Caitlin said. "The bodies shouldn't have been moved. Crucial evidence might have been destroyed."

"I said the same thing to Danyon when I first heard about it," Shauna said.

"He could have called Jagger," Fiona said. "He's underworld. He'd have understood the delicacy of the situation."

"It was more delicate than you think," Shauna said. "Nicole and Simon were still in were-state. Danyon didn't want to take any chances on someone seeing them that way."

"Whoa." Fiona suddenly held up both hands and squinted as if she'd just faced the most horrific sight of her life. "You mean to tell me that two weres were murdered, and you were out in the middle of nowhere with nothing but a flashlight?"

Caitlin looked at Fiona with a puzzled expression. "You're just catching that now?"

"It just hit me now! Good Lord, Shauna, do you realize how much danger you put yourself in?"

"I was with Danyon," Shauna said.

"So? Even if Danyon had the strength of ten weres, what good would it have done if the perpetrator turned out to be a gang of thirty or forty? What would you have done? Run away while Danyon fought them all off? You could have been chased down, captured, and killed for heaven's sake! Danyon should never have allowed you to be there."

"Allowed? He's not my father, and I insisted. My God, you're letting all these wild scenarios get stuck in your head—gangs—captured—it's a wonder why I'm not kept chained to a bed for safekeeping. Fi, look, I know you worry because you love me and don't want to see me hurt, but I'm not a baby anymore. Both of you have to remember that I'm a Keeper, too. Keeper of the weres, and I'm responsible for their well-being. If either of you had found out that two from your community had been murdered, would you have just sat back and done nothing? Wouldn't you have wanted details? Been on the scene so you'd at least know firsthand what you were really dealing with?"

After a long pause, Caitlin shrugged, then nodded. "No question, I would've been in the middle of it."

"Don't make this any harder than it is," Fiona said.

"But she's right, Fiona. You know you would've done the same thing."

"Yes, well…"

"Yes well nothing," Caitlin said. "You'd have been there. Go on, admit it."

"All right, all right. But that doesn't mean I have to like what she did. And it doesn't mean I won't worry," Fiona said. "We're all the blood family we have left. I worry about both of you."

"I know," Shauna said. "But I think you toss a little extra my way because I'm the youngest. And that's not really fair. I do appreciate your love and concern, and I feel the same about the two of you, too, but I'm not a kid anymore. I'm almost twenty-seven."

Fiona offered her a smile. "I know. I'll try to do better. Promise."

Caitlin pushed away from the table. "We need some kind of strategy to tackle these wolven murders, ladies. I think the leaders of the other underworld groups need to know about them and—" A frown suddenly settled over her face. "Wait a minute…Shauna; you said Nicole and Simon were found in *were-state?* Weres always revert to human form when they die. Why didn't Nicole and Simon?"

"Good question," Fiona said.

Although August had told Shauna and Danyon to keep the information about the metaphysical powers inherent to were claws and fangs under wraps, she wasn't certain if that applied to her sisters. She was pretty sure if Fiona and Caitlin had been in the meeting with August, he would have revealed the details to them, as well.

Still, to be on the safe side, Shauna said, "August has

some ideas about that, but he's not one hundred percent sure. He's looking into it."

Caitlin's eyes narrowed, an indicator that she thought the answer smelled a little fishy.

"Regardless, we have to let the leaders of the other groups know," Fiona said.

"No," Shauna said. "Not just yet."

"Why not?" Caitlin asked.

"The more people who know, the more opportunity there is for word to spread, and that might send the murderer into hiding before we figure out who it is," Shauna explained.

"What are we supposed to do, then? We can't just wait around for another murder to happen," Caitlin said.

"That's true," Fiona said. "But it's a double-edged sword. I understand what Shauna is saying, yet at the same time, if word leaks out, and the leaders of the other groups weren't forewarned, we could very well wind up with another showdown. Just like we did with the cemetery murders and the walk-ins. It's a toss up—tell them, don't tell them. Either way, we have a huge problem here."

"I know," Shauna said. "But I'm asking the two of you to trust me and respect my role as Keeper of the weres. All I want is a little time before we get the others involved."

Fiona and Caitlin studied her for some time, and in the silence, Shauna felt a vibration flowing between the three of them. She knew her sisters would respect her space and her place as Keeper. She also knew that they fully understood the severity of the situation. Everyone who knew about the wolven murders so far feared the same thing—the possibility of another great war.

Now that Fiona and Caitlin knew about the crimes, Shauna sensed that the expectation bar in her role as Keeper had just risen exponentially. That bar now looked higher than the Himalayas, and Shauna felt about as prepared to take on that height as a climber with two broken arms.

Chapter 9

Every time Danyon crossed over to New Orleans' West Bank, he not only felt like he'd left New Orleans, but that he'd exited the entire state of Louisiana. There was a different feel to the area and the towns that mapped it. Places like Algiers, Gretna, and Harvey. On the East Bank, where the Quarter was located, there was a sense of continuity. Towns such as Kenner and Metairie *felt* like New Orleans. They were only different parts that made up a whole. Having just driven through Gretna, Danyon didn't get the sense that it was tied to anything other than itself.

It wasn't unusual for an alpha to cross into other territories, but it didn't happen often. Some alphas didn't understand the meaning of borders. They were hardwired to believe that whatever ground their feet touched was up for grabs territorially. To limit the number of fights that came with that mindset, August had issued an addendum to the laws that governed the weres. The official postscript stated that in order for an alpha to cross into another alpha's territory, he had to get August's permission. He was also required to provide a valid reason for crossing into that territory. Since trouble makers rarely had a valid reason for anything, the number of problems and fights dropped significantly. This was the first time since the new law was implemented that any alpha had been given free reign over all territories.

Just as Danyon and Shauna were leaving August's office yesterday, the elder had given him a directive. He was to contact all the alphas in south Louisiana and inform them of the recent murders. Each alpha was then to choose a few of their strongest, most trustworthy weres and have them stand sentinel around the perimeter of their own territory. And they were to stay there until whoever or whatever was responsible for the murders had been captured.

Danyon had already notified four of the alphas. One in Lake Charles, another in Lafayette, and the two who were responsible for Baton Rouge. The only one left on his list was Kara Matiste, alpha of New Orleans' West Bank.

Kara was alpha by default. Not that she wasn't strong in her own right, but her husband, Carl, had been the true leader of the West Bank for many years. Kara assumed the leadership role when Carl died eleven months ago in a tragic car accident. He had been traveling home from

Atlanta, where he had been summoned by the magistrate for questioning regarding the whereabouts of funds that had recently disappeared from the community treasury. Carl had obviously provided satisfactory answers. The magistrate and council would not have released him otherwise. He was only five miles from the Alabama border when an eighteen wheeler loaded with gasoline T-boned him at an intersection. Carl's vehicle had exploded on impact.

At the time of an alpha's death, it's customary for his mate, always an alpha female, to take responsibility for the pack. She retains that leadership position until her death or until she pairs with another alpha male. If she does choose another alpha, then she is to relinquish the leadership role to him immediately. That particular circumstance was extremely rare, however.

When an alpha chooses his mate, it's for life. The bond between them is fierce. Indestructible. Granted, when one mate died, it didn't mean that the survivor didn't have sexual relations with other weres. But when he or she did, it was usually to maintain or increase the population of the pack, and that would be the extent of the tryst. Rarely, if ever, would he or she call another were their mate.

It was possible for a were to mourn for a lifetime. In the beginning, when the death is fresh and the wound deep, it wasn't unusual for the surviving mate to become incapacitated by grief. That is when the pack is most vulnerable. At first, many members of the pack act like children, rejoicing that no one is watching their every move. But soon, when they realize how big and bad the outside world really is, they grow fearful and sometimes angry because they no longer feel safe. That never appeared to be the case with Kara's pack.

Kara had changed significantly since Carl's death, which was understandable considering how close they had been. Carl had doted on her. Always surprising Kara with jewelry, roses, or whatever he thought she might fancy at any given time. Being vice president of Regent's Bank, Carl's income had afforded them the luxury of a three-story colonial in Algiers and matching Corvettes. Now, Kara lived in a two-bedroom apartment and drove an eight-year-old Chevy Malibu.

Danyon hadn't had many dealings with Kara since Carl died, but he'd heard that her mourning period was unusually short, and that she ruled with a firm hand, did not tolerate slackers, and was obsessively territorial. He supposed those traits were good for the pack in that they established black-and-white boundaries. But those same traits might prove problematic when it was time for her to take orders from someone else. Danyon couldn't help but wonder if Kara thought she had to be tougher because she was female and younger than most of the alpha males who led other packs. He wondered if Shauna, being the youngest Keeper, thought the same.

Danyon exited off the expressway and headed south toward Estelle, a small town that sat at the feet of the Jean Lafitte Wildlife Preserve. As he drove, Danyon found his thoughts awash with Shauna. It was difficult for him to see her as the Keeper of an entire race for the city of New

Orleans. She was so young and beautiful. He remembered how she had stood up to him, defiant, wanting to be part of the murder investigation. How she never once faltered in her commitment to that decision, no matter how frustrated or angry he became. She was certainly from MacDonald stock—hard-headed, loyal, fiercely passionate in her beliefs and, of course, stunning.

All three MacDonald sisters were breathtakingly beautiful, but there was something about Shauna that hooked into his senses and refused to let go. When they had sat across from each other at August's conference table, it had taken a massive amount of will power not to sit and simply stare at her. Watch her move, talk, blink, breathe. The struggle to control his attraction to her had been as great as his battle to fight off the anger that forced his transformation. As difficult as it had been, however, Danyon thought he'd managed it relatively well.

Until last night.

He had only to take one look at her wrapped in that bathrobe, her freshly scrubbed face, bare feet, long hair, wet and tousled, and something so powerful welled up inside him, he feared he'd transform on the spot. It was more than desire, more than common sexual attraction. She looked like a waterfall to a man dying of thirst. Somehow, he'd still managed to control himself, act as if everything was normal—even though he stirred a pot he could not see—heard only the melodic sound of her voice, her laughter. He'd kept reminding himself that she was human, he was were, and the difference between them was too vast to bridge.

Not that sex hadn't tried to shove its way to the fore-front of his mind. There was no question he was sexually attracted to her. Any man in his right mind would be. But Danyon had had more than his fair share of sexual encounters, with most of them beginning and ending the same way. A little spark of chemistry—a tangle of arms and legs—a physical need met, but a soul left empty. Intuitively, he knew that any man lucky enough to be intimate with Shauna MacDonald would be satiated in ways he never thought possible.

His intuition had been right.

Danyon knew he was tempting fate when he'd helped Shauna retrieve the plates from the cabinet shelf. And fate did not disappoint. When he'd leaned over to grab the plates, her scent, a heady mixture of musk and lilacs, nearly shattered his resolve. His undoing, however, had been when she'd turned around, and he first tasted her lips. From that moment on, the rest of the world had ceased to exist.

He lost count of the number of times they had made love, but it hadn't taken him long to figure out he was already in way over his head. She had left him feeling filled and emptied at the same time, which was nirvana in its purest form. But the sure sign of his demise had been the ache in his heart, when he'd watched her leave this morning.

Danyon was still lost in thought when the smell of blood caught his attention. Puzzled, he glanced down at his hands and then up into the rearview mirror to check his face. No blood. He slowed the car and lowered the driver's side window. The scent of blood slammed into his nostrils. He swerved to the shoulder of the road and hit the brakes. Fortunately, the road he'd been driving on wasn't heavily traveled. Aside from an old pickup that had passed him some time ago, his car was virtually the only vehicle on the road.

Following his nose, Danyon inched the car back onto the road, then drove another mile or so before the scent of blood led him to a graveled road on the left. He turned and followed its meandering path to the base of a forest that was part of the Jean Lafitte Wildlife Preserve. The road eventually ended at a small boat launch on a lake.

Danyon parked the car and got out to further investigate on foot. The blood trail led him around the short end of the lake, then deeper into the woods. It wasn't long before he heard voices. The loudest belonged to a female, and he recognized it almost immediately.

It was Kara Matiste.

"When I tell you to pick it up, that means now!"

"I tried," a male voice cried. "It makes me—"

"I don't care if it makes you sick."

"Swear to God I tried!"

"Quit your sniveling. What kind of man are you, crying like a girl?"

"But I—I can't."

"There's no such thing as can't. Do you understand me?"

Danyon stepped into a clearing and saw Kara shove

one of her weres, who he knew— Lawrence Castille—
so hard, the were stumbled backwards and nearly fell.
Standing a short distance away to Kara's left, was James
Darbonne, another were from her pack. Lawrence and
James had been two of Carl's top men. Both stood a little
over six feet tall and had average builds. In human years,
they would have been closing in on their mid-thirties.
Although James and Lawrence were twice Kara's size
and topped her by at least four inches, they cowered away
from her like frightened puppies.

Kara's long black hair was pulled back and held in
place by a gold barrette, and she wore jeans with the pant
legs tucked into black cowboy boots. Her short-sleeved
blouse was blood-red with white snaps running down the
front. She did a double take when she spotted Danyon.
Obviously, she'd been so wrapped up in verbally bashing
her weres, she hadn't caught wind of his approach.

"What are you doing here?" she asked him, sounding
a little unnerved.

Lawrence and James looked away shame-faced.

"I have news from August," Danyon said. The smell
of blood had grown so thick, he actually tasted it. From
between Kara and Lawrence's legs, he spotted something
on the ground behind them. He suspected it was what led
him here. He wanted to walk over and see for himself,
but out of respect for Kara's role as alpha and the fact
that he was in her territory, he stayed put.

"Is that so?" Her dark eyes flashed with anger.

Danyon glared at Kara long and hard, making sure she
understood— *If you think you're big and bad enough to*

*get me to fold at your feet like the other two, you need
to think again.*

Evidently getting the message, she broke eye contact
first. "How in the hell did you find me way out here?"

"I smelled blood. Followed it here."

She put her hands on her hips. "Well, you're just a
regular effin' Sherlock Holmes now, aren't you?"

Danyon glanced down at her legs, a signal to let Kara
know he'd spotted something behind them. Then he
asked, "Anything I can help with?"

Her eyes became black, cold marbles. "Not unless
you can raise the goddamn dead." With that, she shoved
Lawrence back, then turned to one side, giving Danyon
a better view.

A were lay on the ground about ten feet away. He was
in full were-state, wrapped in cable, covered in blood,
minus claws or fangs—and was most certainly dead. A
roll of plastic sheeting lay on the ground beside him.
From the looks of it, Kara had probably been trying to
get Lawrence and James to move the body onto it.

"Who is he?" Danyon asked.

"Why in the hell does it matter to you who he is? He's
one of mine."

Danyon narrowed his eyes, felt his nostrils flare. "It
matters because he's were, Kara. One of us."

She rolled her eyes. "Yeah, whatever."

"His name is Theodore Price," James said, taking a
tentative step toward them. "But everybody called him
Teddy."

"Did anybody ask you?" Kara snapped.

James bowed his head submissively and retracted his step.

"When did you find him?" Danyon asked.

After a long pause, Kara sighed, evidently sensing that she wasn't going to get rid of him that easily. "About an hour or two ago. I'm not sure of the exact time. Can't keep track of every damn thing. Been trying to get the body moved before all hell breaks loose out here. If the rest of my pack sees this, they're going to panic like a bunch of effin' coyotes."

Danyon nodded. "I know what you mean."

She let out a sarcastic snort. "You don't know jack."

"I know more than you think."

She frowned. "What the hell are you talking about?"

With an almost imperceptible aim of his chin, he signaled that he didn't want to discuss the matter in front of James and Lawrence.

Kara turned to James. "Get your ass to town and take the sniveling fool with you. But I want you back here in thirty minutes, no later. Got that?"

"Yes," James said, head down, eyes averted.

"And this time, bring somebody with you who's got a set of balls. Now get outta here, both of you."

In a flash, the two weres darted off, disappearing into the forest on the opposite side of the clearing.

Once they were out of sight, Danyon turned to her, knowing he would get blasted for the question he was about to ask. "Why do you treat them that way, Kara?"

Her face clouded, and her lips tightened into a thin line. She took a step toward him, and he saw the muscles in her forearm begin to ripple. "What kind of pussy alpha would ask a question like that?"

"Being alpha doesn't mean beating the dignity out of your pack."

Kara's feet widened to a fight stance. "Let me tell you something, Danyon Stone—I don't know how you lead the marshmallows you call wolven over on the East Bank, but I keep a strong hand on mine. If you don't, they'll run all over you, doing and saying whatever they want, whenever they want. I'm alpha of the West Bank, and I make damn sure my pack never forgets it. You've got to keep your weres tough, sharp, ready for anything." She pointed to Teddy. "If you don't, crap like this happens." She turned away, but not before Danyon saw her eyes well up with tears.

He gave her a moment to compose herself, then said, "I know where you're coming from because I lost two yesterday."

Kara whirled about, mouth agape. "Two?"

"Yes. Same way, too. Cables, claws and fangs torn off—"

"Human? Had they turned?"

"No. Both still in were-state, just like Teddy."

Kara brushed a hand briskly over the top of her head. "What the hell's going on here? Have you ever seen anything like that before? A dead wolven still were, I mean?"

"Not until yesterday."

She shook her head slowly. "I'll tell you this much, if some asshole thinks he's gonna just come out here to the West Bank and pick off my weres, he's got another thing coming. The sonofabitch better think twice."

"Whoever or whatever does not seem to be targeting any specific pack. Remember, it happened on the East Bank, too."

"Anywhere else?"

"Not that I know of," Danyon said. "I've already seen the other alphas, and, thankfully, nothing's happened within their packs."

"August sent you to warn us about this, didn't he?"

"Yes. That and he wants all of us to pick out a handful of our strongest weres and post them around the perimeter of our territories. They're to stay there until the murderer is found."

Kara threw her hands up. "I'm busting my ass, trying to keep this quiet, and now I've got to stick some of my weres on watch? Just what the hell am I supposed to tell them to watch out for while they're out there picking their noses?"

"Have them keep an eye out for unusual activity. Anyone new or suspicious in the area."

She exhaled a loud breath of frustration. "Can I get any more vague? They'll look at me like I've lost it."

"Tell them whatever you have to," Danyon said. "With as tight a reign as you have over your pack, I'm sure all you'll have to do is tell the weres you choose to stay put, and they'd stay put. They don't have to have a reason."

Kara sucked on the back of her front teeth and nodded. "True. Good point. Very good point." Still nodding, she glanced over at Teddy. "You see that? If you had only listened to me. If you hadn't been so damn weak. How many times did I tell you that you had to toughen up?"

Danyon felt awkward, as if he was eavesdropping on a private conversation. "Want some help moving him?" he asked.

"Nah, I got it." Shoving her hands into the back pockets of her jeans, she stared up at Danyon and offered nothing more.

After a few minutes of uncomfortable silence, Danyon finally said, "So I can tell August you'll be setting weres at post?"

"Yeah. I'll set 'em up."

"Good. I'm sure August will summon everyone together in a couple of days, so we can compare notes. Unless something comes up before then, of course. If you notice anything unusual, no matter how slight, give me a call, would you?"

Kara arched her brow.

"All right, so don't call me. At least call August. He'll send reinforcements."

"I don't need backup," Kara said. "If anything, or anyone, is brave enough to come out my way, my best weres will definitely mark it—or him. Trust me, if I have to call August, it'll be for him to send over a grunt to pick up a body." With that, she turned away and walked over to Teddy.

Taking that as his exit cue, Danyon left Kara alone with her dead were and headed back to his car, following the trail he had created on his way to the clearing.

Mission accomplished. All of the alphas in south

Louisiana had been alerted, and in short order. He should have felt some sense of satisfaction about that. Instead, he felt uneasy. Kara's obvious anger issues, combined with her my-way-or-the-highway attitude, was a recipe for disaster.

She was an explosion waiting to happen.

And that was the last thing any of them needed.

Chapter 10

Fiona's idea for the three of them to take some time off yesterday in preparation for the Nuit du Dommage tourist rush had been spot on. So had been her suggestion to pick up additional inventory from Keeno's. Without those extra supplies, most of the shelves in the shop would have been empty hours ago.

It was mid-afternoon, and Shauna had managed to steal only one bathroom break since they'd opened that morning. So many customers were wandering in and out of the shop, that Caitlin eventually shoved a plastic wedge beneath the front door to keep it open and stop the trio of small bells that hung over the threshold from ringing every other second. Her feet and head throbbed; even her face ached from forcing a smile every time someone came to the register. She needed food, another trip to the bathroom, and sleep. If she had gotten an hour of sleep at Danyon's, it had been a lot.

She was still standing behind the register, ringing up a large number of items for an elderly man, when a black-haired woman wearing too much perfume and a skintight blouse with a neckline that plunged down to her navel, shoved a bag in Shauna's face.

"What's these for?" the woman asked.

Shauna held up a finger, signaling the woman to wait, then finished keying in the last series of numbers from a product code.

With that done, Shauna looked over at the woman, forced smile in place. "I'll be glad to help you as soon as I'm finished with this gentleman."

"Aw, c'mon. All I want to know is what they're for. Look, he don't mind if you help me. You don't mind, do you, mister? You don't care if I get a couple questions answered, huh?" She smiled at him, rested an elbow on the counter and leaned forward, giving him a close up of her cleavage. To Shauna's surprise, and the woman's shock, the man completely ignored her.

Good for you, Shauna thought.

Refusing to be deterred, the woman leaned over the counter and shook the bag under Shauna's nose.

"Puhlease? I just want to know what this is."

"I'll help you—in a minute," Shauna said, keeping her eyes on the elderly man's purchases. She despised bullies and people who whined and threw tantrums until they got what they wanted.

"I thought y'all were supposed to help people," the

woman said. "I'm staying with a friend at the Bienville House, and he told me to come over here because he's feeling poorly and said y'all had natural stuff that would make him feel better. He told me to get some kind of shriveled up berry thing…seesaw or sawmill or something stupid like that. I can't remember what the name of it is, but if I heard it, I'd probably remember."

"Saw palmetto berries," Shauna said.

"Oh." The woman pulled the bag back with a snap, a huge smile on her face.

Shauna was about to total the man's order, when the woman shoved the bag under her nose again.

"So what are they good for?"

Shauna glanced up at the man apologetically, then said to the black-haired nuisance, "They're used for colds, hay-fever, bronchitis, mainly upper respiratory problems."

"Oh." The woman snapped the bag back again.

Not two seconds later, the bag was in Shauna's face.

"So what you got to do with 'em? Eat 'em?"

"Ma'am, please. Just give me a minute to finish helping this man, and I'll answer all of your questions," Shauna said.

"All I wanna know is what I've gotta do—"

A large hand appeared out of nowhere, grabbed the woman's arm and yanked it down so the bag was no longer in Shauna's face. Lurnelle Franklin had arrived to save the day, and she had come in style. She wore a plum-colored, V-neck pullover that reached her mid-thigh, tight black pants, and gold, strappy sandals.

"You got a problem with you ears, Miss Thing?" Lurnell snapped. "The lady here said to hol' up, and she even asked you nice."

Shauna smiled a thank-you to Lurnell and finished bagging the gentleman's merchandise. The black-haired woman with the bag of palmetto berries took a couple of steps back to put some distance between herself and Lurnell. "Well, I never—"

"That's right you never, and you never gonna neither with them titties hangin' out like that," Lurnell said. "Go cover that up, girl. Ain't nobody tryin' to see them old nasty things anyhow."

The man Shauna had been waiting on, the one who had refused to be swayed by the display of cleavage earlier, burst out laughing.

Obviously shamed, the black-haired woman threw the bag on the counter, spun around on her heels and stormed out of the store.

Shauna handed the man his bag of goods. "I'm so sorry about all of that."

"Oh, don't be," he said between chuckles. "It's the best laugh I've had all year. I like this place. I do believe I'll come back."

"You a smart man," Lurnell said. She gave him a big grin.

No sooner did he leave the store than Fiona came out of the reading room, where she had been reading tea leaves for an Asian woman, and walked over to the counter.

"I thought I recognized that voice." Fiona smiled at Lurnell. "How are you doing, honey?"

"Oh, I'm all good," Lurnell said.

"Glad to hear it." Fiona turned to Shauna. "And what about you? It sounded like things were getting a little carried away out here."

"No, it's all cool," Lurnell reassured her. "Some old, nasty hussy was shovin' stuff in my girl's face here, so I put a little play on her. I be figurin' that the hussy's gots to go, you know what I'm sayin'? You feelin' me?" She shook her head. "I swear, I don't know what's wrong wit' all the people in the world today. They crazy."

"I hear you," Shauna said. "I appreciate you stepping in the way you did. That woman would probably still be waving that bag in my face if it hadn't been for you."

Lurnell tsked and flapped a hand at her. "Aw, ain't nothin' but a thing, girl."

"Well, I think every good heroine deserves a reward," Fiona said. "I've got fresh baked chocolate cookies back in the office. Think you can handle a few?"

"A few? Sheee, I can handle a lotta few." Lurnell slapped a hand to her belly.

"You bring 'em, and Lurnell's gonna eat 'em. I love chocolate!"

Fiona laughed. "You've got it. I have to help Caitlin with something first, but as soon as I'm done, I'll get those cookies for you. It shouldn't take long."

"Oh, I ain't goin' nowhere," Lurnell said, bright-eyed.

As Fiona headed for Caitlin, four girls who appeared

to be in their early teens, came rushing up to the cash register, giggling.

"Can I help you?" Shauna asked.

More giggling. Whispering. Then each girl stretched out a hand. One held a piece of citrine, another hematite, the third, a piece of amethyst, and the fourth, a beautifully cut quartz.

"Are these, like, magical?" the girl holding the citrine asked.

"Yeah," said the one with the amethyst. "'Cause, like, we have a friend, you know, who told us they were real magic. And, like, we were supposed to come over here and get some, and you'd be able to tell us, like, which ones might bring us boyfriends and stuff."

All four girls started giggling again.

Shauna grinned. She didn't want to burst their bubble by getting technical, but the truth of the matter was that the magical elements in crystals and gems didn't have anything to do with magic at all. The vibration of each stone, united with the energy of focused thought, often times did manifest a person's goal or desire. But that had nothing to do with magic. It was simply the natural law of attraction. She was trying to figure out how to explain that without getting too technical, when Lurnell stepped up to the girls.

"Okay, if y'all wanna know if them rocks is magic, put 'em right here in my hand," Lurnell said. "I'm gonn' feel if they magic, and if they is, I'm gonna tell you they is. If they not, I'm gonna tell you they not."

Looking a little fearful, each girl dropped her stone into Lurnell's palm.

"Now, let's see what we got in here." Lurnell sandwiched the stones between her hands, closed her eyes, then cocked her head like she was listening to something far away. "Uh-huh, I be hearin' somethin'... Oh, yeah, I be feelin' you now." She frowned, squeezed her eyes shut tighter. "Huh? Whatchu said? Oh...okay." With that, she opened her eyes, held out the stones and declared, "They big magic for sure."

"Really?" one of the girls said.

Lurnell plopped a hand on her hip. "What? If I told you they magic, they magic. Now, that's all I'm sayin'."

"Wow," another girl said breathlessly.

"That's so cool," a third girl chimed in.

The girl with the amethyst raised a hand as if she were in a classroom.

"Uh-uh, don't be wavin' no hand at me," Lurnell said. "I ain't got nothin' more to say."

"But how do we make the magic stones work?" Amethyst asked.

Lurnell harrumphed. "All I got to say is they big—*big* magic. The res' is all you."

The girls nodded in unison and couldn't pay for their stones fast enough. Shauna fought with her conscience as she rang them up. She didn't want the girls to leave the shop thinking they had real magical stones, but she didn't want to risk saying anything and embarrassing Lurnell. Besides, the girls did look extremely happy.

As the girls left, whispering and giggling en masse,

Shauna turned to Lurnell. "Why did you tell them that?" she asked, unable to hide a grin. "Now those kids are going to go home thinking they have real magic stones."

"And there be somethin' wrong wit' that?" Lurnell shook her head. "Girl, don't you start climbin' on no high horse, you hear me? You gots to learn how to work you stuff in the shop if you wanna make that green. Them kids is gonna go home all excited, and they's gonna tell they friends, and them friends gonna tell some more friends, and *all* them friends gonna come up in here to get some rocks. You call that—takin' care of bidness."

Shauna laughed. "You're a trip, you know that? Hey, talking about business, why aren't you at Sistah's?"

Lurnell's face lit up. "'Cause I had to come show my girl somethin'. Look here." She held out her right hand, pinky side up. "Go 'head, check it."

Shauna rolled her eyes. "Don't you think it's a little soon to be trying this again?"

"Don't be talkin' like that. Just look when I tell you look."

To appease her, Shauna took Lurnell's hand and examined it. "What the…?" There, just above the thin, pink scar that had come from Lurnell's handy work, was the real deal—a marriage line. It was faint, but unquestionably there. Shauna peered up at her. "It's real," she said, amazed.

"I knowed it!" Lurnell pulled her hand back and clapped. "I seen it when I was brushin' my teeth and hair this mornin', and I says to myself, 'Lurnell Shantelle

Marquetha Franklin, you gonna get married, girl!' Then I says, 'You got to go show her—that be you—'cause she ain't gonna believe it's for real. I swear to gawd, girl, I be so excited, I had to back myself up to the commode before I peed myself."

"I'll bet! I've never known one to appear that fast. Not in one day."

"Yeah, but I know why it come fas'," Lurnell said. Her eyes danced with a secret she couldn't wait to share.

"Why?"

"'Cause I met me a man las' night. His name be Tyree Johnson, and, oh, that man look good. He all the time be sweet talkin' and even got hisself a real job. And he ain't got no baby mamas nowheres, so he ain't gotta pay that child support."

"Where did you meet him?"

"Down to Zydeco Joe's, and let me tell you what, child, that man can for sure bus' a step!"

Lurnell was demonstrating a few zydeco moves, when Fiona appeared with a plate of chocolate cookies.

"Here you go, just like I promised," Fiona said, and handed the plate to Lurnell. "Enjoy." She gave Lurnell a little four-finger wave, then headed for a group of customers standing near the amulet and totem display.

"Oh, yeah!" Lurnell held the plate close as though someone might steal it at any moment. "I'm gonna have a few of these here, then I got to get back to the store. Bidness be good and all, but they got all kinda people walkin' up in my stuff wit' they dirty shoes. I gots to go

pass the vacuum, so the place look good. Tyree comin'
later. He gonna be—"

A blast of rap music suddenly erupted, and it sounded
like it was coming from Lurnell's rear end.

"Hol' up," she said, and dipped a hand behind her
back. It returned clutching a cell phone. She checked the
caller I.D. and broke into a wide grin. "That be Tyree."
She handed Shauna the plate of cookies. "Now don't be
goin' nowheres wit' that. I'll be right back."

Lurnell flipped the phone open and put it to her ear.
"Hey, Tyree, baby, where y'at?" As she listened to his
response, she winked at Shauna, then stepped away from
the counter, evidently wanting some privacy.

Watching Lurnell coo into the phone, reminded
Shauna of Nicole and Ian. How each time they had come
into the shop for tea and scones, Nicole had had that same
over-the-top happy look on her face. Just like Lurnell did
now. Thinking about Nicole made Shauna wonder about
the keening sound she had heard in the shop the day
before. Had it been Nicole crying out before she died or
Ian in mourning? Not that it really mattered. Dead was
dead, and heart-pain was heart-pain. Both carried pitiful
sounds.

Thoughts of the two weres brought Danyon to mind,
and Shauna suddenly realized she had yet to hear from
him today. She figured he had been too busy, alerting
the other alphas, as August had requested, and busy she
certainly understood. Still, it would have been nice if he
had taken the time to call her at the shop, for no other
reason but to hear her voice.

She would give anything to hear his right now. To feel his touch. Last night had been one of the most amazing nights of her life. Shauna still couldn't get over how quickly she had reacted to his touch. She had never felt anything so—right before. To call it electricity or a connection, didn't even come close to describing what had flowed between them. It had felt as though each had reached into the other and took hold of their soul, absorbing not only all they were now, but all they were ever meant to be.

"Excuse me. Can you help me with this?" a woman asked, and thrust a matrix box at Shauna. "How does it open?"

Shaken out of her reverie, Shauna took the box and began to work it open. She felt a bit guilty. In the short respite she'd had between customers, she had let her mind float away on thoughts of Danyon instead of focusing on Nicole and Simon, and how they might go about finding the murderer. It wasn't going to be an easy task. They had found no blaring evidence that pointed them in any specific direction. So far, all they had was speculation—a human couldn't have done it—a shifter, possible, but not likely—a group of glamouring vampires held some possibilities, but weak ones. For all they knew, those assumptions could be wrong. Maybe a vampire or a shifter or even a were was exactly what they should be looking for. She just wished they had more to work with. Anything that might tighten their aim. In some respects she understood why Danyon wanted to hold things close to the vest for now, and why he didn't want to inform the leaders of the other subcultures yet. On the other hand, she saw the benefits that could come from joining forces just as clearly.

"If someone doesn't do something about that kid, I'm going to hog-tie him and toss him out of the store myself," Caitlin said storming up to the register.

"Who?" Shauna asked

The answer came running down the center aisle of the store, arms flapping wildly, like a hummingbird on speed.

It was Banjo Marks.

Some customers yelped and jumped out of his way. Others hurried out of the store, as if the building had suddenly caught fire.

"I smell 'em, smell 'em!" Banjo shouted, then slid toward the counter. His knees smacked into the counter wall—hard. He didn't even flinch. "Lemme have some, girly girl. Now, okay? Where's at? I smell 'em, smell 'em!"

He was chattering at a hundred miles an hour, and the customers still in the store backed away, giving him a wide berth.

"Look at that," Caitlin fumed. "He's scaring our customers off!"

Shauna scanned the store for her muscle, but Lurnell was nowhere to be seen. She'd evidently stepped out to have a private conversation with her new man. He must have truly been a gem for Lurnell to leave an entire plate of cookies behind. The plate still sat near the end of the counter, where Shauna had placed it a few minutes ago—and where Banjo was headed now.

"I knew it—smelt it—knew it! Smelt 'em all the way across the street," Banjo declared, then let out a loud, twittering laugh that made Shauna want to slap her hands over her ears.

More customers scrambled out of the store.

Banjo was about to dive into the plate of cookies with both hands, when Fiona suddenly appeared and grabbed him by the arm.

"Come on, sweetie. Let's go into the office, and I'll make you a sandwich."

"No!" Banjo yelled. "Cookies, cookies. Gotta have 'em, want to have 'em. Cookies!" He wiggled, trying to pull out of Fiona's grasp.

Caitlin slapped a hand to her forehead. "Fi, you've got to quit encouraging him like that. You keep feeding him, and he keeps coming back here."

"Coming back, coming back!" Banjo mimicked, sounding like a hoarse parrot.

"You two go see about the customers," Fiona said. "I'll—"

"What customers?" Caitlin said, frowning. "He's run nearly everybody off."

"Then see to the ones who are left," Fiona said sternly. "I'll take care of Banjo. Don't worry, it'll be okay."

"Not okay—it's not okay!" Banjo squawked. "No sandwich! I want a cookie. Cookie!"

Shauna picked up the plate of cookies, thinking out

of sight, out of mind. The moment she turned away with the plate, Banjo let out a loud shriek.

"No, feed it! It's all good—it's good!"—hehehehehe, squawk-scritch-squawk.

There it was again. That nerve-grating, hair-raising laugh. It made Shauna's teeth hurt.

Banjo plucked his arm from Fiona's grasp and started hopping in place. Then he worked his way around Fiona, bouncing from left to right, so she couldn't get hold of him.

Still bouncing, he made his way to Shauna. "Gimme cookie, give you secret." An ugly grin spread over his face. "Cookie—secret, secret—cookie."

Shauna wanted to punch his high wattage lights out. "Stop bouncing like that. You're making me dizzy."

That twittering laugh again.

"Look, just go with Fiona, Banjo," Shauna ordered, hoping that food would calm him down at least a little.

"No, no. Got a secret. Gooood secret! One cookie, good secret. Two cookie, more secret!"

"What are you talking about? What secret?"

Banjo lifted his head, sniffed three or four times. "Sixteen cookies. Got sixteen cookies on the plate. Sixteen!"

Puzzled, Shauna glanced down at the plate in her hand, did a quick count, and was astonished to find it held exactly sixteen cookies. "How did you know how many there were?"

"Smell it. Can't you smell?"

"Come on, you," Fiona said, finally latching on to Banjo's arm.

"No, not come on!" He leaned way over to the left, closer to Shauna. "Give me a cookie, tell you a secret!"

"Go eat a sandwich or something, Banjo. You're talking out of your head."

He stopped bouncing and squinted at Shauna, as though sizing her up. Then he opened his eyes wide. "Got no teeth. Ain't got no more teeth—no more big fingernails. Nope, none!"

Shauna froze. "What—who has no teeth or fingernails, Banjo?"

Hehehehe, squawk-scritch-squawk—"No teeth, gotta have teeth! Gotta." He hooked a finger on either side of his upper lip and pulled it up over his teeth. Then he tapped a dirty fingernail against a tobacco stained incisor. "Gotta have the teeth."

"Any idea what he's talking about?" Fiona asked.

"I'm not sure," Shauna said, then set the plate on the counter out of Banjo's reach and took a cookie from the top of the heap. "But we'll soon find out." She dangled the chocolate chip cookie in front of him.

With a loud grunt, Banjo grabbed the cookie and stuffed all of it into his mouth in one fell swoop. He closed his eyes, a blissful expression on his face. When he opened his eyes again, he started hopping on one foot then the other.

"Okay, I gave you a cookie, now what's the secret?"

Hehehehe, squawk…

Banjo broke free of Fiona again and took off running through the store. Fiona and Caitlin ran after him, but before either could corner him at the back of the stop, he'd spun around and was halfway back up the center aisle, heading toward Shauna.

The counter caught him at the waist this time, and for a moment, Shauna thought he would flip clean over to the other side.

"One more dead," he hissed, glaring at her, fidgeting in place. "One, two—three. Three dead, no teeth. No big fingernails. Three dead, three dead!"

With her heart thudding in her ears, Shauna grabbed the back of his shirt and held tight. "What the hell are you talking about? Who's dead?"

Banjo suddenly stopped fidgeting and pulled away from her. "Three blind mice," he said, his voice low, robotic. "See how they run. Run with no teeth. So stupid. Three, stupid, blind—dead mice."

"Please, Banjo," Shauna said, keeping her voice low. "Tell me who you're talking about. Who's dead?"

Without warning, he sparked back to life. "Cookie, cookie!" he yelled, then shrieked with laughter and ran out of the store.

Shauna's heart was beating so hard it made her nauseous. Banjo knew about the weres. She was sure of it. But he said there were three.

Nicole, Simon...who else?

Had another were been killed?

And the teeth. How did Banjo know about the teeth and claws?

Shauna felt an uneasiness rising in her gut. An intuitive whisper. And she remembered Banjo and Mattie fighting in front of the store—how Mattie had dented the light pole with her fist.

Too much strength for such a small woman...

And Banjo, who claimed to have smelled the cookies from across the street. With so many tourists clogging the streets, that would have been...should have been... impossible.

August had said that whomever ingested the claws and fangs of a were would take on the traits of a were. Everything but transformation.

Had Banjo and Mattie ingested either? Both?

Fear crept up Shauna's spin.

Three down—no more to go.

It was time to get Jagger and Ryder involved—time to bring in the leaders of the other races—time to enlist reinforcements.

Whether Danyon liked it or not.

Chapter 11

A Little Bit of Magic was so packed with customers that Danyon had to literally squeeze into the shop sideways. Any other time, and he would have backtracked out of there, refusing to be part of the throng. He hated crowds. The collective energy of too many people in a limited space scrambled his thoughts and made him anxious.

There was only one reason he allowed this exception. Shauna. He had to talk to her.

As soon as the West Bank was a dot in his rearview mirror, Danyon had hurried back to the Quarter to find her. That in and of itself had made him feel strange. He had never hurried back to anyone for anything before.

Since their time together last night, Shauna had burrowed into his core, and there was no getting rid of her. He wouldn't have wanted to if he could. His intellect kept telling him that the intimacy they shared had been a mistake. A human and a wolven didn't belong together. Their worlds were too different. It would never work.

His emotions countered, however, telling his brain it was full of crap. He needed to enjoy and treasure the remarkable gift that she was.

Danyon couldn't remember the last time he had felt this alive. And, if the truth be told, it had little to do with the sex they'd had—although to him it scored a thousand on a scale of one to ten. Danyon had had more than his fair share of intimacy with other women, but not once had he left their beds with a total sense of contentment.

Shauna had been different. Being with her had caused a floodgate to open inside him.

The contentment he had felt had been absolute, filling him, yet emptying him at the same time.

Danyon not only wanted to share her bed, he wanted to share her heart and share his with her. He had never felt more emotionally raw, vulnerable or befuddled in his life.

Shauna was the Keeper of the weres, so she had a right to know about the death of Kara's were. That's what he kept telling himself. But it was only half the truth and mostly an excuse. He simply wanted, needed to see her again.

Danyon moved slowly through the crowd, making his way to the front counter. If Shauna wasn't there, working the register, he knew one of her sisters would be. And they'd know where to find her.

When he finally made it to the register, he saw Caitlin

pounding away at the keys. A long line of customers waited their turn. He stood off to one side, waiting for a break in the action so he could talk to her. Caitlin must have sensed him watching her because she glanced over and gave him a hesitant smile.

A moment later, she peered over at him again. But the fifth or sixth time she looked his way, her brow was deeply furrowed. Either curiosity was getting to her or she was worried that she might have a stalker on her hands.

It didn't take long before she gave in and turned to face Danyon. "May I help you?" A middle-aged man, who had been next in line, let out an exasperated sigh.

Evidently hearing the customer's distress, Caitlin quickly turned back to the man and offered her apologies. "Thanks so much for your patience. I'll only be a couple more seconds."

With that, Caitlin faced Danyon again. "Is there a reason you're just standing there staring? Do I know you from somewhere?"

"I don't believe we've met before. My name's Danyon Stone. I'm looking for Shauna." There were too many people around for him to identify himself as the alpha of the East Bank pack.

Caitlin's frown deepened. "What do you want with my sister?"

"I'm a friend of hers," he offered.

At first, his answer seemed to puzzle Caitlin all the more, then a twinkle lit up her eyes and she smiled.

"So you're the infamous Mr. Stone," she said.

Wondering what Shauna might have told her sisters about him, Danyon cleared his throat. "I'm afraid I am, yes." He smiled. "Is Shauna here?"

Caitlin chewed her bottom lip, as though trying to decide if she should divulge any information. Finally she said, "Shauna's in the reading room. Take a left after the row of curios, then head straight back. You'll see a heavy blue curtain. Push past it, and you're there."

"A reading room?"

"Yes…oh, sorry. I figured you already knew. I read Tarot cards, our oldest sister, Fiona, reads tea leaves, and Shauna palms. We do all of our readings back there."

Taking in that nugget of information, Danyon thanked Caitlin for her help and headed for the room with the heavy blue curtain. He wondered if Shauna had read his palm without him knowing it. He didn't know whether to smile or cringe at the thought.

As soon as Danyon laid a hand on the curtain's edge, ready to pull it aside, he heard voices in the room beyond it. It sounded like two men—another woman.

Shauna wasn't alone.

He hesitated. Ordinarily he would have knocked, so as not to seem intrusive, but there was no door.

Caitlin directed you here. If she'd thought you'd be interrupting on a private matter, she wouldn't have…

With that thought in mind, Danyon pushed the curtain aside and stepped across the threshold of the room. Their conversation stopped abruptly when they spotted him a few seconds later, but he heard scraps of their conversation in the meantime. He felt his heart drop to his feet.

The room wasn't very big, maybe ten by twelve and sparsely furnished. Shauna was indeed inside. So was her older sister, Fiona, Jagger DeFarge, the vampire homicide detective and another man, tall, square-faced, someone Danyon didn't recognize.

The collection of people wasn't what made Danyon's heart drop. It was their topic of discussion—his dead weres. He had gone on blind faith that Shauna would honor his request to keep the information about Nicole and Simon quiet for twelve hours. And if he went strictly by the clock, she had fulfilled that request. But after the intimate time they had spent together last night, he had stupidly assumed she would extend that vow of silence until they at least had a chance to discuss the matter again.

He felt betrayed, even though he knew he had no right to the emotion.

Shauna had fulfilled her obligation.

She owed him no more.

His disappointment must have shown because the tentative smile Shauna gave him when she spotted him in the room suddenly collapsed to a frown.

"Danyon, how good to see you again," Fiona said.

He gave a small nod. "Good to see you, too, Fiona." He had only met Fiona twice before, and the last time had been over a year ago. He was surprised she remembered him. "Sorry for the interruption. I was looking for Shauna. Caitlin said I'd find her in here."

Fiona offered a small smile. "Not at all. Please, come

in. I'm sure you know Detective DeFarge…" Fiona motioned to Jagger.

"Yes, of course," Danyon said.

"This is Ryder Mallory," Fiona said, introducing him to the man he hadn't recognized. As soon as Fiona said his name, Danyon remembered that Ryder was the shape-shifter and bounty hunter who had come into town a few months ago in search of the walk-ins. Ryder had been instrumental in bringing that battle to an end. He, along with Caitlin and the leaders of the other subcultures, had literally saved the city from destruction.

Danyon nodded a greeting to Ryder, and he returned it.

By this time, Shauna had made her way to his side. She placed a hand on his arm, her touch tentative. "I heard there was another dead were," she said quietly. "And there was no way for me to reach you. I hadn't heard from you all day and wasn't sure when you'd be back." Her sad, beautiful eyes searched his face. "Three dead in two days…I had to do something. We need back up."

He studied her, hoping his eyes relayed the message in his heart, *How could you possibly believe I wouldn't contact you again? Did you honestly think I would simply disappear?*

Shauna dropped her hand from his arm. "Everyone in here knows about Simon and Nicole, Danyon. We also know there's been a third murder. Who was it? Anyone from here? Where was he or she found?"

"East Bank were," Danyon said tersely, then clammed

up. He wasn't about to share any intimate details about Kara's dead were in front of a vamp and shifter.

Evidently sensing his reluctance, Shauna said, "It's okay, really. Everyone here just wants to help."

Danyon looked from her to Jagger. "I appreciate the offer, but we can take care of our own."

Jagger nodded. "I understand completely. I felt the same way during the cemetery murders six months ago. But I was wrong. Believe me, nobody here is questioning your ability as a leader. We're only offering more manpower to help you get the job done."

"I think it's important for all of us to stick together," Fiona said. "We had major problems with finger pointing during the cemetery murders, and the same when the walk-ins tried to take over the city. The vampires blamed the shape-shifters, the shifters blamed the weres, and so on. Everyone in our respective communities may have calmed considerably since then, but I believe there's still undercurrents of sensitivity and wariness running through the city. We don't need that exploding in our faces."

"I agree," Ryder said, sidling up to Fiona. "I get where you're coming from, Danyon. Just like Jagger, when I came here looking for the walk-ins, I had been tracking them for over two years. The last thing I wanted was anyone's help. Sharing the takedown after all the time I'd spent tracking those bastards was unacceptable to me. But, man, the truth is I had to get over myself. My stubbornness wasn't helping anybody. People were dying faster than I could count. I needed help fast, whether

I liked it or not." Ryder hooked a thumb in the front pocket of his jeans. "Look, the murderer you're looking for could be walking down Royal Street this very minute. Maybe scoping out restaurants and bars for that perfect were. Once he targets one, all he has to do is wait him or her out until the end of a work shift, and he's got himself another victim."

Shauna nodded. "To keep that from happening, we need more eyes keeping watch in and around the city, especially during Nuit du Dommage. More weres will be working overtime at their jobs because of the flood of tourists. We have to protect them. It's our job."

"It's my job," Danyon snapped.

"Not only yours," Shauna shot back. "I'm the weres' Keeper. It's my responsibility to keep them safe, too."

He glared at her and lowered his voice. "You should have discussed this with me before telling them."

Shauna didn't even flinch under his stare. Her expression hardened. "I kept my word. Twelve hours, remember? And, for your information, I would have talked to you about it first, but you weren't around."

"How did you find out about the third were anyway?" Danyon asked. "Who told you?"

"Banjo Marks."

"Who?"

"A local vamp," Jagger said. "The kid lives on the street. Heavy drug user."

Danyon frowned. "How'd he hear about it?"

"I don't know," Shauna said. "Banjo didn't actually come out and say he knew about Nicole, Simon or a third were for that matter. He sort of…it's a long story. I'll have to fill you in later."

"Danyon, we all have a vested interest in this matter," Jagger said. "I know the victims of the murders have only been weres so far, but that doesn't mean it'll remain that way. Members of the other communities might be targets, as well."

"No, they won't," Danyon said, then immediately regretted letting the words out of his mouth.

"What do you mean?" Jagger asked.

Danyon didn't answer. The information August had given them about the rogue were, about the metaphysical powers inherent to were claws and fangs, was proprietary knowledge. The only reason August had shared it with them was because he was the victims' alpha, and Shauna their Keeper. The information wasn't meant for a vampire or a shape-shifter. In fact, August had specifically told them to keep the knowledge confidential.

As though reading his mind, Shauna said, "We have to tell them everything, Danyon. I trust them. All of them. I'd bet my life that whatever we say will never leave this room."

"You have our word on that," Fiona said.

"Have you forgotten what August said about confidentiality?" Danyon asked Shauna.

"Of course not," Shauna said. "But August didn't actually come out and forbid it."

"Semantics."

"Not really. Besides, I'm the Keeper of the weres, which includes you. I'll take the responsibility for what is or isn't said and deal with August myself. You forget that he taught me the ways of a Keeper. Trust me. He'll understand and respect my decision."

Danyon slowly swiped a hand over his mouth. Everyone in the room was staring at him intently—waiting. It was obvious Shauna hadn't revealed everything to them and for that, Danyon was grateful. It left him with a little dignity. Shauna would have probably thought that to be petty, but to an alpha, dignity was paramount. His pride had been bruised when he'd heard them discussing what he considered his business. But the truth was he trusted Shauna. They had only been together for a short time, yet he felt he understood the very core of who she was. And that was more than enough for him to trust her with his life. If she believed that strongly in everyone here, he had no reason not to.

Hesitantly, Danyon began to recount the story August had shared with him and Shauna. How decades ago a rogue were had been captured and sentenced to death, and why a specific manner of death had been chosen.

When he was done, everyone stood silent for some time, evidently trying to absorb all he had said.

Finally, Ryder asked, "Is this common knowledge amongst your people? The special powers in the claws and fangs I mean. And that if they're stripped away, the were's heart will burst?"

"No," Danyon said.

"Now I see what you meant when you said the other cultures weren't at risk," Jagger said. "But you're still going to need help. I think we should get the leaders of the subcultures together and let them know. If—"

"No. This needs to stay low profile," Danyon said.

Jagger held up a hand. "Please, hear me out. If what you're saying is true, then the wolven in and around New Orleans aren't the only ones at risk. This is much bigger than any one group in one city. Weres around the world could be in danger. The only way this is going to be stopped is if we all band together."

"Whether the other leaders are told or not, this information has to remain in this room," Shauna warned. "If it gets out, other scumbags may decide to jump on the bandwagon right away. The problem gets out of control then."

"Good point," Fiona said.

"Danyon, I only offer my opinion on the matter, about including the leaders, so everyone can pitch in and help," Jagger said. "But we'll take your lead on this. If you want to keep it just between us, then we'll honor your decision, and the four of us—Ryder, Fiona, Shauna and I—will do everything we can to support you."

All eyes were on Danyon now.

As much as he hated to admit it, Jagger was right. He had been so focused on the weres in and around New Orleans that he hadn't seen the broadness of that scope. Weres in other parts of the United States—around the world—in danger. The vastness of that changed everything.

There was only one answer he could give them.

Any other response would make him an irresponsible leader.

And that was unacceptable.

Danyon agreed to calling the leaders together for a meeting, but kept one thing in mind and to himself. He wasn't going to just sit on his hands and wait for everyone to join hands in a council meeting. It might take hours, even days, before they got all the leaders together.

Even an hour was too long to wait. Something had to be done now, before another were died.

And he planned to be the one who took care of that something.

Chapter 12

Attending a meeting at three in the morning was not something Shauna's body or mind appreciated. Both had to be forced into compliance. She was surprised they were able to gather everyone so quickly. The leaders of the three major subcultures in New Orleans owned their own businesses, which made them difficult to pin down even with extended notice. Compound that with the record number of tourists swarming the city right now, and this morning's meeting was nothing short of a miracle.

Since the business to be discussed was about the weres, August had offered his conference room for the gathering. The elder's response to having the meeting in the first place had been Shauna's second surprise. She'd expected August to be miffed that she had taken matters into her own hands and leaked word about the murders, along with some of the confidential details surrounding them. To her amazement, August took the news very well. In fact, he even commended her, saying that keeping the twelve hour vow of silence she had made with Danyon, then carefully deliberating matters before making the decision to get the others involved, showed initiative and integrity, all signs of an excellent Keeper. She had been taken aback and humbled by his praise.

Shauna and her sisters usually met with August and the leaders of the other subcultures at least once a year. The purpose of that meeting was to share basic information about city business, as it pertained to each race, and to generally keep tabs on one another. In the past year, however, they had had to meet multiple times due to major problems plaguing the city.

Six months ago, it had been the cemetery murders. Two women were discovered lying across tombs in a local cemetery, each dead and completely drained of blood. The exsanguinations heaped suspicion onto the vampires, then fingers pointed to the shape-shifters since they were able to mimic a vampire in appearance and action. Not much was said about the werewolves then, because weres are basic black-and-white. When they kill, they usually slaughter, and the bodies of both women had been in pristine condition. Regardless, that hadn't stopped one race from accusing the other. Everyone had been on edge.

The situation worsened three months later, when a group of rogue walk-ins tried taking over the city. It was then that Ryder Mallory came into town. Ryder was a bounty hunter and a shape-shifter, and he had been tracking the rogue walk-ins for quite some time. The number of casualties from the walk-in invasion exceeded those from the cemetery murders. So did the number of suspects. This time every race was subject to blame, and the accusations flew at lightning speed. Had it not been for Ryder, Caitlin and Jagger, the entire city of New Orleans might have been destroyed.

Now, here they were again.

Another crisis. More death.

Had there ever been a time when the world was quiet? When no blood was shed because of someone or something's greed or anger? When no one had to fight to protect some small corner of the earth they called home?

And what about the future? Was it possible to have one without strife and pain? Wars were still fought in the name of peace, and strife still flowed through the streets of the world in the name of equality. Every generation basically did the same thing as the one before it. If the definition of insanity was doing the same thing over and over but expecting different results, then Shauna figured the future was pretty much doomed right out of the gate. All anyone could do was the best they could do with the life that was given to them. Everything else seemed up for grabs.

Shauna was just settling into a chair at the table in August's conference room, when Rita, August's assistant, ushered Danyon inside.

They exchanged smiles as Rita rearranged a tray of

pastries. Danyon paused near the empty chair beside Shauna, then moved to the opposite side of the table and sat across from her. At first, Shauna didn't understand why he had purposely chosen not to sit beside her. Then it struck her...

When Andy Saville had arrived at the scene of Simon's murder, the were had given her a look that said, 'You're a woman—a kid—what the hell are you doing here?' Had it not been for Danyon creating an environment of acceptance, her presence would not have been tolerated, and she never would have been taken seriously. He was doing the same thing for her now by choosing that particular position at the table. Ninety percent of the attendees would be male, and Danyon knew if he sat beside her, any time one of the leaders had a question, they would direct it to him simply because he was male and an alpha. She might have been a Keeper, but she was still female and young, and the leaders weren't used to her being a front-runner at the council meetings. Fiona always took that position. Today would be different, though. Everyone would be discussing weres, which were Shauna's responsibility—and that meant she would be plopped right on top of first base. Danyon was giving her the room she needed to be a real part of the team.

Within a couple minutes of Danyon's arrival, Fiona and Jagger appeared, and following them, Caitlin and Ryder. Jagger and Ryder didn't carry leadership titles in their cultures, but Jagger's experience as a homicide detective and Ryder's as a bounty hunter made both invaluable assets, so they had been asked to attend.

Next in line was David Dulac, leader of the vampires and the owner of a club called The Underworld, which was located on Esplanade. It was unlike any other bar in the city. The building was a deconsecrated church, and it still sported stained glass windows, a cavernous main section and multiple balconies and private rooms. David never did anything in a small way.

Trailing David was Armand St. Pierre, the acting head of all the shape-shifters and the owner of Muriel's, one of the higher-end restaurants in New Orleans. Save for August, Shauna found Armand to be one of the more elegant leaders. He had an aristocratic air about him. To those who didn't know Armand, he might have been considered snobbish, when that wasn't really the case. He was simply a very private man.

August arrived last, and he immediately surveyed the silver tea and coffee pots in the center of the conference table, along with the fresh croissants and pâtè, shrimp puffs and beignets. Evidently satisfied that there was plenty for all to eat and drink, August dismissed Rita with a nod.

As soon as the conference room door closed behind her, August said, "Please be seated at your leisure, everyone." Even at three in the morning, August looked rested and ready for business. His black Armani suit had not one wrinkle, and his long, silvery-white hair was combed away from his face, not a strand out of place.

He took his place at the head of the table. "I want to thank all of you for clearing your calendars so we could meet quickly, and for your willingness to attend at such an early hour."

"No problem," Ryder said.

"I'm terribly sorry for your losses, August," Armand said.

"Same here," David Dulac said. "It's good that you've called us together. Things might look like they've settled down in the city after the disaster we had with the walk-ins, but to tell you the truth, my people have been riding on the edge of panic ever since."

"Anyone in your group stick out as particularly jumpy or nervous lately?" Ryder asked.

"What makes you ask that?" David said, his tone defensive. "Why pick on my group? I'm sure every leader here can testify that their communities are just as antsy since the walk-ins. We've gone through a lot this year."

Ryder held up a hand. "Hang on, I didn't mean to single out your group. One of the reasons we're here is to figure out what to do about this situation, right? In order for us to do that, we need to be able to lay everything out on the table. That includes looking at the possibility that someone in our own community could be the murderer. I'm sure that's uncomfortable for everyone here, but it's necessary if we're to get to the bottom of this quickly. Right now, it appears that weres are the murderer's target, but we don't know how long it will stay that way. All of our people could be in danger. So, please, don't take my question personally. I just thought it would be a good jumping off point since you mentioned your group was still edgy from the last crisis."

"I was just stating an observation," David said.

"Fair enough," Ryder said. "No harm, no foul."

"I think everyone is still on edge," Jagger said. "In my opinion, we not only have to figure out a way to find the murderer, we have to do it without adding more tension between our people. One way to do that is by keeping the investigation low profile, although I suspect word has already gotten out about the deaths. Regardless, you, as leaders, can do a lot to minimize the tension, but, as Ryder said, it has to start *here*. The doors to this office are closed. No one outside of this group will know where the clues are leading us or if they're aiming at a specific group. It doesn't matter—human, shifter, vampire…" He looked over at Danyon, then August. "Even were. In this room, all bets are off when it comes to getting to the truth of this matter. Outside of this room, we have to be supportive of one another and encourage our people to do the same."

August laced his arms together and rested them on the table. "Jagger and Ryder are right. As leader of the weres, I know how much pride a leader takes in his people. It is always easier to look at someone else, another race, another culture, and label them suspect. But it is very difficult to look at our own and do the same because it feels like a personal insult. In this case, however, if we don't put our pride aside and be willing to look at everything, even our own, we could be setting ourselves up for the war of the century."

"Don't you think that's a smidgeon over the top, August?" Armand said, while pouring himself a cup of coffee. "Certainly the death of three weres is not to be taken lightly, but you, Jagger and Ryder are making it sound like we've had a massacre, or the commencement to one. Why is that?"

"If I may…?" Jagger said, looking to August for permission to answer the question posed to him.

August nodded his consent.

"Because of extenuating circumstances," Jagger said to Armand. "They lead us to believe that the stage *is* being set for an all out massacre, particularly of weres. The evidence has lead us to conclude we're not only looking at the possibility of that occurring, but that it's inevitable."

"What are the extenuating circumstances?" David asked.

Shauna held up a hand before Jagger could answer. "I'm sorry, David, but for safety's sake, the circumstances Jagger referred to can't be revealed. It would endanger too many more lives."

"Now wait a minute," David said, crossing his arms over his chest. "You call us together to help, but you're not going to give us all of the details? What's that about?"

"How absurd," Armand said. "If you expect us to develop a strategy to end this plight, then the sharing of information is quite necessary, my dear."

Shauna had to bite her tongue to keep from shooting off at the mouth. She hated when a male, human or otherwise, took the liberty to call her "dear" or "honey." To her, it sounded so damn patronizing. Armand's tone didn't help matters either. He might as well have said to her, "Go play, little girl. The grownups have real work to do."

Fiona suddenly stood up, leaned over, and pressed her fingertips to the table. She peered at each male in the room before her eyes settled on David Dulac. "David, I'd like to ask you a few questions."

David cocked his head, his brow furrowing. "Okay, shoot."

"As Keeper of the vampires in this city, do you trust my judgment?"

"Implicitly."

"Do you think I am loyal to our race?"

"Absolutely."

"Do you believe the decisions I make for our race are made with the vampires' best interests at heart?"

"Of course."

"And why is that?" Fiona asked. "Is it only because I carry the title Keeper?"

Armand tsked. "Oh, Fiona, now please. You know you're held in high regard by your entire race. It is the same for the shifters, and how we feel about our Keeper. Caitlin earned our trust a long time ago. We believe in her loyalty because she proves it time and time again. And we know the stock she comes from. Heavens, your mother and father were strong, wise leaders, so adored by all. No one ever doubted their word or intentions. Now granted, your parents' reputation alone gave Caitlin carte blanche to our hearts, but it is being who she is, along with all she does for the shifters, that truly connects her to the very soul of our race."

"Sucking up for a larger Christmas gift this year, aren't you, Armand?" Caitlin teased.

He grinned impishly. "www-dot-tiffanys-dot-com."

Fiona winked at Caitlin and Shauna. "That was eloquently put, Armand. Thank you. I think Caitlin is extraordinary, as well. And so is Shauna—which brings me to my point. I would ask that all of you remember that just because she's the youngest Keeper, does not mean she deserves less respect. As Keepers, our word is our bond. It means everything. And when we, as Keepers, address you, the leaders of the cultures we are responsible for, it is *always* with your best interest in mind, not ours. So, David—Armand, if Shauna says that revealing certain information would endanger more lives, her words should be taken as fact. The information is not being kept from you as a power play."

With that, Fiona sat down and busied herself with a croissant. Shauna wanted to reach over the table and hug her sister for standing up for her, literally and figuratively. It was the first time she truly felt like their equal. Not just Fiona and Caitlin's little sister.

"Now, if we can get back to the business at hand," August said, placing his elbows on the table and steepling his fingers.

From where Shauna sat, she could see the small smile hiding behind his fingers. He was obviously pleased, as well, that Fiona had stood up for her.

"Unfortunately, at the moment, we don't have much to work with in respect to clues," August said. "Alphas from Lake Charles to New Orleans' West Bank have been instructed to place their strongest, most loyal weres at post. They're to keep an eye out for any unusual activity or people, beings, what have you. The challenge is we don't know what we are looking for, which brings us to one of the main questions in this case. Who or what has the strength to restrain a were once he's transformed? If we knew that answer, it would at least give us a target to aim at."

"I hope this won't be taken the wrong way," Armand said. "Like I'm unwilling to offer up my own as possible suspects, you know? But honestly, I seriously doubt the murderer is a shifter. Most of us are my size, tall and slender. Just a willow in the forest of life."

Shauna turned her head, so Armand wouldn't see her rolling her eyes.

Armand sighed heavily. "My point is that not even a dozen shifters cemented together could hold down a were."

"But what if those twelve shifted into something larger than a were?" Ryder asked. "Wouldn't it be possible then?"

Armand shot him a look. "Whose side are you on, Mr. Mallory?"

"He's on the side of justice," Caitlin said. "Haven't you been listening to what's been said? Each of us has to be willing to put our own on the table for examination. Even shifters."

This time Armand was the one to roll his eyes. He tsked and looked away, all but saying, "Go away, little gnat, go away," despite all the virtues he'd just proclaimed about Caitlin.

"They could have shifted into something bigger than a were," Jagger said. "But when a shifter changes, doesn't he or she have to mentally map what they're changing into?"

"Yes," Ryder said. "Unless they go into auto-shift."

"What's that?" Shauna asked.

"When a shifter is young and shifts for the first time, nine times out of ten, it's random, almost accidental," Ryder explained. "One day a dog, a cat, a bird, whatever, catches their attention, and, in that moment, for some odd reason, mother nature decides it's time for their first shift. So whatever they're focused on gets imprinted on their brain, and they never have to mind map that particular thing again. For many shifters, whenever they get frightened or sense danger, their shifter nature goes into automatic response and shifts them into whatever imprinted itself in the very beginning."

"If they have to mind map something or someone before changing into it, what or who is bigger than a full grown were in this area?" Shauna asked.

"Andy Saville," David said.

"Man, that guy *is* big," Ryder said.

"And he's also wolven," Shauna said.

"Doesn't matter," Jagger said. "Everything gets put on the table, remember?"

Shauna nodded hesitantly. She would have bet everything she owned, or ever would own during this lifetime, that Andy was not the murderer.

"Well, I think a vampire is completely out of the question," David said. "A vamp can't shift into just anything they please. If one did attack a were, the fight would have been fang to fang. A vamp wouldn't bother wrapping silver around a were, only to remove his claws and fangs. He'd simply rip his throat out."

"If the vamp could catch him," Danyon said, with a lopsided grin.

"Touché."

"But what if a group of vampires glamoured a were?" Caitlin asked. "Is that possible? Could they glamour a were long enough to restrain him? Once he's secured, all they'd have to do is release the glamour, and the were's anger would force his transformation."

"It's...possible," David said, after giving it a moment's thought. "But I don't think it's probable. What would they have to gain? From what we've been told, the murdered weres lost a lot of blood. Vampires wouldn't have wasted an opportunity like that. The were would have been drained dry."

"What about humans?" Fiona asked.

"I don't know how a human, or even a group of them, could have done it," Danyon said. "They would have had to subdue the were in human form, and any attempt to restrain him would have caused the were to transform. Once that happened, no human would stand a chance. One swipe of a paw, and the were would literally claw the human's face off, or rip his heart out."

"I see what you mean about the unlikelihood of it

being a human," David said. "But humans *can* be very stupid sometimes. No offense, ladies."

"None taken," Fiona said.

"I can just see some drunk yahoo and his buddies suddenly thinking they have superpowers and deciding to add a were-head to their trophy wall back home." David shrugged. "Not hard to imagine with humans, is it?"

Armand snorted in disgust. "With humans? No. Stupid is as stupid does."

"Talking about stupid," Jagger said. "Word has it that some new biker gang rode into town about a week ago. They call themselves BGW."

"What does that stand for?" Armand asked. "Big, gold watch?"

Jagger grinned. "From what I've heard, it's supposed to stand for Blood, Guts and Women."

"How original," Caitlin said, shaking her head.

"They haven't had any run-ins with the eighth precinct yet, so I don't have much information on them. I do know, though, that the gang leader's name is Frank Macina, but the members of his gang call him Big Frank. And with good reason. The guy is six-five and weighs about four hundred pounds. A stereotypical biker, even down to his bald head, which has naked women tattooed all over it."

"Oh, how tacky," Armand said.

"The word on the street is they plan to upstage the Bloods and the Crips."

"Fat chance of that happening," Ryder said, "The Bs and Cs are two of the most hard-core gangs in America.

If this so called BGW gang plans to nudge into their territory, they'd better go armed with Uzies and lots of them."

"It might not be a bad idea to talk with Macina," Jagger said. "I could be pointing at shadows here, but it seems a little too coincidental that the murders happened about the same time Big Frank and his gang got here. Might be worth checking out."

"Something else we may want to check out," Shauna said. Everyone turned to her, which made her nervous, so she looked at August and kept her focus on him. "Banjo Marks came into the store yesterday."

"Banjo Marks?" August asked.

"Yes," David said. "He's a vamp from an old bayou family who never quite fits in anywhere. Banjo does his own thing and is always high on something. To be honest, I think the kid is some sort of a half-breed and don't ask me how that's possible, because I don't have a clue. I know he's a vamp because I've seen his fangs, and I've seen him feed. But I've also seen him eat food and sleep so hard at night he'd snore. There is just something really off about the guy. He's homeless, as far as I know. Walks the streets and begs for loose change."

"Banjo just needs someone to tend to him, to care about him, that's all," Fiona said. "The kid comes into the shop a couple of times a week, and he always looks half starved. I know what you mean about him eating, David, because Banjo does eat and drink whatever I give him, just like a human. When he first started coming to A Little Bit of Magic, I didn't even know he was a vamp."

"It would be you to feed tea and cake to a junkie vamp," Jagger said, the adoration on his face blatant.

"Oh, she'd take in a stray skunk if it crossed our threshold," Caitlin said. "She'll mother anything."

"Now what about this Banjo Marks?" August asked Shauna.

"He came into the store yesterday, acting really weird."

"Banjo always acts weird," David said.

"Weirder than usual," Shauna explained. "Fiona had brought cookies to the shop that morning, and Banjo claimed he smelled them from across the street, and he wanted some. He was creating such havoc in the store, Fiona tried bringing him back into the office, offering to fix him a sandwich, but he refused to go, yelling that he wanted cookies instead. He was really wired, like he'd taken a mega dose of cocaine. Then he fixated on me, sing-songing that he'd trade me a secret for a cookie. When I finally gave him one and he ate it, he started talking about three dead blind mice, no teeth, and something about no big fingernails, and his voice changed when he said it. Sort of low and monotone. Not the chitter talk he'd been doing since he arrived. When I tried to get more information out of him, he ran out of the store. In Banjo's jumbled up way, I think he was trying to tell me that he knew about three dead weres and that their claws and fangs had been removed. I only knew about two of the weres then. How could he have possibly known all that?" Shauna wanted to tell them more—elaborate about Banjo's heightened sense of smell, about Banjo and Mattress Mattie's fight, and how she'd dented the light pole with a fist. But she didn't. She couldn't. Not without revealing what August had told her and Danyon about the metaphysical powers in were claws and fangs.

"I don't think you can trust anything Banjo says or does," David said. "Half the time he can't even remember his name."

"You may not be able to trust him," Armand said, with a flap of a hand, "but I'd love to have a little of whatever he was on right about now. I've been so exhausted lately. Probably becoming anemic. I could use the energy boost."

Caitlin glared at him, and Armand tsked and turned away.

"All I ask," August said, "is that you stay alert, keep an eye out for unusual activity, whether it is within your circle or outside of it, human or some other subculture. Nuit du Dommage is tomorrow, and all of you know how crazy it gets during that time. Because of the holiday, many were will be working longer hours, especially at night. That concerns me. With so many tourists in the city, it will be difficult to discern the unusual from the drunken norm."

"Eyes wide open here," David said.

Armand nodded. "Same for me."

"I know you probably have an alpha who's already stationed weres to keep watch on the West Bank, August," Jagger said. "But I have a friend on the force there. Really sharp guy. I'll ride over and talk to him. Find out if he's seen or heard anything."

"Are you talking about Luke Simms?" David asked.

"Yes."

"You're right. Luke's a very smart vamp. Not much gets past him."

"If you're taking the West Bank, then I'll take a couple of shifters with me Lakeside," Ryder said. "We'll check out that area, then head north."

"I've got the Quarter covered," Danyon said. "I want to find this Banjo character and the leader of that new biker gang, Big Frank."

"You may want to let me take Frank," Jagger said. "His gang might not have a lot of muscle yet, but that can make them twice as dangerous. They still have to prove to everyone how tough they are, you know? Don't get me wrong, I'm in no way saying you can't handle Frank. I'm just thinking that if he sees a badge, it might temper his mood."

Danyon smiled, but the gesture looked more menacing than pleasing. "I'm wolven, remember? I think I can handle Big Frank."

"I'll cover the Quarter with you," Shauna said.

Danyon's head snapped back as though he'd been shot. "No, you won't."

"And I'll go with you Lakeside," Caitlin said to Ryder.

"No, you're not," Ryder said adamantly. "I know you and Shauna want to help, but it's crazy enough out there.

The last thing I need is to be worrying about you getting hurt, while I'm trying to dig up a killer."

"I agree with Ryder and Danyon," Jagger said. "I think—"

"You may want to think again," Fiona said. "Because I'm going with you to the West Bank. I know I don't have to remind you that the three of us are Keepers. We protect and look after our race."

Jagger shook his head, held up a finger. "But—"

"No buts," Fiona said. "The end."

After ten more minutes of round table debates, the men finally conceded—as Shauna suspected they would.

When they finally adjourned, it was with the understanding that everyone would meet back in the conference room the morning after Nuit du Dommage so they could compare notes and share any new evidence.

As they stepped out of August's office complex and onto the street, Danyon took Shauna by the arm and pulled her closer to him.

"I know toward the end there I said it was okay for you to come with me, but I really don't want you to," he whispered. "There'll be so many people out tonight. If I end up chasing a lead, I could lose you in the crowd. Shauna, I don't know what I'd do if you got hurt."

She leaned against him and whispered back, "I promise, I won't get hurt."

He sighed heavily, and Shauna closed her eyes and breathed in deeply, taking in the air he had exhaled. She felt her body flush with heat. The response seemed inappropriate, considering the seriousness of the matter they had met about only moments ago. But she couldn't help it. She was no more in control of her body's reaction to Danyon, than she was to the cloud cover overhead.

He touched her cheek, then lifted her chin gently, until her eyes met his. Under his gaze, every molecule inside her sprang to life.

And, as was always the case when Danyon touched her, the rest of the world simply vanished.

She only wished when it returned again, it would be sans a murderer.

Chapter 13

Shauna actually felt hope as she stepped into the shower.

The meeting at August's had gone better than she'd hoped. Everyone in attendance seemed eager to help. With Jagger and Fiona working the West Bank, Ryder and Caitlin going Lakeside, and she and Danyon covering the French Quarter, they would have New Orleans pretty well covered. August had taken care of the rest of South Louisiana by having the alphas post sentinels around their territories. David and Armand would keep an eye on the traffic that flowed through their bar and restaurant. The Underworld and Muriel's were famous hot spots in the city, and eventually every tourist wound up visiting one or both. If anything new or unusual, aside from the standard freaks, who showed their behinds during Nuit du Dommage, David and Armand would either see it or hear about it.

They still didn't have any solid clues to work with, but with so many eyes and ears on alert, they stood a far better chance of finding some than they did when it was only her and Danyon.

Danyon had not exactly been forthcoming during the meeting with the leaders of the other cultures. But she admired the fact that he had put aside his reservations for the sake of the were community.

It had to be difficult being an alpha. She knew the challenges that came with being a leader, but an alpha carried much more. Not only did he have the responsibility of his pack, he had a take-charge-and-fix-it switch that never shut off. He always ran ahead, taking bullets for those behind him. It had to have felt awkward for Danyon as he stepped to one side and allowed others to join him in the lead.

At first, when all of this began, Shauna had thought pride kept him from accepting help—hers or anyone else's. Though there may have been a little truth to that; it wasn't the kind of pride that made for glory-hounds. Danyon wasn't about basking in the glory of anything. He really cared about his pack, about wolvens as a whole. She found him to be honest, honorable and a bit hard-headed—but who was she to talk?

It was impossible for Shauna not to notice that each time she thought about him, her heart thumped a bit faster and her body grew a whole lot warmer. There was no question that little Miss Stay-in-Control was falling out of control fast, and there didn't seem to be a way to stop it—not that she would have wanted to.

She wasn't a prude by any means. There had been other men in her life, even though they were few. Some she had gone out with because they were funny or intelligent, or both. Most had been decent sex partners. But every one of them had lacked something that kept her from fully committing to them.

Danyon was different.

He simply *got* her.

And he did it without her having to explain a thing to him. He seemed to intuitively know what she was about, who she was at her core. She saw it in the way he looked at her, talked to her, made love to her. She could be herself with Danyon and not be afraid that any part of who she was would be rejected.

Shauna considered herself lucky, because there had been one point in her life when she probably wouldn't have even given herself a chance to get to know him.

About two years ago, she'd gone to a party with a guy named Lance Miller, a smart, right-out-of-the-gate successful entrepreneur, who she'd been dating for about a month. The party had been for his younger cousin, Brian's, birthday, and it was packed with younger people whose music of choice had been heavy metal. The music had been cranked up so loud Shauna had thought her eardrums would burst. She had to get out of there and fast. When she told this to Lance and tried to explain how sensitive her hearing was, he had looked at her as if she had grown an additional head and three extra nostrils.

Even worse, he had been drinking rather heavily, which was obviously all he had needed to convert back to a juvenile. He started making fun of her in front of his cousin's friends, who in turn made certain to shout whenever they spoke to her, crank up the music another ten decibels, and intermittently blow air horns in the house for over an hour.

She had stormed out of there, leaving Lance to play with the rest of the juvenile delinquents. It was the last time she had spoken to Lance, much less saw him. After that experience, it had taken her a while to gather up enough courage to date again.

For Shauna, physical attraction only played a bit role when it came to relationships. There were so many other things far more important. Like enjoying each other's company, valuing each other's uniqueness—being able to laugh together, play together, appreciate similar things and having mutual interests and values.

Danyon was right on the mark in all those areas...

She turned the knob on the shower head, intensifying the spray. Standing anywhere thinking about Danyon was distracting for her. Standing naked in a soothing shower and thinking about him was downright physical torture.

She grabbed a loofah and a bottle of body wash, and was about to start scrubbing away when she thought she heard the chimes of the doorbell.

Puzzled, Shauna turned off the shower.

In order for someone to reach the doorbell, they had to get past a ten-foot tall, wrought iron gate. The only way for them to get through that gate was to be buzzed in by someone in the main section of the house. Fiona and Caitlin had left over an hour ago to meet Jagger and Ryder, so neither of them could have buzzed anyone through. It was possible that whoever went through the gate last may not have closed it all the way, then left, thinking it had latched.

Shauna waited a few more seconds, listening, but heard nothing more.

She was about to turn the shower back on, when she heard the chimes go off again.

"Who the heck can that be?" she asked aloud, and stepped out of the shower.

After wrapping herself in a towel, she padded out of the bathroom and her apartment, quickly heading for the main section of the house and the front door. Danyon wasn't due to meet her for another hour and a half, and she wasn't expecting any other company. She figured she'd look through the peephole to make certain it wasn't some kind of emergency—like someone standing out there on fire, but unless that was the case, she had no intentions of letting whoever it was into the house.

When she reached the front door, Shauna was surprised to see Danyon standing on the other side of the peephole. A thought occurred to her, and she bit her bottom lip. They had discussed the possibility of one or more shape-shifters being responsible for the murders, and although the idea had been given little merit, no one knew for sure if they weren't. What if the man standing outside her door was a shifter posing as Danyon?

She would have to let him in to know for certain. A shifter might be able to take on his appearance, but not Danyon's natural scent, which was something she knew very, very well. The only problem was she had to be close enough to him to smell it, which meant letting him into the house, which defeated the purpose. Then she remembered something…

Shauna pressed an ear to the thin crack between the door and the door frame, near one of the hinges. She squeezed her eyes shut, concentrated and prayed that her hypersensitive hearing wouldn't fail her now.

It didn't.

In a matter of seconds she heard it—the sound of his breathing. The same sound she had heard when Danyon had whispered her name—the same that had followed his moans of pleasure. She would know it anywhere—and knew that a shifter could not mimic breathing patterns.

Now that she was certain it was Danyon, Shauna suddenly felt a rush of panic, and her eyes flew open. What if he was bringing news about another dead were? She quickly unlocked the door and threw it open, forgetting she was dressed only in a towel.

"What's wrong?" she asked, not bothering with the standard hello.

"Nothing," he said, looking a little surprised—and amused.

"Then what are you doing here?"

"Do you greet all of your guests this way?"

Shauna leaned to one side, looked past his left arm,

and saw that the wrought iron gate was closed. "Just the ones I work with on murders scenes. How did you get past the gate?"

Danyon looked down at his feet. "Uh…long legs?"

"The wall and gate are ten feet tall."

"Okay…I took pole vaulting in high school?"

Shauna smiled and motioned him inside. It wasn't until she closed the door that she realized she was wrapped only in a towel. She clutched it tightly to make sure it stayed closed.

"Sorry, I'm not dressed yet," she said. "Was in the shower. Besides, you said you'd be here at ten. It's a little before eight-thirty."

"I thought we'd get a bite to eat before hitting the Quarter."

"You could have called to give me a heads up, you know."

He grinned. "Spur of the moment thing."

"Are you always this spontaneous?"

"Now that you mention it…not really. It just sounded like a good excuse for being early."

Shauna laughed softly. "Fair enough. Come in then. You can have a seat in my apartment while I get dressed."

As soon as they left the foyer and entered commons central, Danyon let out a low whistle of appreciation.

"Very nice," he said, taking in the two curving stair-cases, the wall tapestries, the chandelier and heavy oak furniture.

"Thanks," she said. "My sisters deserve all the

credit, though. I have the interior decorating talent of a porcupine."

"Oh, I bet you have a great sense of style."

"Not even close. If they had left me to decorate this place, it would look like an oversized garage." She grinned. "Fiona lives over there, in the west wing, and Caitlin lives in the east wing. My place is straight ahead."

"I think it's great that each of you have your individual space, but still live under one roof."

"Me, too. I mean don't get me wrong, I love my sisters dearly, but we'd probably get on each other's nerves if we had to live in the same space every day."

When they finally reached her apartment, Shauna signaled for him to follow her through the open door. She had obviously forgotten to close it in her mad dash to see who was at the main entry. "Here we are," she said.

She watched him look over the place from the corner of her eye. Judging by his smile, he evidently approved.

"Did your sisters decorate your apartment, as well?" Danyon asked.

"Unfortunately, no," Shauna said, closing the apartment door.

His smile broadened. "You see? I was right. You do have style."

Shauna felt herself blush. "Yeah, well…" She glanced away before he could see her turn red and waved a hand toward the couch. "Make yourself comfortable. I won't be long," she said, then turned to head for the bathroom.

"Shauna?"

Something in his voice brought her to a halt in mid-step. The tone of it had changed, and she suddenly felt like a million butterflies were fluttering in her chest. She held the towel in a death grip and turned slowly around, only to find him standing inches away from her.

The smile had faded from his lips, but his eyes were soft and warm. He reached out and gently cupped her face in his large hands.

"The real reason I came early was because I wanted to try and talk you out of coming tonight."

"We've had this discussion already. I'm—"

Danyon placed a thumb over her lips, silencing her. "I already know what you're going to say. Look, hear me out, please."

She saw worry in his eyes and nodded hesitantly.

"Everyone knows your loyalty and commitment to weres is exemplary," he said softly. "You really don't have to prove anything to anyone."

She tried to speak, to let him know that her desire to be involved had nothing to do with proving herself to anyone, but he kept his thumb firmly in place.

"It's bad enough that it's Nuit du Dommage," he continued. "You know how it brings out all the crazies. But we're looking for a murderer here, Shauna—a sick psychopath. Remember what he did to Simon and Nicole? If he can do that to two young weres who would've never harmed a soul—I don't even want to imagine what he might do to you."

She tried once again to speak, and he placed his other

thumb over her lips, obviously determined to finish saying what was on his mind.

"I understand that as a Keeper you have to look out for the safety and welfare of the weres in this city. But who takes on that responsibility if something happens to you? Think about it." He held her face a little tighter and looked deeply into her eyes. "I meant what I said when we were leaving the meeting this morning, Shauna. I really don't know what I'd do if something happened to you."

She wanted to reassure him, but his lips replaced his thumbs, and she lost the words.

His kiss was tender, and his tongue soon parted her lips, seeking the warmth of her mouth. She felt his hands in her hair—he pulled her closer.

And she melted into him.

Cupping the back of her head with one hand, he lowered his lips to her neck and lightly brushed them against her skin. The heat emanating from him set her body ablaze. She moaned, desire flooding her and bringing with it a need so great it made her tremble. Her moans soon became small gasps, as his lips moved lower. He kept his touch light and traced the edge of the towel that covered her breasts with his tongue.

She didn't realize she had let go of the towel until she felt it fall away from her body. His free hand moved surely over the swell of her left breast and gently stroked her nipple. It was already hard and aching for his lips— his tongue. She held her breath as his mouth moved toward it, then gasped when he suddenly scooped her up in his arms. She'd been so consumed and blinded by need, she hadn't seen that coming.

He carried her over to the couch, laid her on it, then leaned over her and pressed his lips to hers once again. Her mouth opened to him, and his kiss quickly matched the hunger of her own. She held on to him as his hands caressed her body, one sliding down between her legs and gently urging them open. His long, thick fingers were sure but tender as they pressed against her swollen, wet mound. She arched her back, urging his fingers inside her. But he would not be rushed…

His lips traveled slowly down the length of her neck while the tip of one finger teased her hungry lips below, pushing past them, but barely, only enough to drive her mad. Her moans became a constant, her breathing nearly non-existent. She dug her fingernails into his back, lifted her hips. His finger slipped inside her just a little, as he slowly licked his way to her breasts, down her stomach…

By the time his mouth and tongue replaced the fingers between her legs, it took but a second for her body to unleash a massive orgasm that felt as if it had been building since the beginning of time. She screamed from the force of it, bucked her hips against him, and his tongue deftly lapped all she had to offer.

Everything became a blur except him—he stood, and in less than a moment he was naked, and the thick hardness between his legs visibly throbbed, revealing his own need. She reached for him, ravenous, took him into her mouth, her tongue tingling with delight at the taste of him. He groaned loudly and she could tell by the swell of him that he was trying to contain the explosion desperate to leave his body.

It wasn't long before he pulled her away, leaned over and kissed her hard. Then his body was stretched over the length of hers, his hands on either side of her head, keeping the full weight of him off of her. She felt the bulk and length of him, hard and hot, rub against her, and she wrapped her legs around him possessively.

She cried out when he finally entered her, thrusting against him. Their bodies quickly fell into a fast, hard rhythm, neither able to control the fire raging inside of them any longer. His lips found hers, and his tongue moved in tandem with his long, deep thrusts, muffling her cries of pleasure. Her release sent her bucking wildly against him, contracting around him. He lifted his head, let out a loud groan, and she felt his hot release filling her.

Then he shifted his body carefully, slowly, until he was lying beside her in the narrow space. He held her close, both of them sweating, panting, trembling.

She closed her eyes, relishing the utter satisfaction washing over her.

Then, without thinking, she pressed a hand to his chest over his heart. Its soft, steady rhythm pulsed beneath her palm, and she marveled at how familiar it felt. As though she had known the beat of him for many lifetimes and would treasure it for many more.

Chapter 14

Danyon had made some stupid decisions in his life, but deciding to walk down Bourbon Street the night of Nuit du Dommage with Shauna in tow, weighed in at the top of the list. There were so many people walking the streets, he could barely turn in any direction. Had Shauna been any shorter than five foot eight inches, he would have had to tether her to make certain she wasn't swept away by all the pushing, shoving, and stumbling.

Even worse was the noise level. There was music, voices, shouting, car horns, police whistles, even the clop-clop-clop of horse hooves as the rental carriages went by. All of the sounds rose and fell in pitch and volume, and it pained his ears.

Danyon knew Shauna was having the same problem with the noise from the way she flinched from time to time and lowered an ear to her shoulders as though to block the sounds. He was surprised to find her so vulnerable. But lately, he often found himself surprised by her. He found his thoughts drifting back to her apartment, where they were only a couple hours ago, to the feel of her body, her lips… Before long, he had to literally shake his head to get his mind back on track.

He forced himself to think about Banjo Marks, and all Shauna had told him about the drugged out vamp. How his senses appeared to be heightened when he'd gone into A Little Bit of Magic, demanding cookies and claiming that he had smelled them from across the street. Danyon also remembered what Shauna had told him about a woman named Mattress Mattie, and how she had fought with Banjo in front of the shop, then punched a heavy metal lamp post instead of the vamp, and dented it.

If August was right about anyone being able to ingest a were's claws and fangs simply by pulverizing them, and through that ingestion, they would gain certain were attributes, like speed, heightened senses—strength, then was it possible that Banjo—and Mattie—had stumbled on to a supply? If they had, that meant a supply source—a supplier—the murderer? He had to question Banjo to find out more.

But how were they supposed to search him out in this chaos of people?

Being a natural tracker, Danyon's first instinct was to use his sense of smell to find Banjo. He didn't have a direct link to his scent, like a jacket or shirt, but he wasn't too concerned about it. A vampire gave off an acrid odor that he could usually smell a mile away. The same held true with a drug addict. Even if they had just stepped out of a shower, their bodies emitted a chemical scent, similar to gasoline. Since Banjo was both vamp and addict that narrowed his scent range considerably. But it still didn't make it easy.

Everyone walking the streets carried their own scent. Mix that with spilled alcohol, a little blood, piss and vomit, and the combined odors overwhelmed his sense of smell. It had made his nostrils flare, then constrict— flare, then constrict, as if they were confused and trying to sort and decipher the smells, so they could be placed in appropriate categories. It hadn't taken long for them to give up and roll all of the odors into one huge ball and label it "sour." Now, no matter which way he turned, hoping that a different wind direction might disintegrate that ball, it was all he smelled.

Shauna suddenly tugged on his left arm to get his attention, then pointed to a lamp post on the opposite side of the street.

"I know her," she yelled over the music blaring behind them. "She might know where we can find Banjo."

Still holding on to his arm, she took off for the other side of the street.

Danyon didn't know which woman Shauna was talking about. There were hundreds strolling Bourbon Street and at least a dozen clustered around that lamp post. Shauna seemed confident in her direction, though, so he just kept his mouth shut and followed.

He was a little surprised when she finally walked up to a large creole woman. The woman was dressed in leopard print tights and a bright orange dress or blouse—Danyon couldn't tell the difference. But he didn't have to be a clothes designer to know that if the woman raised her arms, she'd flash the entire state. Topping off her ensemble was a wide, gold lamé belt that she had cinched around her very thick waist. She had an arm wrapped around a tall, well-dressed, black man, who was looking down at her with unabashed pride.

The woman broke into a huge smile the moment she spotted Shauna.

"Girl, whatchu doin' here?" the woman asked. She disconnected herself from the man and planted both hands on her hips. "Since when you be out partyin' like—? Whoa, uh-uh, hol' up…girl, who that good lookin' hunk you got wit' you? That's your man?"

"This is Danyon Stone. Danyon, this is Lurnell Franklin. She's a regular at the shop," Shauna explained.

"Oh, yeah, that's right. I is a reg'lar. I goes there all the time, sugah. See her? That's my people right there, that be my girl." She waggled her head at Shauna. "Now what be up wit' you? All the time I go down to the shop, and you never even told me nothin' 'bout no Mr. Hunky. Where you been hidin' him, girl?" Lurnell's eyes suddenly widened. "Hol' up. Looka here…"

Lurnell turned, grabbed the arm of the man she'd been standing next to, and pulled him up alongside her. "See here? This be my man, Tyree Johnson." She leaned closer to Shauna. "He's pretty, huh?"

"He sure is. You might want to hang on to this one."

Lurnell snapped her fingers. "Girl, that ain't nothin' but a thing. I gots that man on lock." Grinning, she straightened and tugged on Tyree's arm. "Look here, Tyree, this be my girl, Shauna, from down to the shop on Royal, and that be her man, Darrin."

"Dan-yon," Shauna said louder, enunciating his name.

Lurnell's brow wrinkled. "What's wrong wit' you? You los' you hearin? That's what I said—Darrin."

Shauna glanced over at Danyon and winked. Then she turned back to Lurnell. "We're looking for Banjo. Have you seen him around here?"

"Whatchu want with shrimp bait?"

Shauna shrugged, as though it really didn't matter to her if they found him or not. "Just want to talk to him about coming into the shop all drugged up, like he was the last time he came in."

"That boy went down to you shop waxed?" Lurnell asked. "I didn't see nothin'. Where I was at?"

"You were on the phone, remember?"

"Oh…yeah," Lurnell said, then grinned up at Tyree. "I was on the flip talkin' to you, baby."

He smiled and rested a hand on her shoulder.

Lurnell shivered hard, like a dog shaking off rain water. "Lawd, look at you givin' me the want-tos like that." She fanned her face with a hand and refocused on Shauna. "So what shrimp bait do to your store? Mess it up?"

"Not really. Freaked a few customers out, though."

"That little, scrawny motha f—" Lurnell slapped a hand over her mouth, then dropped it and said to Danyon, "You gots to 'scuse me, Darrin. Sometimes I get a bad case of potty mouth when I has too much to drink. Know what I'm sayin'?"

Danyon grinned. The woman was loud and brassy, but he couldn't help but like her. "No problem," he said. "So have you seen him? Banjo?"

"Oh, hell no. With all the people trashin' 'round here, that piece of shrimp bait could of run up my damn nose, and I wouldn't have knowed it."

"Any idea where we can find him?" Danyon asked.

Lurnell blew out a raspberry. "Piss-ants like him they stay over to the weird-ass bars down to the other end over there. They got Under the Stairs—that be on the other end of Bourbon, then they got a place called Rush. That one's a couple more blocks down the same side of Bourbon. If shrimp bait ain't in neither one of them, then he probably be stuffin' his beak wit' batter, you know what I'm sayin'? Either that or the po-po done got him."

Danyon leaned over to make sure Shauna heard him. "Batter? Po-po?"

"Cocaine," Shauna explained. "And po-po means the police."

"Oh, uh-uh," Lurnell exclaimed. "You don't know what batter and the po-po is? Don't tell me somebody pretty like you is slow on the uptake, huh?"

Shauna intercepted quickly, cocking a finger at her. "Girl, he's not slow on nothin', you hear what I'm sayin'?"

"Yeah, you right!" Lurnell said, with a huge grin and slapped her hands together.

The two women laughed, and Danyon had to smile at how easy it had been for Shauna to fall into rhythm with Lurnell's street talk.

"Hey," Lurnell said. "We goin' down to the Cat's 'cause I got to do me some karaokin'. Y'all wanna— what the hell…?" She suddenly stood at attention on tiptoe, gawking at something over Shauna's shoulder. "Well, I'll be damn. Looka that sumabitch."

Danyon and Shauna turned and looked in the direction she indicated. All Danyon saw was a sea of people.

Shauna evidently caught sight of what Lurnell was talking about, because she glanced back and shouted over the crowd noise, "I've never seen him out at any of these things. You?"

"No, me neither. But that dog sure steppin' out to-night."

"Who are you talking about?" Danyon asked Shauna.

She took him by the arm and pointed straight ahead. "See the man in the purple shirt?"

"Yes…"

"And the woman to his right dressed all in red?"

"Yeah?"

"Look between them and to the right a little. See the big guy standing a few feet in front of them, the one in the white shirt? He's got a—"

"The heavyset guy with the boa constrictor hanging around his neck?"

"Heavyset?" Lurnell said. "That man be dressin' four-fifty on the hoof for sure."

"Right," Shauna said to Danyon. "That's Papa Gris Gris. He owns the voodoo shop next to Sistah's, which is Lurnell's store. They've been competitors for years."

"Any idea what would make him come out tonight?" Shauna asked Lurnell, who was now standing beside her.

"Hell, yeah, I got a idea. Look at that skank rubbin' up against him."

Next to the man Shauna had identified as Papa Gris Gris, Danyon saw a very skinny younger woman rubbing her nearly exposed breasts across the fat man's left arm.

Shauna must have spotted her, as well, because she asked, "Who is that?"

"Girl, that be Trish I-gots-the-crabs Deveraux. She work down to the Hustle Club, and that skank be heavy on the batter. She out there doin' the nasty wit' Gris Gris 'cause he gots some blow, you know?"

"You mean he deals cocaine?" Shauna asked.

"There be only one reason why she'd be be hangin' on that fat man. He either got the blow or the dough. She tryflin', that's what she be doin'. Now that's said, yeah. She already don't got a pot to piss in or a window to throw it out of."

It was easy to see that the woman was putting the moves on Gris Gris, and that all four hundred plus pounds of him thoroughly enjoyed it. She was playing the tease, and he had jumped into the game with both feet.

Danyon turned away. He needed to get out of here. Not that any place else would be any less crowded, but at least moving would help circulate the air around him. They needed to move on with the night and find Banjo.

He inched forward through the crowd with Shauna still holding on to his arm and glanced back over his shoulder just long enough to say, "Nice meeting you Lurnell—Tyree."

"Oh, you, too, baby. When you down to Rampart Street, you come to Sistah's and see me. I'm gonna give you a good discount to whatever be up in my store."

Danyon gave her an obligatory thank-you, waved, then pushed ahead through the crowd. Shauna was evidently still watching Gris Gris because her head was still turned in that direction and she hadn't said goodbye to Lurnell.

Inching ahead, he detoured around a guy in a clown suit and was about to detour left, when Shauna suddenly dug her fingernails into his arm.

Something in the way she gripped him told Danyon that it had nothing to do with controlling the direction he was heading or stopping him.

It felt more like a reflex, and judging by the look on her face, what prompted it was fear.

Chapter 15

"Digging your way to China with those nails?" Danyon asked, patting Shauna's hand.

She threw a quick glance his way. "Huh?"

He motioned to her hand on his arm.

"Oh...sorry." She released the pressure, but didn't let go.

She hadn't realized how tightly she had been gripping him because her complete attention had been on Papa Gris Gris and Trish.

Not long after Lurnell had pointed them out, Shauna found herself being slowly sucked into a weird sound tunnel, something she had never experienced before. It happened gradually at first. So gradually she didn't notice.

She remembered asking Lurnell if Gris Gris was a

cocaine dealer, but not much more after that. For some odd reason, she became fixated on Gris Gris and Trish's mouths, watching them move whenever they spoke. Before long, she started to pick up a word or two that fell in sync with the movement of their lips. When that happened, Shauna took notice of what had changed and was changing around her.

The jumble of faces that belonged to the mass of people crushing them from all sides had grown blurry, while Gris Gris and Trish remained sharp in her line of sight. The noise that had reached inhuman levels had lessened a little in volume. It was still earsplitting to her, but it had dropped enough so that if she turned just so, she was able to hear a few more words.

And what little she had picked up so far was scaring the hell out of her.

"You okay?" Danyon asked.

"I'm…not sure."

"What do you mean, you're not sure?"

Shauna hitched a thumb in Gris Gris' direction. "See the man and woman Lurnell was talking about a little while ago?"

"Nasty snake man and Trish? Yeah. What about them?"

She peered up at Danyon, praying he wouldn't think she was crazy. "Can you…uh…can you hear anything they're saying?"

"Hear them? There's so much noise out here, I can hardly hear you. Wait…don't tell me you can hear what those two are saying from here. Over all this noise?"

"Well—"

"Hey, lookee here, Joe, I found us 'nother one!" A short, skinny, drunk guy, wearing a camouflage T-shirt with GET 'ER DONE! stenciled across the front, suddenly stepped up to Shauna. Even in the glow of the street lights, she could see the red spider veins that covered his cheeks and the end of his bulbous nose.

"Excuse me," Shauna said, and peered over his left shoulder. She didn't want whatever sound connection she had picked up with Gris Gris and Trish to get lost.

The drunk laughed until he nearly fell backwards, then he held a fistful of Mardi Gras beads up to her face. "Hey, you, purty lady—"

"Time to move on, friend," Danyon said to him.

With his timing off a few beats, the drunk looked over and up at Danyon. "Damn, you a big boy, ain't ya?"

Danyon glowered at him. "I said you need to go."

The drunk's brain was either two Gherkins over-pickled or he was just plain stupid, because he turned back to Shauna and dangled the beads in her face again.

"Hey, you, purty lady. You want you some of these here Murdi Gass beads? 'Cause you can have 'em if ya show me them there purty little boobies of yours."

Before she had a chance to respond, Danyon grabbed the guy by the scruff of the neck and literally yanked him up off his feet. He jerked the guy up close, nearly nose to nose.

"I want you to apologize to the lady for what you said," Danyon said.

The drunk blinked, looked around, obviously confused. "Where's Joe?"

Danyon shook the little man, and the guy appeared to suddenly wake up. Fear widened his eyes.

Shauna saw the muscles in Danyon's arm begin to ripple. She reached out to him. "Please, don't. It's okay."

Not breaking eye contact with the drunk, Danyon said, "No, it's not okay." He gave the guy another little shake. "Is it, buddy? Now apologize to the lady."

"I'm sorry," the drunk cried. "Sorry, sorry, sorryer'n I can be!"

"Danyon..." Shauna touched his arm. "Please."

His jaw muscles tightened, then relaxed. Then he opened his hand and let the drunk drop to the ground. The guy landed on all fours, and he stayed that way, scrambling away like a crab.

"What's wrong with you?" Shauna said. "You could have really hurt that guy."

"He's lucky I didn't kill him for talking to you like that."

"He was just drunk. I could've handled him."

"I don't care if he was drunk. I'm not going to have anybody disrespect you that way, especially when I'm around."

Suddenly remembering Gris Gris and Trish, Shauna stood on tiptoe and scanned the crowds until she spotted them again. The weird sound tunnel that had connected her to them earlier was no longer there. All she heard was street noise.

Shauna squinted and was about to concentrate on Gris Gris and Trish's mouth like she had before, when she felt Danyon's hand on her shoulder and his breath against her left cheek.

"You never got a chance to answer my question," he said. "Can you really hear those two over all this noise?"

"Right now? No. But earlier…I don't know if it had something to do with the direction of the wind and where I was standing, but…" She peered up at him. "Yes, I heard a little of what they were saying."

Danyon arched a brow, evidently impressed. Then he looked in Gris Gris and Trish's direction, cocked his head, and squinted as though to get a bead on their voices. Shauna found it curious that he did the very same thing she did whenever she wanted to identify a particular sound or find its origin. She couldn't help but wonder if he too experienced the emotional pleasures and pain that came from acute hearing.

Shauna had discovered young that most sound carried an emotion to the listener in some form or fashion.

Fear—curiosity—comfort—heartache—joy—relief—panic.

Being a kid with overactive myringi and living in a never silent world, she'd had a hard time figuring out what to do with the constant influx of sound and emotion. Each seemed to beg so many questions. Should she keep this emotion that came with that sound? Or should she shelve it? Was there something to learn from that sound or this emotion? Or should she sweep it under a rug and hope she'd never have to hear it and feel it again? Was that sound and that emotion supposed to spur her to action? Or was it calling for inaction and silence?

As she grew older, Shauna learned that the noise of the fast paced world in which she lived often evoked more negative emotions than positive ones. She had discovered ways to temper the onslaught, but still, even now, it wasn't always easy to keep them balanced. More times than not, she had to search for the sounds that gave her peace and comfort. Like a soft giggle hidden behind the hand of a small, shy child—the gentle purring from a contented cat as it threaded its way around her legs—the sound of a breeze heading her way to cool the heat of the day. Whenever she found these treasures, she stored them in memory and pulled them out whenever the bad became too much to handle, which seemed to be too often. Sounds like—the last, ragged breath of the dying—the crunch of metal and the snap of bones that came from a car accident too far away to be seen—the cry of a heartache muffled in a pillow by someone who had been taught that the strong don't cry—the whimper of a sick child too pained to move—the keening of a dying, mourning wolven.

"Hearing anything?" Shauna asked Danyon.

He shook his head hesitantly. "Maybe a word or two, but I can't really tell for sure if it's coming from them. With all this noise, the couple of words I think I'm picking up are garbled and don't make sense. As far as I can tell, it's just a fat guy being hit on by a junkie who's looking for either money or a fix. I don't get why that's such a big deal. What am I missing?"

Suddenly, a pot-bellied man wearing an oversized diaper fastened at the hips with ridiculously large safety pins stumbled by. He was sucking on a huge pacifier when he bumped into Danyon. The pacifier popped out of his mouth and hit the street. "S'cuse me," he said, and a plume of whiskey and onion breath hit Shauna full in the face. She gagged and quickly turned her head away. The guy leaned over to pick up the pacifier and stumbled sideways. The dozen or more Mardi Gras beads he had hanging around his neck slapped against his hairy chest.

Shauna gave Danyon a "take it easy on this one, will you?" look.

He responded with a half-smile, then helped the guy stand upright. "Careful, buddy."

After sending the drunk on his way, he asked Shauna, "Has your hearing always been that sensitive?"

She shrugged. "Ever since I can remember."

He studied her for a moment, and Shauna saw wonder in his eyes. She looked away, suddenly embarrassed. "It's no big deal. More a pain in the rear than anything. You should try being in the Superdome during a Saints' football game with ears like mine. All those people cheering and screaming…"

"Can you make out what snake man and his girlfriend are saying now?" Danyon asked.

Shauna turned toward Gris Gris and Trish. Since she didn't know how the sound tunnel was formed the first time, she didn't know how to recreate it. So, she did what she always did when zeroing in on a sound—Shauna tilted her head, squinted, and concentrated. She watched the movement of their mouths.

Trish Deveraux's voice came through almost immediately, but, as before, her words were choppy, disjointed.

"—give you—money. I…it, honey."

Trish rubbed up against Gris Gris provocatively. It didn't take someone with great hearing to know she was hitting on the man.

"Anything?" Danyon asked.

"Sounds like a drug deal's going down."

"That's no surprise. Lurnell told us she was a user. We really don't have time to bother with those two right now, anyway."

"I know, but Gris Gris is talking about some weird stuff."

"Maybe so, but from what you said about Banjo, how he acted in the shop, smelling the cookies from across the street, then the whole thing with Mattie—I think he's our best lead so far. Let's—"

Shauna held up a hand. "Wait. Gris Gris just said… 'Gonna make you feel—you God—makes you God—it does—ain't got—but I can.' Now Trish is saying, 'Gotta have…bad.' Gris Gris again—he's saying, 'Thousand dollars—ounce—clean—pure—fresh ground.' Now Trish is saying, 'Ain't got thousand—give blow—for it.' Okay, Gris Gris again, 'Only me.'"

Then their conversation was interrupted by a couple

who stopped to coo over the snake. She saw Trish begin to fidget, pace, evidently agitated that the couple had stolen Gris Gris' attention.

Oddly enough, Shauna heard the couple talking about the snake so clearly, they might as well have been standing two feet away. The woman was doing most of the talking. Her accent had a twangy, southern lilt to it, very different from the Creole and Cajun accents from south Louisiana.

"I swear, I ain't never seen a snake that big," the woman said. "Back home, in Valdosta, my PawPaw always taught me not to touch snakes 'cause you never know which of 'em is poisonous and which of 'ems not. And you know, back home in Valdosta, we have these here kinda snakes we call egg-suckers. They ain't big like your snake, but they'll crawl right on up the fence of the coop and help themselves. They take them baby chick eggs right out from under the mama chicken. She can peck 'im and peck 'im and squawk 'til the cows come home, but that don't bother that ol' snake none. Can I touch your snake?"

Although Shauna didn't hear Gris Gris' response, he must have given the woman permission because she reached out and poked the boa with the tip of a finger.

"Oh, my, she's dry," the woman said. "I heard snakes was slimy and all, but I never held one before so I didn't know for sure. I think she's pretty, though."

The man standing near the woman, took her by the arm and was urging her to get moving.

"Oh, okay, then—well, bye-bye now," the woman said to Gris Gris. "Thank you for lettin' us look at your snake."

No sooner did the couple walk away, than Trish glued herself back to Gris Gris' side. She saw Trish slide a hand over the big man's belly, all the way down to his groin. A sneer crossed Gris Gris' face. Shauna didn't know what made her more nauseous, seeing that or the guy with the whiskey-onion breath. Then Trish stepped in front of Gris Gris, and from the way she moved, it was a sure bet that she was rubbing her breasts against the man's chest.

Shauna shook her head. "I can't hear anything now. Not with Trish in front of him like that."

"I don't know about them," Danyon said. "To be honest, what you said they were talking about didn't sound that weird to me. I think you're right about it being a drug deal, but they could be talking about anything, heroin—cocaine—meth."

"A thousand dollars an ounce?"

He shrugged. "Like I said, I don't know. They could have been talking about more than one thing, and you might have picked the words up out of sequence. I mean really, Shauna. Take a good look at the guy. He's so big he probably loses his breath just crossing the street. Can you really picture him trying to hold down a were?"

"No…but I think he knows something—they both know something."

"I think you're pulling at straws."

She shook her head. "I don't think so."

"All right, I'll keep everything you've said in mind, but humor me for now, will you? Let's find Banjo first. I think he's a more solid lead, and we need to follow through with it. It's not going to get any easier with this crowd. The later it gets the more crowded it'll become. And crazier. I don't know how we're going to find Banjo in this mass of people as it is."

"Okay, but I want to stay here for a few more minutes. Maybe we'll hear more."

"We're wasting time. Look, Rush is only two or three blocks from here, and according to Lurnell, it's one of Banjo's regular hangouts. So we'll start there." He turned, ready to leave.

Shauna tugged on his arm. "Wait. What if we move a little closer to Gris Gris and Trish? We'll hear more if we're closer."

"We can't go over there," Danyon said. "Not with all these people. To get anywhere out here, you have to flow with the foot traffic, not against it. We'll get to them next if we need to, but I really don't think Gris Gris makes a solid candidate. Besides, if he was dealing some new drug, or any drugs at all, don't you think Lurnell would know since her store isn't far from his?"

Shauna wanted to argue back, to plead her case. Something in her gut was telling her to pay attention to what Gris Gris had to say. But Danyon was already in motion, his mind evidently made up that they had to get to Banjo first.

With little choice but to follow, Shauna squeezed

through the crowds after him. She had a sneaking suspicion that Gris Gris was somehow involved with the were deaths, and she planned to find out why, how, and with whom.

And she'd do it with or without Danyon's help.

Chapter 16

Shauna wound up clinging to the back of Danyon's shirt as they made their way down Bourbon. He had been right about the crowd getting worse as it got later. Even now, they weren't able to walk side by side, so she had to trail behind him.

From the safety of Danyon's height and width, she saw men and women hanging off of balconies on the second floors of restaurants and bars, most of them dangling Mardi Gras beads of different shapes and colors over the railing, offering them as prizes to anyone on the street below brave enough to show a little skin. The alcohol flowed, breasts were bared, pants were yanked down, offering a full moon view to whoever had the biggest, brightest beads. Some people were dressed in costumes that ranged from cartoon characters to horror movie headliners like Freddy Kruger, Jason in the infamous hockey mask and, of course, Leatherface, only this one carried a plastic chainsaw. Some were dressed in street clothes, others barely wore clothes at all. Many wore Mardi Gras masks that were decorated with purple plumage and sprinkled with green and gold glitter.

To many people, New Orleans was the party capital of the world. They loved coming to the city because they knew she would open her arms wide, no matter their race, sexual preference, or political beliefs. Most of the tourists who came for Nuit du Dommage and Mardi Gras loved wearing the costumes and masks because it gave them an outlet to shed their inhibitions and do things they normally wouldn't do. Shauna saw the city in a slightly different light. To her, New Orleans was a safe haven—a mother, a lover, a friend, one who would accept you without judgment when you removed the mask you wore in everyday life. People love New Orleans for different reasons, and although she welcomes all who come to her door, there are only a few that she truly loves back. Shauna could always spot those fortunate people. They were the ones who saw beyond the booze and glitz and free-for-alls. They truly *got* her.

It seemed to be taking forever for them to cover the two blocks needed to reach the Rush club. They had been inching along so slowly, that it took Shauna a few minutes to realize they had come to a dead stop.

She tugged on Danyon's shirt, and he leaned toward her.

"Why did we stop?" she asked.

"Best I can tell, the police are breaking up a fight up ahead."

"This is ridiculous," Shauna said. "We're not making any progress. Let's go back to where Gris Gris and Trish were. I just know there's something going on there."

He shook his head. "It'll be even more difficult going back than it is going forward. And we can't be everywhere at once. Besides, you only heard bits and pieces of their conversation. If we took that trail instead of the one we're on with Banjo, we might be led down a never ending rabbit hole. You heard Banjo clearly. You said he talked about no teeth and no big fingernails—I want to start where I think we'll have a decent shot of at least getting more information. We can get to the snake man later. He's not going anywhere. A four-hundred pound man who uses a boa constrictor as an accessory can't have that many places to hide."

"Maybe not, but—Hey…that's him! There he is!"

Danyon snapped to attention. "Who? Where?"

"Banjo. Over there in the orange shirt!" She pointed ahead and to the right. It was by chance she had caught sight of him. Out the corner of her eye, she had spotted something orange popping in and out of view. It caught her attention long enough for her to see that it was a person with a pointed head and long, greasy, brown hair and was wearing a bright orange shirt. The person appeared to be jumping up and down, like they were spring-loaded, and it wasn't until the person turned slightly that she saw Banjo's face just as he jumped on the upswing.

A couple of seconds after she pointed him out to

Danyon, Banjo was no longer jumping in and out of view. Fearing he had spotted her, as well, Shauna pushed aggressively through the crowd, trying to reach the spot where she had seen him. But the more she pushed and shoved, the tighter the crowds wrapped around her.

"I think we lost him," Shauna shouted to Danyon.

"No, we didn't," he said, then grabbed her hand and forged ahead. "I saw him run into Opal's bar."

Shauna soon found herself trotting to keep up with Danyon. He didn't have to push anyone out of the way. People saw him charging ahead, and they simply parted to make way.

In a matter of minutes, Danyon veered left, still pulling her along, then crossed the open doorway into Opal's.

Like any other bar on Bourbon on a busy night, Opal's was dark, save for the neon beer sign over the bar and a couple of blue and red spotlights that showcased a blues band playing in one corner. The small joint smelled of booze, sweat and cigarette smoke, and was as packed as the street outside. The loud thump of music, glasses clinking, people laughing and talking, the noise was almost more than Shauna could bear.

Still holding her hand in a vice grip, Danyon led her to the long stretch of bar on the left.

The bartender was a short, sweaty man wearing a bad hairpiece. He was running from one end of the bar to the other, replacing empty beer bottles with fresh cold ones and pouring shots of bourbon, vodka, and tequila. Danyon signaled him over.

"Get to ya when I get to ya, Bubba," the bartender said as he rushed past Danyon to deliver a drink to a woman sitting at the other end of the bar. As he raced back in the opposite direction, Danyon leaned over the bar, grabbed him by the shirt tail and pulled him up close.

"Hey, man! Get your hands off me. What the hell you…" It was about this time that the bartender appeared to get a really good look at who he was talking to and the size of the hand that held on to him. "Yeah, okay, whatever. What you gonna have, man?"

"Nothing," Danyon said. "Have you seen a guy running through here? Bright orange shirt, long hair, skinny?"

The bartender shook his head. "Dude, you're talking about half the drunks in the city right now."

Danyon pulled him up a bit closer. "Do I look like a dude to you?"

"Uh…no. No, man, no. I'm just saying. Shit, I'm just doing my job. There're so many people in and out of here, everybody starts looking the same after a while. I don't know if the guy you're looking for has even been in here. Look, help yourself—look around the joint if you want. Maybe he's out back or something. You a cop are what?"

"Or what," Danyon said, then pointed to an open door on the other side of the bar. "What's back there?"

"Bathroom, storage space, that's it. Hey, uh…you mind letting go of my shirt?"

Danyon gave him a hard look before releasing his hold on him. "Got a back door?"

"Naw, man it's an old building. No place for a back-door."

"What happens if a fire starts in here?" Shauna asked. "How do people get out?"

The bartender shrugged. "Some do, some don't."

While Danyon and the bartender continued their little "tete-a-tete," Shauna glanced about, searching through the crowd for Banjo. A flash of orange suddenly darted in front of the bandstand, then it wiggled through the crowd and slipped between the wall and the door jam, like a cockroach running for cover under a baseboard.

"Over there!" Shauna shouted, then pulled out of Danyon's grip and took off after Banjo. Fortunately, Danyon didn't waste time by stopping her to ask for clarification. Within seconds, he was beside her and forcing a path through the throng of people.

As soon as they got outside, Danyon asked, "Which way?"

Shauna looked from left to right. "I'm not sure. I saw him slip out the door on the left, so…maybe this way?" She pointed left.

"No, right there!" Danyon grabbed her hand again and took off running.

Before Shauna knew it, they were barreling into "Bare-ly, Barely, Barely," one of the many strip clubs on Bour-bon that redefined the term, "adult entertainment."

The place was much bigger than Opal's, with three circular stages in the main room. A metal pole rose from the center of each stage, and attached to each pole was a gyrating woman wearing nothing but a glittering

G-string and stilettos. Shauna was surprised that she wasn't undone with embarrassment, especially with Danyon beside her. She couldn't help but watch the women, fascinated by how effortlessly they stretched, climbed and wrapped their bodies around the poles.

As the woman in the middle finished her routine, she slid down her pole, slowly winding her body around it as she lowered herself. When her stilettos hit the platform, Shauna spotted Banjo on the opposite side of her stage. His body was pressed against it, and his arms were spread out wide. It took a second or two for Shauna to realize that Banjo was dry humping the stage.

Taking advantage of Banjo's preoccupation, Shauna tapped Danyon on the arm and pointed him out as inconspicuously as possible. She felt his body tense, as though ready to spring into action. She signaled for Danyon to lower his head so she wouldn't have to yell to be heard and possibly risk alerting Banjo again.

"We're going to have to sneak up on him," Shauna said, when he lowered an ear to her. "If we try to charge him, he'll see us and take off again for sure. You stay here in case he goes for the front door. I'm going to slip around the stages and see if I can come up from behind him."

"You trap that wild thing from the back, and you're going to have a hell of a fight on your hands," Danyon said. "I'll get behind him."

"No way," Shauna said. "You're too tall. He'll be able to see you coming from a mile away."

"And you're short?"

"No, but I'm shorter than you."

With that, Shauna made her way stoop-shouldered through the male dominated crowd, then took her time going around the stages until she was directly behind the center platform. Banjo was still preoccupied, evidently determined to impregnate the stage.

The crowd that stood between him and Shauna was at least four rows deep. She sneaked past the back two rows without anyone taking notice, then braved the third. Most of the men in the place appeared singularly focused, their eyes locked on the swaying breasts and gyrating hips. No one paid any attention to her, and she wanted it to stay that way. She continued to inch forward, keeping an eye on Banjo. The last thing she wanted was to lose sight of him again. She didn't even bother looking for Danyon to make certain he was standing guard at the door in case Banjo bolted. She simply trusted that he was where he needed to be.

By the time Shauna reached the last row of men, the one closest to the stage and the only obstacle left between her and Banjo, she was holding her breath.

So close now…

All she had to do was duck around the last row of men, and she would be home free. She was determined to get hold of Banjo, even if it meant taking him down with a flying tackle. But she had to get close enough to him to make that happen.

She turned sideways and gently pushed past two men who stood gaping at the live version of what had probably been their greatest sexual fantasy since puberty. Her right foot had barely touched the open space between the stage and those men, when she heard the whistling and catcalls begin.

"That's right, girl! Go on up there and show them how to work it!"

The place erupted with whooping and hollering, cheering and clapping.

"Take them clothes off, girly!"

Worrying that Danyon had heard that last request and might come storming through, looking for blood, Shauna shot through the last row of men and took off for Banjo.

She wasn't two feet past the starting line, when Banjo spun around, spotted her, and bolted for the front door of the club. Shauna ran after him and saw Danyon standing in the doorway like a linebacker, arms outstretched and ready to catch the slippery little worm.

Banjo evidently noticed Danyon, as well, because he darted left, then right, then left again, like he was trying to come up with an escape strategy.

Shauna raced past the first two dance platforms and the cat calls grew louder. The noise sent Banjo whirling about, and when he saw how close she was, he began to serpentine right, then left, circling, circling. She heard him laugh, that horrible, twittering sound that hammered on her nerves, and gritted her teeth.

Still laughing, Banjo darted hard to the left, then dove into the crowd that had gathered to watch.

Fearing they might lose him, Shauna raised a hand over her head and signaled Danyon to Banjo's location.

Obviously understanding what she meant, Danyon
sprinted in the direction she had indicated. Seconds later,
when Shauna came to a stumbling stop beside Danyon—
Banjo was no longer in sight.

"No way!" Danyon said, incredulously. "Where in the
hell did he go?"

"Over there!" a man standing in the doorway shouted.
He pointed outside and to the left.

"There! He ran that way!" a handful of men yelled,
all of them pointing in the same direction as the man
before them. They were obviously anxious to see this
ordeal through to its conclusion.

When Shauna and Danyon reached the street, a tall
guy wearing a new Orleans Saints' ball cap and a Dallas
Cowboys jersey was standing on the sidewalk, pointing
and yelling. "He ran inside the Lightning! Over in the
Lightning!"

Puzzled, because she didn't know of any bar or restaurant in the area with that name, Shauna shouted over
at the guy in the ball cap. "Where's the Lightning?"

The man raised both hands over his head and pointed
adamantly to his left. "There—there!"

Concerned that she might be dealing with another
drunk who didn't know his rear end from a hole in the
ground, Shauna scanned the street as best she could with
so many people in the way, to see if any of the blinking,
multi-colored business signs on either side of Bourbon
read Lightning. As far as she could tell, none did.

"Got it," Danyon suddenly shouted, then grabbed

Shauna by the hand and pulled her along as he pushed forward.

Half a block down, he pointed to a small swinging sign that hung over the threshold of a narrow entryway. The sign read, *UNDER the STAIRS,* and the logo beside it was a yellow lightning bolt. As soon as Shauna read it, she recognized the name. It was one of the dives Lurnell had told them that Banjo frequented. Shauna let go of Danyon's hand and quickly took the lead through the entryway.

Immediately upon entering, she was surprised to find a short flight of stairs instead of the main room of the bar. With Danyon following close behind, she took the stairs two at a time only to find herself in a narrow hallway once she reached the top. The walls were black and splattered with orange, green, red and blue neon paint that came to life under a black light. At the end of the hall was another set of stairs, which led them to a narrow landing, then another set of stairs, and yet another landing.

"This is like a maze from a horror movie," Shauna said.

The last hallway ended at the top of a longer flight of stairs. Shauna went down first, following the stairway down, down, down. The maze of stairways and landings, then the final set of stairs heading down, had been built to create the illusion that you were going further below ground than the first floor. Shauna thought that odd, since anyone who lived in, or had been to, New Orleans knew going below ground was impossible, given most of the city was at or below sea level.

At the bottom of the stairs was the entrance to the club. It was no bigger than Opal's, but just as dark and dank. The place wasn't nearly as crowded, though, and the jukebox playing in the corner was at a moderate volume. An Asian couple swayed slowly together beside it, and it looked more like they were holding each other up than dancing. A pool table stood at the back of the room, and a few lopsided wooden tables with accompanying plastic chairs of various colors had been placed haphazardly about the bar. People were clustered into small groups here and there, most of them hidden by shadows.

"See any sign of him?" Danyon asked.

"No," Shauna said through gritted teeth. Anger was rolling its way to fury inside her. How was it possible for that scrawny twerp to keep slipping out from beneath them? A thought suddenly struck her, pitching her anger right past fury to a tsunami of rage.

What if Banjo had purposely led them on a wild goose chase so real business could be taken care of elsewhere? Had he been sent as a diversion? What in the hell was his connection to this? Shauna wanted to wrap her hands around Banjo's scrawny neck and choke the answer out of him.

"Anybody here see a scrawny guy in an orange shirt run through here?" Shauna asked loudly.

The answer was the clack of billiard balls being racked and set—the *schtack* from a pop top—the screech of a chair shifting on a concrete floor. No one else said a word.

"Unless there's an exit door we don't know about," Shauna said to Danyon, "there's no way Banjo could've gotten out of here without us seeing him. We would have passed him on the stairs."

Danyon nodded and walked over to the bar. She followed, hoping he had picked up the same feeling she had—that the people in this bar might not take too kindly to their bartender being grabbed by the collar.

When they reached the bar, Danyon rested an arm on it, then asked the middle-aged guy standing behind it, "You have a back door here?"

The man's eyes stayed flat as he shook his head. Then he turned his back to Danyon and started rearranging bottles on the shelf by the register.

"Was that a no?" Danyon pressed.

The bartender didn't respond.

Exhausted from being pushed and shoved on the street for hours, tired of not being any closer to answers than when they started, and furious that Banjo had managed to slip past them again, Shauna quick-stepped to the bar before Danyon could stop her, then leaned over it and slapped a hand on the Plexi-glass top.

"He asked you if there was a back door," she declared. "If you can't answer the damn question, I'll go looking for it myself."

The bartender turned and looked at her, and for a moment, Shauna expected him to either burst out laughing or pick up the phone and call the police. Instead, he cocked his head toward the pool table.

Thinking he may have just given away Banjo's hiding place, she spun about on her heels.

But it wasn't Banjo.

It was a huge white man about Danyon's height, but at least two and a half times his weight. He had an acne scarred face, dark eyes that were too small for his face, and a bald head that not only looked like it was a transplant from a bulldog, it was covered with tattoos of naked women.

He stared at Shauna and leaned over the pool table, stick in hand as if preparing to shoot. His thick lips curled into a sneer, that all but said, *"You're one good lookin' piece of prime rib, and I'm hungry."*

The man had to be Big Frank Macina, the leader of the BGW gang that Jagger had told them about, the biker gang that thought they were big and bad enough to take over some Blood and Crip territory.

She wanted to laugh at the absurdity of it. Macina didn't look big and bad. He looked like he needed a bath, a dentist, and a hard-hitting weight loss program.

It suddenly struck Shauna as she stared at his tasteless tattoos—what better way would there be for a new gang to take turf from one of the toughest gangs in the country than to be the sole provider of the most potent drug in the underground market?

The answer to that was simple.

None.

Without giving it a second thought, Shauna stormed toward Big Frank.

She was a Keeper and was responsible for the safety and well-being of the weres in this city. She was also responsible for helping to keep peace between her weres and every other race living in the city.

However, there was one race she could not have cared less about maintaining peace with—assholes.

In her book, anyone out to harm her weres, directly or indirectly, fit into that category.

Being a Keeper wasn't her job. It was her purpose in life. And if that meant tackling a three hundred and fifty pound, tattooed, yeast-colored piece of crap like Macina, then so be it.

Whatever it took to protect her weres.

And nothing and no one was going to stop her.

Chapter 17

Danyon had one eye on the bartender, wondering if a quick jab and a nose realignment might re-circuit the guy's attitude and sharpen his memory, when he spotted Shauna heading for the pool table.

"Hey!" he called after her, meaning to get her attention, to stop her.

It didn't work.

He saw that her hands were balled into fists at her side and knew big trouble was on the way.

Danyon took off after her, intending to steer Shauna toward a quick exit up the stairs, but he was two steps too short. Shauna was already leaning over the pool table, confronting the bull mastiff who was holding a pool stick.

Earlier, he had been so focused on finding Banjo and

keeping Shauna out of trouble, that he hadn't noticed the tattoos on the big man's bald head. The entire lumpy sphere was covered with ink drawings of naked women in different poses. Danyon remembered the description Jagger had given them of the leader of the BGW biker gang that had recently come into town. Although there were a lot of people in New Orleans right now for Nuit du Dommage, he seriously doubted he would find more than one man who fit the gang leader's description. He had no doubt he was about to meet Big Frank Macina.

Shauna kicked that meeting off with all the grace and charm of a MacDonald ready to take on the world.

"So, what's your game?" Shauna asked.

Danyon stood about six feet behind her, trying to figure out if he should just scoop her up now and get her out of here, or let her get out whatever she had in her system. He also had to consider that she was a Keeper, which meant he needed to respect her space and abilities, instead of jumping at every turn to protect her, the way he had with the drunk on Bourbon earlier. Standing back and just watching was far from easy. His basic nature and instinct wanted to toss Shauna over his shoulder and haul her outside. But who was he kidding? Even if he did haul her out against her will, she would just turn around and head right back in. What concerned Danyon even more, was that he knew even if he wasn't standing right behind her as backup, Shauna would still be up in Big Frank's face.

Frank's grin was wide and nasty. He tossed the pool

stick on the table and laid his big hands palm down on the felt.

"Say again?" he said to Shauna.

"I said, what's your game?" Shauna repeated. The Travis Tritt song that had been playing on the jukebox went silent, and the entire bar fell into an eerie hush.

Frank glared at Shauna, his eyes unwavering. "I'd say the game's you, Missy."

"You run with some skinny chick named Trish and a guy who goes by the name Banjo Marks?" she asked.

Frank's grin grew wider, and he stood upright and sauntered over to the corner of the pool table, then leaned a hip against it and folded his tree trunk-size arms across his chest. "What's it to ya?"

"Simply asking a question."

"And I just gave you a simple answer."

"No, you didn't. You gave me another question," Shauna said.

Frank laughed, a deep rumbling sound that had no humor in it at all. "Little girl, I think it's past your bedtime. You best be gettin' home."

Danyon flinched. Now why did the guy have to go and call her a little girl?

As he suspected would happen, Shauna popped to attention, bristling.

Frank snorted, and his eyes traveled over Shauna's body, pausing in places that made Danyon want to rip the massive guy's eyeballs out of their sockets.

"The *last* thing you're looking at is a little girl," Shauna declared.

"Yeah?" Frank uncrossed his arms, then grabbed his crotch with a hand. "Then why don't you come on over here and prove just how little you aren't?"

Danyon wanted to pounce on the guy and yank his heart out through an ear canal. But he held his ground, allowing Shauna to keep the lead.

She didn't disappoint.

"I don't have to prove jack to you," she said.

"Then maybe I'll let big ol' Frank here," he pointed to the thick bulge in the crotch of his jeans, "be the one to do the provin'."

She harrumphed.

Frank folded his arms again, appearing to grow bored. "So what the hell's your game? You just bored and out to start some shit?"

"I hear you're the head of some new biker gang," Shauna said.

That must have pushed Frank's pride button, because his chest expanded another two inches. "Yeah, well, you heard right."

Shauna pursed her lips and nodded, and Danyon had a sinking feeling that things were getting ready to go from bad to worse.

"And the name of your gang is BGW?" Shauna asked.

"Somebody give the lady a stuffed penguin for getting two right in a row," Frank said sarcastically.

"Better make it one of those big stuffed bears," she said, "because I'm about to hit you with a third."

"Go for it," Frank said, obviously amused now.

"Word has it that you plan on scarfing some territory from the Bloods and the Crips. Is that right?"

At the mention of the Blood and the Crips, four men from a nearby table got up and slowly made their way behind Frank, forming a semi-circle.

"I asked if that was right," Shauna pressed.

Frank's eyes grew hard. "You one of their bitches?"

Appearing far from deterred, Shauna glared at each man standing behind Frank, then set her sights back on the big man. "Get real," she said. "Do I look like I belong to either of those gangs? Quit acting like a punk and call off your goons."

One of the guys standing behind Frank took a step toward her.

Danyon countered it.

"Back off, Tee," Frank said to the front man who appeared to be getting a little ahead of the game.

Tee was about Frank's size, and he had long brown hair that he kept flipping over his shoulder like a girl. Even though he'd been told to stand down, he took his time about it, all the while staring at Shauna.

Frank leaned toward her. "You listen close. If you're looking for information on this 'Banjo' dude, you came to the wrong place. But if you're looking for trouble, you've hit the mother lode," Frank warned. "There's no business in here for you."

"This is a public bar. I have as much right to be here as you."

Frank rubbed a hand slowly over his bald head.

Even from where he stood, Danyon felt anger radiating off the guy, like heat from a sunlamp.

"Know what else I heard?" Shauna asked, taking a step toward Frank.

Frank narrowed his eyes, tucked a thumb in his belt loop.

"I heard you picked up on some new stuff, and that you plan to push it, use it to take over some B and C turf."

"And just what new stuff did you hear we got?" Frank asked.

Danyon had no idea what Shauna was talking about. When Jagger had told them about BGW, he didn't say anything about them bringing drugs into the city. In fact, Jagger had claimed that, so far, the gang had been laying pretty low. Shauna was obviously fishing for something.

Shauna shrugged a response to Frank. "All I heard was 'new.'"

Frank gave her a crooked smile. "I don't know what the hell you're talkin' about. We're just here for a little Mardi Gras fun."

Weighing Frank's reaction, Danyon couldn't figure out if the guy knew exactly what Shauna was talking about, or if he was simply determined to fuel her temper.

If his intention was the latter, it appeared he had accomplished the job...big time.

"Listen up, creep. I really don't care what gang you lead. For all I know, the whole damn lot of you probably ride Schwinns. And what kind of gang name is BGW anyway? What does it stand for? Balloons, gumballs and watermelon? Grow up. You, the Blood, the Crips, all of you strut your stuff like you own the world, but all you bring with you no matter where you go is your dope and a pile of crap. People are dying because of what you put out on the street. I'm going to put a stop to your little boy's club, even if I have to do it myself!"

Frank stood up straight, dropped his hands to his side. "Bitch, you don't know what the hell you're talking about. Your mouth is about to get your face smashed in."

Much to Danyon's dismay, Shauna snapped back, "Oh, that's a big man for you. You're going to hit a woman? Is that how you're used to getting your way? Is that your exercise regiment for all that blubber you're hauling around?"

Frank aimed a finger at Shauna but glared at Danyon. "Dude, if this is your bitch you'd better grab her ass and get her out of here, before my foot winds up in her face and yours, too."

"So, who did your tats?" Shauna asked, evidently determined to get herself killed. "Some kindergartener with a green crayon?"

Frank lowered his head ever so slightly. If looks could kill Shauna would already be at the morgue.

"Oh, come on. Spill it," Shauna demanded. "Be a man and say what you've got. What's your game? What's your stuff? What are you going to use to take over that Blood and Crip territory? Your gumballs? Your watermelon? Are you using Banjo to run your junk? Is that what you're doing? What's the matter? Your balls aren't big enough to talk to a woman? You can't tell it like it is?" Shauna took another step toward him.

All Frank had to do was lean over a couple inches, stretch out a hand, and he would be able to grab her by the neck and snap it. She was going too far.

Shauna jabbed a finger in the air, right in front of Frank's face. "I've got people dying out here because of scum like you. And I'm tired of it, you hear? I'm tired of my people always having to watch their backs because of dogs like you. You and the rest of your punks need to get on your tricycles and just get the hell out of town."

"That's enough, bitch!" Frank roared. His right hand shot up, then swung out, heading for Shauna's face.

In a flash, Danyon sprang forward and grabbed Frank's arm. "I don't *think* so," he said through clenched teeth.

By now, all of Frank's goons had circled in tight.

"You don't have any idea who you're messing with," Frank said to Danyon. His eyes had narrowed into slits, and he bared his teeth.

"Oh, I think it's the other way around," Danyon snarled.

"That little slut of yours is the one who started all this shit," Frank said.

The second Danyon heard the word "slut" fly out of Frank's mouth, his entire body began to vibrate, and his muscles rippled from his calves to his thighs—from his arms to his chest. He wanted to rip the man's face off. Rip his heart out of his chest. Even if it meant transforming to were right in front of everyone in the bar.

Shauna appeared, seemingly out of nowhere, and forced her body between his and Frank's. He thought he saw her mouth move, but he couldn't hear any words. The fury inside of him had grown too loud.

When her voice finally came through, it was panicked. "I just saw him! He's out back—Banjo!"

Danyon didn't know if she was making this up to prevent him from transforming to were, or if she was telling the truth. By the way she kept jabbing a finger toward the stairway, he suspected it might be the latter.

"We're going to lose him again if we don't go now. I just saw him dart up the stairs. We've got to hurry!" She pulled Danyon's arm, and he allowed her to lead him back to the stairway.

As they rushed up, two steps at a time, Danyon heard a roar of laughter behind them. He knew the men were laughing at him, because he had been yanked out of the bar by a woman. Under any other circumstances, Danyon would have gone back and changed their tune, possibly slaughtering them all—his fury was that great. But he had an entire pack to take care of. They had to come first. They were always first.

"There!" Shauna said, as soon as they'd stepped into the street.

He spotted a flash of orange dart between two buildings about seventy feet away. This time Banjo was *not* going to slip past him.

Danyon ran.

So much tension had built up inside him, that Danyon quickly reached a speed he only acquired when he was were. He wondered if he had transformed without even realizing it.

In a matter of seconds, he caught up to Banjo, grabbed him around the throat with one hand and wrapped the other hand in his hair. Then he yanked Banjo into a side alley and slammed his back against a brick wall.

Shauna appeared immediately after and stood at the entrance of the alleyway, which would have been Banjo's only hope of escape, since the opposite end of the alley was blocked off by a ten-foot brick wall.

Banjo's eyes were wide and darting up, down—left and right. Danyon knew he was looking for an escape. Anything, anywhere—if he could scale the walls he would have. His face held nothing but stark fear when he realized he was trapped.

Banjo laced his fingers together and put hands on top of his head. He started rocking back and forth, then dropped to his knees. "Whaddaya want, man? Whaddaya want? Look, she know me." He aimed his chin at Shauna. "You know me, huh?"

"Oh, I know you all right," she said. "You were in my shop, telling me secrets, remember? Trading secrets for cookies—does that ring a bell?"

Banjo rolled his head from shoulder to shoulder and squeezed his eyes shut for a couple seconds. "Aww, man, aww, I be takin' stuff, ya know? Takin' stuff—I—I don't know." As he jabbered, he got to his feet, lowered his hands, and took a step forward.

Danyon grabbed him again and threw him back up against the wall. Banjo dropped into a squat and clasped his hands together as though he were praying. "Don't kill me, okay, man? Please, don't kill me. I didn't do nothin', I don't know nothin', I swear!"

"If you don't know anything and didn't do anything," Shauna said, "then why did you take off running when you saw me?"

"I don't know. I do that—I just do that."

A street light near the entrance of the alley cast muted white light over Shauna's shoulder and had settled on Banjo. Danyon saw he had broken into a heavy sweat, and his body was shaking violently. Either he was really nervous, or Banjo was going through withdrawals. Whichever it was gave Danyon an advantage.

Wearing heavy black boots, Danyon lifted a foot and parked it between Banjo's legs, right on his groin.

"Oh, no, man, not them! You can't do that, bro. It ain't right—it just ain't right!"

Banjo squirmed beneath his foot, and Danyon added a bit more pressure to the guy's genitals. "We need some information, and we need it fast. And you're going to cough it up."

"I don't know what you're talkin' about! I already told you I don't know nothin'. I swear, nothin'! Why you been after me?"

"Because you came into my store, wanting to trade secrets for cookies, talking about three dead mice—no teeth—no big fingernails," Shauna fumed. "I know you were talking about the weres, and I want to know what you know about them. How did you know they didn't have fangs or claws? How?"

"I don't know whatchu talkin' about. I went in the store 'cause, like, I was hungry, and the other lady that's there, she always feedin' me and stuff. I was—I was hungry. I thought I could get a cookie if I said that. I was hungry, so I said it, you know? They smelled so good and—"

Danyon pressed his foot down even harder.

"Whoa, whoa, whoa, man! You gonna bust 'em. Stop! I told you the trut'. I was just hungry."

"How did you know about the weres?" Danyon asked. "What was all that about? The three blind mice and no teeth? You knew about the weres, didn't you?"

"How did you know?" Shauna added.

Banjo shook his head, greasy brown hair falling into his eyes. "Word on the street, just word on the street."

"Whose word?" Shauna asked. "Who told you about the weres?"

He shook his clasped hands, an adamant prayer for mercy. "Look, I swear to Gawd, I don't know nothin'. I musta been talkin' out the side of my neck. I swear, I don't know!"

Danyon smelled fear wafting up from Banjo. And he also smelled a lie. He lifted his foot and tucked the toe of his boot under Banjo's crotch, making sure it jabbed him in the most sensitive spot.

"Aw, no!" Banjo started crying. "I'm not gonna have nothin' left. You can't take 'em from me, man! Like I ain't gonna be able to have kids or nothin'. Ain't gonna even be able to do it no more. I swear to Gawd, I don't know nothin', I didn't do nothin'. Just don't kill me, okay? Don't kill me."

Danyon twisted his foot to the right, jabbed the toe of his boot in a little harder—deeper.

"Okay, okay! I'll tell ya, okay? Ease off, okay?"

"Spill it first, then I'll let off."

"Aw, man…okay, yeah, they got a new drug. I heard about it on the street. Everybody talkin' about it. Big stuff called Lacodah. People sayin' it make you strong, keep you buzzin', like you all wired and stuff, so you can see and smell and hear good. And you can run fast. It's the shit, man. It's the shit."

"So you've taken this new drug?" Shauna asked.

"Me? No, no. Not me, no. Like I say, I just heard about it on the street."

"Bullshit," Shauna said. "The last time you came to the shop, you were on it. How else could you have smelled those cookies from across the street? With all the people out there, the food smells and alcohol—for you to smell those cookies over all that, I'd say you have a pretty sensitive nose."

Danyon gave his foot another sharp twist. "Tell the lady the truth."

"Okay! Yeah, okay, I tried it! Once, though. One time."

"And what about Mattie?" Shauna asked. "I saw the two of you fighting in front of the shop. She dented a light pole with her fist. That much strength, she's got to be on it, too, right?"

"I don't even know who you talkin' 'bout," Banjo said. "Who be Mattie? I don't know her—I swear to Gawd."

Danyon grabbed a handful of Banjo's hair and pulled, forcing the guy to look at him. "If you keep lying, I'm going to make sure you walk and talk like a girl for the rest of your life. Do you understand me?"

Tears streamed down Banjo's cheeks. "Yeah…yeah, I heard. Okay—okay, yeah, Mattie, she takin' Lacodah, too. I share, you know, share a little bit wit' her."

"Since when does a junkie share anything?" Shauna asked. "You're dealing it, aren't you?"

"Oh, no!" Banjo held his hands out as if to block her words. "I ain't sellin' nothin'. That's sample stuff, you know, sample stuff."

"Where did you get it?" Danyon asked.

The young vamp looked up at him, and there was no missing the terror in his eyes. "Man, I can't say—I can't do—they gonna kill me. They gonna kill me for sure."

Danyon removed his boot from Banjo's crotch, then parked it on his left shoulder and pushed down until he sat flat on the ground. Then he repositioned his boot between his legs, only now it was in a prime position. He had leverage to work with. Concrete, a heavy boot, and testicles between them. The man was in a bind. Danyon rocked his body forward, so the pressure increased between Banjo's legs.

"Mutha—mutha…" Banjo gasped. Danyon pressed down a little harder, and Banjo's mouth fell open. He looked like a fish out of water, gasping for air. When Danyon released the pressure on his testicles, it was as though Banjo's body needed time to absorb the knowledge that it was no longer restricted. He sat frozen, his mouth hanging open for a four-count before he finally blinked.

"Next time they're going flat," Danyon said. "Unless you tell us what we need to know."

Banjo started weeping loudly. He put his hands over his face, sobbing. "I can't! Man, you don't know what you're sayin'—I'm gonna be dead!"

"You're going to be dead either way," Danyon promised. "Tell me what you know. Who's in this with you?" He forced Banjo's head up by the hair again. "And this is the *last* time I'm asking."

Keeping the pressure on his genitals, Danyon squatted in front of Banjo and rocked his body forward so that he was only inches from his face. The pressure from his boot evidently shot the pain level up to excruciating, because even in the dim light Danyon saw the guy's face turn purple.

To make sure he got his point across, Danyon lowered his head, allowed some of the anger he had been holding back to rush through him. He concentrated on one section of his body and soon felt the muscles in his neck begin to ripple and move up to his cheek. He shifted his head to one side to regulate the mutation—snout elongating, fangs bared.

Banjo jerked his head back so hard he smashed it against the brick wall behind him.

"Holy mother, not that! Okay, yeah, okay, it was the voodoo man! The fat man. He's got somethin' to do wit' it, but that's all I know. He get that voodoo stuff going wit' that snake, and—I—that's all I know. That's all. He's the one call it Lacodah—not the snake, the stuff. The stuff that makes you run fast, that's Lacodah. That's him, man, I swear—that's all I know. Okay—don't tear my face off, okay? Don't kill me!" Banjo wailed at the top of his lungs, "Oh, God, don't kill me!"

Danyon had to wonder what breed of vampire would take this much pain and not transform.

"Please, I don't want to die!" Banjo cried.

Danyon drew in a deep breath, held it, closed his eyes for a moment, and felt his human features return. Then he removed his foot from Banjo and stood, leaving the guy in a sniveling, blubbering heap.

Without another word, Danyon walked the length of the alley, took Shauna's hand, and headed north.

"Where are we going?" she asked.

As keen as her hearing had been with Gris Gris and Trish earlier on Bourbon, he was surprised that she hadn't heard what Banjo had said.

"Where are we going?" she asked again.

Eyes forward, his mind's eye locked on a vision of his prey, Danyon lengthened his stride.

"We're going to see a man about a snake."

Chapter 18

Papa Gris Gris' Voodoo Shop was located on Rampart Street, on the ground floor of a two-story shotgun house. The foot traffic on Rampart wasn't anything near what they had just come through in the heart of the Quarter, but it was still heavier than a standard business day.

Gris Gris' shop was teeming with customers, even at this late hour, as was T-Boy's T-Shirt Shop, Bailey's Praline Store, and Sistah's, Lurnell's mystic shop. All three stores were on the same side of the street and attached at the hip, Sistah's being on the end. Shauna could only imagine what Lurnell's reaction would be if she knew she was going into her competitor's store. The last thing Lurnell had to worry about, though, was her buying anything from Gris Gris, especially after Danyon had told her what he had gotten out of Banjo and why they were all but racing to Rampart.

Danyon had asked her how she had not heard Banjo squawling about Gris Gris and Lacodah when she had heard Trish and Gris Gris in the middle of Bourbon. Shauna had managed to dodge the question by claiming she had been preoccupied guarding the alleyway entrance, making sure no one else came in—and no one went out. That hadn't been the whole truth. All of the truth was that she had indeed been guarding the alley entrance, but her thoughts had been preoccupied with how stupid she had acted back in that bar with Big Frank Macina.

What on earth had possessed her to confront such a bear of a man that way? It had been tacky, unproductive and just plain stupid. The excuse she had given herself about why she had done it was that she had thought a direct approach—a blatant confrontation—might shake some information out of Macina. It had really started out that way, then something inside of her just sort of snapped, and she became a runaway train. Fortunately, Danyon hadn't confronted her about it or reprimanded her like she was a child. She could only hope that it was because he had accepted what had happened, knew she couldn't go back and change it, and that she was mature enough to see how she could have handled it differently.

There were two signs attached to the screen door that was the entrance to Gris Gris' shop. One read Open and the one beneath it Push, which she did.

She had never been inside the voodoo shop and was surprised to see that it looked nothing like A Little Bit of Magic or Sistah's. She couldn't understand why Lurnell saw Gris Gris as such a threat. The only merchandise he sold were voodoo masks, altar supplies, a few books on the history of voodoo, and some wooden statues that looked as though they had been carved by a second grader. Gris Gris sold them as totems, guaranteeing that they would strengthen any spell offered on any practitioner's altar.

Shauna suspected that Gris Gris' biggest income generator was himself. He wasn't shy about claiming to be one of the most powerful voodoo practitioners in the south, as well as a psychic with extraordinary abilities. She suspected that his steady customers were people stuck on the road to hopelessness that appeared to have no end, and they saw Gris Gris as their last resort.

Within ten feet of the entrance of the shop, was a narrow stairway that led to the second floor and a voodoo museum that you could tour for an additional five dollars.

There may have been fifteen people in the shop when Shauna and Danyon entered, but it felt like many more in the cramped space. The customers who were there talked in hush tones as they walked about, examining pictures on the wall and different pieces of merchandise, all of which, Shauna noticed, didn't carry a price tag. It was a shake-down technique used by some small shop owners. Without a price tag, they were able to size up the customer examining the merchandise. Then, when the customer asked about cost, the shop owner would wing a price off the top of his head, basing it on the quality and size of the customer's clothes and jewelry. The bigger the jewelry and the higher end the clothes, the higher the price for the piece of merchandise. It was a practice Shauna and her sisters abhorred.

Gris Gris sat behind an old wooden desk in a double-wide, ladder-back chair at the rear of the room. He probably claimed that both the chair and desk were antiques, but Shauna would have bet her own shop that both came from Goodwill.

The chair creaked as he rocked, his eyes ever watchful as customers picked up and examined different items. He appeared quite content, like someone who had discovered the secret to peace while still living in a chaotic world. Either that, or someone really stoned who lived in total oblivion. He wore a long-sleeved, billowing white shirt and heaven only knew what else, because the rest of him was hidden under the desk. Shauna wasn't surprised to find that seeing Gris Gris up close was no different than seeing him from afar. He looked the same—ugly. His eyes, nose and mouth were too small for his face, and his fingers looked like stubby, albino sausages, and he smelled…moldy.

Like Gris Gris didn't have enough going for him, the boa constrictor served as the pièce de résistance. Only rarely, if ever, did anyone see Gris Gris without that six-foot boa draped about his neck, and either one or both of Gris Gris' hands were always in motion, stroking, petting the snake as it slowly coiled its tail up, then relaxed it.

Its head and at least a third of its body would undulate over Gris Gris' rotund stomach. The sight was not for the faint of heart—or stomach.

Using subtle body language and eye signals, Shauna and Danyon made up their minds to stall in the front section of the shop and wait for most, if not all, of the customers to leave before they confronted him. They pretended to be looking at the different pictures and masks that hung on the wall.

"Remember, you're leaving this guy to me," Danyon whispered, when they found a moment of privacy.

Shauna nodded, felt her face grow hot and knew she must have been blushing different shades of crimson from embarrassment. She didn't blame him for wanting to handle Gris Gris after the way she had dealt with Big Frank Macina.

"Well, Ms. MacDonald, what a pleasant surprise," Gris Gris said, when she and Danyon finally approached his desk. The boa lifted its yellow-striped head, as if curious to see who Gris Gris was addressing. "Mmm… and who's your handsome friend?" he asked.

Surprised by the lecherous look Gris Gris was giving Danyon, she said, "This is Danyon Stone. Danyon, this…" She paused, realizing she didn't know Gris Gris' real name, then decided to use what she did know. "This is Papa Gris Gris."

"Charmed," Gris Gris said, and held out a hand.

Danyon didn't reach for it.

Gris Gris retracted his hand slowly, resumed petting the boa in long slow strokes and smiled.

"How may I help the two of you this evening?" Gris Gris asked Shauna.

"We need some information from you," Danyon said.

Gris Gris rested his head against the back of his chair and rocked steadily. "And what information might that be, Mr. Stone?"

Danyon stared at the fat man, and Gris Gris returned the stare. They held eye contact for so long, Shauna thought both had fallen into a trance.

"I think you already know what kind of information I'm looking for," Danyon finally said.

Gris Gris laughed. "Well, I must admit that my psychic abilities are indeed acute, but, unfortunately, not in every situation or circumstance."

"Oh, I don't think you have to be a psychic to know this."

Gris Gris grinned, rocked back, then said, "Mr. Stone, please do get to the point. As you can see, I have customers to tend to. If you insist on playing these guessing games, I'm afraid I'm going to have to ask you to leave."

Shauna was standing at Danyon's side, and she felt the muscles in his arms tense against her body. No question he wanted to punch the fat man square in the face. She had to admit that she was curious to see how Danyon was going to handle this. Gris Gris was human. Wolven, vampires, and shape-shifters maintained an unspoken rule—they didn't openly admit their true nature to a human. If Danyon found out Gris Gris was involved in the wolven deaths, however, she was confident he would make an exception to that rule.

"I'm certain you've heard that there have been three murders recently," Danyon said.

Gris Gris arched a brow. "Really? Three—is that all?"

Danyon scowled. "How dare you—"

"Oh, Mr. Stone, relax. You take life much too seriously. I do watch the news you know. Since Katrina, it's common knowledge that New Orleans is viewed as one of the top five cities in America with the highest murder rate per capita."

"The three I'm talking about happened not far from here."

"I see," Gris Gris said. "And your point?"

Danyon's face grew darker. "I was curious as to whether you had heard anything about them. Knew any information about the murders."

"Now why would I be privy to such information?" Gris Gris asked.

Danyon allowed a long pause to follow Gris Gris' question before answering, "It's often surprising what some people are privy to."

A light twinkled in Gris Gris' eyes. "Very true, Mr. Stone." He glanced around Danyon to Shauna. "Do forgive me for not asking earlier, Shauna, but how are your sisters, Fiona and Caitlin?"

"They're well, thank you," Shauna said.

"And your business? Thriving I hope?"

Shauna answered with a curt nod.

"Splendid. I'm so glad to hear it."

"Excuse me, are y'all in line?" Two middle-aged women wearing matching floral dresses stepped up behind Danyon. One was sweating profusely and fanning herself with a small piece of cardboard.

"Yes, we are," Danyon said sharply, and both women stepped back immediately.

"I'm sorry… I apologize for…we didn't mean to interrupt," the woman with the fan said hastily. "I wanted to make an appointment for a reading and thought the gentleman sitting behind the desk was the person I needed to make the appointment with."

"I am indeed, and you may," Gris Gris said to her, then narrowed his eyes at Danyon.

No one moved.

"If you will excuse me, Mr. Stone—Ms. MacDonald. I have clients who need my assistance—paying clients."

Shauna slid a hand into the front pocket of her jeans, pulled out two twenty-dollar bills and tossed them on the desk. "Yes, you do indeed have paying clients."

With a slight shake of his head and roll of his eyes, Gris Gris turned to the two women. "Ladies, I will be happy to assist you as soon as I'm done with these… two."

The woman without the fan suddenly gasped. "Oh, my word—it moved! Is that a real snake around your neck?"

Gris Gris smiled broadly and stroked the boa. Even his teeth were too small for his head. "Oh, yes, Simone is quite real. Isn't she lovely?"

Danyon cleared his throat loudly.

Gris Gris tsked, "Ladies, if you will excuse us—and in exchange for your patience, I would like to offer you a free tour of our voodoo museum, which is right at the top of that stairwell. Please, take your time and enjoy the artifacts. I am certain my business here will conclude…" His eyes fell on Danyon. "…shortly."

The women thanked him profusely and headed up the stairs.

Once they were out of sight and hearing range, Gris Gris' calm, nonchalant demeanor abruptly changed.

"All right, what do you want, Stone? Why are you here busting my balls like this? I've never done anything to you. Hell, I don't even know you."

Shauna did a double take. The few times she had heard Gris Gris speak, his high-brow style and diction had been superfluous. His sudden "home-boy" talk took her aback.

"I can only guess what else you're faking," Danyon said to him. "But what I really want is more information about the new product line you've got out on the street right now."

Gris Gris frowned. "What are you talking about?"

"The name 'lacodah' mean anything to you?"

As hard as Gris Gris worked to keep his expression neutral, Shauna noticed the flicker of surprise in his eyes.

"I don't have the slightest idea what you're talking about, man."

"Yeah? Well, there are a couple people on the street telling me different."

"What's with you? You a cop?"

"No, but I know quite a few."

"What the hell does that have to do with anything? I don't know anything about no locodi, Bonighnigh, whatever the hell you called it."

"That's strange," Danyon said. "Because the way I've heard it on the street, you're the man and the direct connection to it."

"I don't know who you talked to, and I really don't give a damn. All I know is you've got the wrong person."

Simone, apparently sensing Gris Gris' growing agitation, began undulating rapidly, the bottom half of her body coiling in tighter. Her tail curled around Gris Gris' neck, the tip of it overlapping her head.

"It's all right, baby," Gris Gris said, stroking her head calmly. "Daddy's fine. These bad people are going away now. It's okay." As he petted her and spoke soothingly, Simone began to relax, her tail dropping away from around Gris Gris' neck. "There you go…you're such a sweetheart."

When Simone had calmed completely, her head gently bobbing from side to side, Gris Gris looked up at Danyon.

"As I was saying, Mr. Stone. Feel free to search this place. Call the police if you must. But if I may offer one piece of advice, as in any area of life, you should always be careful about what you ask for and look for. Because you just might find it."

Chapter 19

"I'd call today a bust," Danyon said, leaning against the grave of Gustav Henry. They were sitting in St. Louis I Cemetery, across the street from Gris Gris'. They had hit a stalemate. At the moment, keeping an eye out for any unusual activity coming in or going out of Gris Gris' shop, anything that might direct them toward their next move, was about all they could do.

"The night's not over yet," Shauna said, sitting on the concrete lip of a nearby crypt. "And besides, it wasn't a total bust. We linked a couple of things together."

"I'd say you're being pretty optimistic. And even if we did link one or two things together, I wouldn't try pulling anything with it. The links would break. They're too weak."

"So what about the whole thing with Banjo and Gris

Gris? I mean, he fingered the snake guy for heaven's sake. Don't tell me you're just going to dismiss that?"

Danyon shrugged. "Really, when you think about it, Banjo could have been blowing hot air up our rear ends. He's a junkie, I know, but he's a conniving junkie. He might have rattled off the first name that came into his head just because he was scared."

"Even if he did, can you blame him?" Shauna said. "You were pretty convincing back there. If I would have been the one trapped under your boot like that, I would have spilled my guts in a nanosecond."

He gave her a half smile. "Hey, you know, that brings up something that's had me stumped since we left the alley."

"What's that?"

"If I would have confronted a regular vampire, like I did with Banjo back there, don't you think he would have at least flashed his fangs or something?"

"I'd bet on it."

"Then why didn't Banjo? What kind of vampire is he?"

"I don't know what breed of vampire he is. David Dulac had said something about Banjo during the meeting. He knows the vamp is different, but said he wasn't sure if that was due to him being the product of a cross-breeding, or if it had something to do with the drugs he's been using for years. I really don't have a clue myself. Fiona would probably know more, since she's his Keeper."

Danyon shook his head. "Now that I think about it,

I should have handled things differently back in the alley."

"How so?"

"What I should've done was as soon as Banjo fingered Gris Gris, I should have grabbed the little weasel and brought him here with us. Then force him and Gris Gris into a face-off."

Shauna laughed.

"What's funny?"

"Sorry, I couldn't help it. I know a face-off between the two of them would probably get serious quick. But when you first mentioned it, I suddenly got a picture in my head of Laurel and Hardy. You know, fat guy, skinny guy?"

Danyon grinned. "How do you know about Laurel and Hardy? Even the reruns of their movies stopped playing long before you were born."

Shauna shrugged. "I like old movies, and they do make DVDs you know."

Her smile made Danyon's heart flip-flop in his chest. He forced himself to look away. He had to keep his mind on business. "Have you heard anything from Fiona, Caitlin, Jagger, anybody?"

"No," she said, her smile quickly fading. "I won't know anymore than you do until I see them again."

"Wouldn't your sisters call if they found anything?"

"Probably," Shauna said. "But I don't carry a cell phone, so they have no way to reach me."

He cocked his head, surprised. "I thought everyone carried a cell phone these days."

"I don't."

"And why is that?"

"Because wherever I go, I like to be where I am. A cell phone only divides your attention—all the texting, beeping, buzzing, call-waiting, call-forwarding, voice mail. It's no wonder that there is so much anger in the world. No one has a moment's peace to regroup their thoughts, to really think through their problems so they can find a solution."

"Smart girl."

"I know."

Grinning, Danyon stood up and stretched, working out the kink forming in his lower back.

"You know, you may be right about something," Shauna said.

"Me? Right?"

She smiled. "What you said about Banjo blowing hot air—that sort of ties in to what you said earlier about Gris Gris being in no physical condition to hold down a were."

"Wait—are you saying I may be right about *two* things? We should call the local paper. That's headline news!"

Shauna tsked, then chuckled. "I know, I know. But let's think this through for a minute. Banjo ratting out Gris Gris doesn't make very much sense when you take into account the big man's physical liabilities. Banjo might be screwed up on drugs, and he might be conniving, but I don't think he's stupid. If he was lying, I think he's sharp enough to have picked a much more likely candidate.

Either that, or he figured we were stupid enough to fall for anything."

"Maybe, but since we're thinking this through—you know, the two things I was right about? Banjo could have been telling the truth, only we're looking at it from a physical perspective. Gris Gris may not be doing the physical work, like restraining the were, wrapping him in cable. Maybe he's orchestrating the whole thing. Who the heck knows?" Danyon walked over and sat beside her. "It very well could have started out one way and wound up another."

"What do you mean?"

"Remember when August said that the murderer's motive might be similar to a trapper's? Someone who hunts alligators and bear, specifically for their claws and fangs, because they make jewelry out of them?"

"Yes, I remember when he told us."

"Well, what if the murderer started off that way, you know, harvesting were claws and fangs to make expensive jewelry, it would have to be expensive because they're rare. Then somehow, the murderer winds up ingesting a few granules of either the claws or fangs when he's grinding them down for jewelry. He ends up with a serious buzz, one a lot different than he's felt from any other drug. He discovers he's stronger, faster, more agile. By process of elimination, he figures out where the buzz came from, and he's off to the races from there."

Shauna shook her head. "I don't even like thinking about what those races might look like. People are so beyond their own limits now. Even a hint of something that powerful being available on the street—it would be like August said. The death toll would become astronomical. Weres might even become extinct."

"It's a scary thought for sure."

Shauna propped her arms on her knees and lowered her head. "Do you think that it's only happened in this area? Do you think there are other weres in other states going through this right now?"

"I haven't heard news about it happening anywhere else," Danyon said. "And I hope we don't. If similar were murders show up anywhere else that would only confirm what you just said—it would be the beginning of the end. I try not to think about how big the problem could get. I just want to focus on this area and our weres right now."

Danyon glanced over at the voodoo shop. The lights were still on, and he saw shadows from people walking back and forth in front of the screen door. He had seen some customers leave the shop and new ones come in, but nothing out of the ordinary. No suspicious looking characters, only curious tourists.

"What do you think Gris Gris meant when he said you should be careful about what you look for?" Shauna asked. She was looking toward the shop, as well. "Idle threat?"

"I'm sure that's all it was. The guy's good at pulling off a con. Look how his accent and entire manner of speaking changed when he was pressed to the wall."

"I know," Shauna said. "I couldn't believe it. I mean, it's not like I know him well. I've seen him around a time or two, occasionally cross him on the street in the Quarter, but I've never heard him roll into street talk that way. He always came across rather highbrow. You know what I mean?"

Danyon nodded, but didn't offer more.

It was getting late and traffic was slowing on Rampart. The praline shop next to Gris Gris' had already closed for the night. He felt frustrated and as useless as a spigot on a rock. Too many maybes had sent them chasing shadows that led them nowhere.

Maybe the claws and fangs were being pulverized and sold as a drug. Maybe Big Frank was tied to it simply because he wanted his gang to upstage the Bloods and the Crips. Maybe Gris Gris was involved. Maybe Banjo had been telling the truth when he had fingered the snake man after Danyon had put the squeeze on him. Maybe all of this was about a new drug, but then again…maybe not.

Danyon was used to addressing problems at the root cause. The challenge he had here, though, was that he had no roots to work with. His frustration and desire to do something, to find whoever, or whatever, was responsible for the murders, grew by the hour, and that was causing him to make bad decisions.

It would have been smarter had he taken a more subtle approach to Gris Gris, instead of confronting him head on. If the slime ball was responsible for the were deaths in any way, all Danyon had done was alert him to the fact that they suspected him. If anything, Gris Gris would be more cautious now about where he went and who he spoke to. The same applied to Big Frank Macina, since Shauna all but shoved an accusation up his nose.

Banjo didn't really concern Danyon. The guy stayed so drugged most of the time, he probably had trouble remembering from one hour to the next what he had said, much less what he had heard or done.

If he was going to be truthful with himself, then Danyon had to admit that neither he nor Shauna knew what the hell they were doing. If drive and heartfelt passion to save and protect the weres were the only two things necessary to solve this case, then it would have been solved long ago.

The bottom line was easy to sum up. He wasn't a detective. Neither was she.

He wondered if Jagger, Fiona, Ryder or Caitlin had had any luck in the areas they were monitoring. If they had uncovered any clues that might lead everyone in a different, more productive direction.

And what about the weres? Had the sentinels who were assigned to post by the remaining Southern alphas spotted anything? Something that might shed more light on the case, offer some clarification?

If everyone returned empty-handed, then they would have no choice but to bring in additional help.

That wasn't an easy thing for Danyon to admit. He took great pride in being an alpha, and never once had he ever considered his role as leader, protector, defender a burden.

It was his purpose in life.

Pride would have to take a backseat. The only thing

that mattered was the safety of the weres, protecting them against the psychopath who had already killed three of their own.

If it took a boatload of vampires, a battalion of shifters and every breed of were in North America to find the murderer and stop him from killing again, then bring them on.

Since the final directive to call in additional, outside help had to come from August, Danyon planned to speak to him about it as soon as everyone met up again. And they were scheduled to gather in August's conference room in the morning.

He swiped a hand over his face, wishing he could wipe away the fatigue that weighed him down, and the sense of defeat that wanted to drown him.

In that moment, he felt Shauna rest a hand gently on his arm.

So reassuring and soothing. So calming. It was as though she had heard his every thought.

Danyon closed his eyes, and allowed himself to get lost in her touch. And in that one blissful moment, he found absolute peace.

Chapter 20

After quietly slipping back into her clothes, Shauna grabbed her sneakers and snuck out of Danyon's bedroom, where he still lay sleeping, then out of the penthouse. She rode the private elevator down to the back entrance, then put on her sneakers and headed outside.

It was a little after 4:00 a.m., the only time of day when New Orleans' streets were relatively quiet. This morning she heard a chorus of hydraulic hisses from trash trucks cleaning the streets down in the Quarter. She certainly didn't envy their job this morning. No doubt the mountain of trash left over from a half million people celebrating Nuit du Dommage would rival Mt. Everest.

Shauna glanced up at the dark, clear sky and saw that the moon was nearing its apex. She didn't worry about Danyon's wolven during a full moon because they were a breed of werewolves whose transformation trigger wasn't dependent on the moon. But she did worry about humans, because their emotions seemed to be at the mercy of any full-faced moon. Any policeman or hospital worker would testify to that. During a full moon cycle, the number of crimes blew through the roof, and emergency rooms overflowed with victims, as well as perpetrators, of gunshot wounds, stabbings, cuts and broken bones from fights, and a myriad of injuries from car accidents spurred by road-rage.

A full moon always made Shauna restless. Add to that restlessness her worry about a murderer targeting her weres, and she wound up with a bad case of insomnia.

Although she hadn't said anything to Danyon, Shauna feared he was right. They had been running after shadows and were making little to no progress. Even worse, she had an unsettling feeling that all hell was about to break loose. She had turned all the few, ragged pieces of information they had collected over the last two days over and over in her mind until they made even less sense than they did before. The only way she knew to clear her head was to move—jog—run.

The predawn air was crisp, and the humidity low. Shauna breathed in deeply, then began to stretch her back, arms, and legs. There were very few street lights along Burgundy, almost non-existent when compared to the heart of the Quarter, but, with the help of the moon, she had plenty to light her way.

After a few minutes of stretching, Shauna started off with a slow jog. She quickened her pace after two blocks, then broke into a full run after four. The wind in her face, heart rate rising, the sound of her sneakers thumping rhythmically on the sidewalk—this was her safe haven. The rest of the world was welcome to all the Xanax on the market. This was her drug of choice.

Soon, the worries that clogged her mind began to slip away.

Shauna was only a few blocks from Esplanade, which she planned to take south to the French Market, when she caught sudden movement off to her left, out of the corner of her eye. It barely had time to register in her brain before she found herself abruptly slammed to the ground by a flying tackle.

In a flash, a hand clamped over her mouth and a knee dug into her back. Shock kept Shauna immobile for a moment or two, then she started kicking, tried to scream, flailed her arms in an attempt to throw her attacker off balance. Something cold and metal was slapped across her left wrist. Then it tightened and clicked.

Handcuffs?

In a full blown panic now, Shauna screamed into the hand covering her mouth and swung her right arm wildly to keep it from being restrained. The struggle proved futile, however. Her attacker pinned her arm and cuffed it so quickly she might as well have been paralyzed.

Shauna kicked out with both feet, jerked her body from side to side, frantic to escape. Another hand grabbed a fistful of her hair and yanked hard, forcing her to her feet. She had yet to catch even a glimpse of her attacker.

With one hand clamped over her mouth and another wrapped tightly in her hair, Shauna was shoved into motion. She kicked backwards, first with her right foot, then with her left, wanting to connect with a knee, a shin, testicles. When that failed, she tried to run, but was immediately jerked back by the hair, then shoved forward faster.

Soon she was forced into an alley on the right, then left, behind a building—left again into another alley. Tears streamed down Shauna's cheeks, which made her angry. The last thing she needed to do right now was cry. With a hand over her mouth, if her nose got stuffed up, she wouldn't be able to breathe. And what good would crying do anyway? She had to keep her head clear and figure out a way to break free.

The hand over her mouth pressed harder over her lips, but Shauna still managed to open her mouth just wide enough to bite down on a small pad of flesh. She bit hard into the palm, and twisted from side to side, like a dog with a bone.

It was then that something hard and heavy slammed down on Shauna's head. And the moon went from full… to black.

When Shauna's eyes fluttered open, it didn't take long for her to realize she wasn't waking from a bad dream. Her hands were still cuffed behind her back, and she was standing, bent in half, the upper part of her body lying on a sheet of plywood that appeared to be some kind of makeshift table. The left side of her head throbbed terribly, and she felt something sticky on her neck and left cheek. She figured it was blood.

Shauna tried to stand up and realized that her legs had been pulled back and spread wide apart, and her ankles restrained. She lifted her head and looked about, trying to figure out where she might be. But she could hardly make out a thing. Her eyesight was blurry, and two huge spotlights that stood about twenty feet or so in front of her blinded her all the more.

She pressed her right cheek against the scratchy plywood and turned her head to the left. Even without the light in her eyes, she only saw shadows and darkness. But there was depth to that darkness, indicating a vast space. She turned her head to the right and saw the same. Whatever this place was, it smelled of dirt, rust, and motor oil.

Suddenly, a loud clatter echoed around her. It sounded like a heavy tool, like a pipe wrench, falling to a concrete floor. The sound jump-started Shauna's heart and sent it racing. She lifted herself as high as she could and yelled, "Help! Somebody, help! Hel—"

Her head was slammed to the plywood, sending a shower of shooting stars before her eyes. Someone held her face down, smashing her nose, forehead, and chin into the plywood. They pressed harder, harder still, fingers digging into the wound she already had on her head. The throbbing pain she had felt only moments ago was turned into an excruciating fireworks display in her mind.

Shauna felt herself fading to black and fought it.

Can't lose consciousness! Can't! Have to fight!

The shooting stars returned briefly, then blinked out, only to return seconds later in multiples of a thousand.

Somewhere between dark and light, Shauna realized that her shirt and been pushed up, almost under her arms. And someone was tugging on the waistband of her jeans.

Tugging—pulling…

Oh, God, no…not that! Please, not that!

She had to scream—needed help. Heard a ripping sound—felt a sudden breeze on the back of her thighs.

Her jeans had been cut off!

That realization fueled Shauna's struggle to remain conscious, enough at least for her to open her mouth—to scream.

Her hair was grabbed again, her head slammed hard against the plywood.

Now the stars weren't only before her eyes, they surrounded her—they were her. Nothing else existed.

Except one sound.

One…familiar…sound.

A high pitched, twittering laugh. That laugh. That horrible, wretched laugh snapped Shauna back to consciousness, like a bullwhip coming out of high flight.

"Banjo!" she yelled. Shauna wanted him to know that she knew he was the one behind her.

He laughed.

She felt hands on her bare back, rough clothing rubbing against the back of her thighs. And the laughter grew louder and louder.

"Banjo, stop! It's Shauna MacDonald. Stop!"

He began to singsong and wiggled his body against her thighs, her buttocks. "Gonna get me some—get me some—get some!"

"Shut the hell up, Banjo!" a woman's voice shouted. It sounded like it came from a distant place, and it was immediately followed by a metallic echo, as if her voice had bounced off metal walls—aluminum walls…

Was she trapped in a warehouse? Who was the woman?

"Hehehe, SQUAWK!" That laughter again, then, "She ain't gonna give it up, give it up. So Banjo's gonna take it! Take it—no give it up—I take it!" Banjo squealed like a school kid excited over Christmas.

"I said shut your goddamn mouth, you little turd!"

Shauna screamed, "Help me! Help!" If Banjo wasn't able to hear her because he was too doped up, she had to hope that someone, somewhere would hear her screams.

"Shut that bitch up!" the woman yelled.

"Ain't nobody gonna hear. Nobody gonna. Too far—too far in the middle of nooowheres!" Banjo sang.

"Stop with your 'effin singing and just do it already!"

"You leave me alone!" Banjo said, his voice suddenly clear and his words sharp. "You understand? Leave me *alone!*"

"Screw you, you sonofabitchin' half-breed. You wanna dick around with me? Fine, then consider your turn lost, asshole. Get the hell away from her. He'll take his turn *and* yours, too."

He? Someone else besides Banjo and the woman?

Shauna prayed for a miracle. If Banjo was that clear-headed now, maybe she could get through to him. Maybe he would hear her and realize what he was doing and who he was trying to do it to.

"Banjo, it's Shauna! Don't—help me get out of here!"

A dirty, oily smelling rag was suddenly shoved into her mouth. Shauna gagged against it. She shook her head frantically and pushed her tongue against the rag, trying to force it out of her mouth.

It was shoved in farther.

"I said back off her. You lost your turn!"

"And I said leave me the hell alone, bitch! It's about damned time somebody started giving *you* orders, Kara Matiste!"

"What the hell is wrong with you? You just said my name! She's not deaf, you dumb shit!"

"Whoa ho ho—scare now, are you?" Banjo's piercing laughter was the one thing that didn't change. His voice and words may have found a balanced cadence, but *not* the laughter. The change in Banjo's diction reminded her of how Gris Gris had gone from his usual snooty repertoire to "home talk" in a matter of minutes.

And Kara—alpha of the West Bank—one of her weres had been a murder victim. Why was she here? How did she tie in to Banjo? And why was she encouraging him to do the unthinkable?

"You are going to do what I say, when I say it!" Kara yelled at Banjo.

Banjo pressed his body firmly against Shauna's naked thighs, then began to hump them, the way he had dry-humped the stage in the strip club.

"Who's got the power now, Missy Pissy Kara?" Banjo said. "You're the one who's the goddamn idiot. The biggest mistake you made was giving me a sample of that mojo. See what it did? Who's in control now? Guess who's got all the power now? Oh, and looky, looky who's gonna get some of this sweet, sweet stuff." Banjo wriggled against Shauna, and she feared she would vomit and wind up smothering in it.

"If you don't shut the hell up, I swear I will take a tire iron and shove it clear up your ass, all the way up to your ugly, pointed head," Kara screamed.

"Yeah? Then whatchu gonna do? Who ya gonna get to lure your little weres to a special place so that fat freak over there can do his hoodoo? Who ya gonna get to bait 'em, if I ain't around, huh? Ain't nobody else gonna do your dirty work for a little Lacodah and a piece of ass. They gonna want cold cash, baby. Something you and that fat snake freak ain't never gonna wanna part with. Noo, you gotta save up that blood money for new digs, like you had when old Carl was around, ain't that right? Tell me, whatchu gonna do, Kara Matiste, when everybody finds out you two been killin' off weres? How you gonna explain that, Miss Badass? Killin' 'em off for the power trip, 'cause only the strong survive, right? Power, man—it's the power trip rush. It's the money rush. You stuck in it, tangled all up in its web. You're one sick bitch."

A monstrous growl echoed through the building.

"You'd better get your head out of your ass and remember who's still in charge of this operation," Kara said.

Shauna couldn't believe what she was hearing. If what Banjo was saying was true, Kara had genocide planned for her own species! And all for money? How was it possible for anyone to do such a horrible thing to their own kind?

Banjo began to sing a crippling tune…"Money-money-money, yeah! You don't have me to use as bait, and you not gonna be rolling in the dough no more, baby. Stashin' all that blood cash away." Banjo tsked. "Uh-uh, no more, no more Lacodah to sell, not without old Banjo."

Another growl, this one so loud and menacing it hurt Shauna's ears and seemed to make the building vibrate. Then she heard a loud *thump,* then…silence.

And then came the horrid, twittering laugher—that wretched shriek of a laugh told her that Banjo was about to take possession of his final payment for being such a good and helpful boy.

Shauna tried to scream, but the rag muffled it to a mumble. She shoved her tongue against the nasty piece of cloth again and again, but was only able to move it a fraction of an inch. She had to stop him somehow. Call out his name again—hope he'd hear her, really hear her. Her brain had trouble processing all that was going on. This was the same guy who came into the shop regularly, the one Fiona fed, and now he was trying to rape her? How could he allow himself to do this? Why? What made his jitter talk change? Did he have a split personality? Was it that Lacodah? Or was it the same quirky, unknown thing that made Banjo so different from every other vamp?

It was evident by Banjo's frantic movements, that he wasn't up for hearing another word from anyone. He was in another world, and right now he was working his way toward the next one. The one right between Shauna's legs. Her tears refused to be held back any longer. They streamed down her cheeks, made her nose clog up.

Shauna no longer heard Kara and feared she had been left alone with Banjo, who seemed to have gone completely mad. Had he gone mad? Or was this who he really was? Shawna felt like she had been thrown into another dimension without warning, without any knowledge of how to survive in it, or the tools to even try. She was at its mercy.

She had never known this level of vulnerability before. Hopeless, helpless, useless.

Banjo grunted behind her, and Shauna squeezed her eyes shut, saying a silent prayer to the universe, begging for this not to happen. It *couldn't* happen.

She shoved against the dirty rag in her mouth with her tongue, once again trying to push it out. This time her efforts were rewarded with a little more movement.

Then to Shauna's horror, she felt skin against skin. Banjo had taken his clothes off. He was obviously finished playing games and intended to take care of business now.

"Hey, shit for brains!" It was Kara again.

Shauna shifted her head slowly, as inconspicuously as possible. She wanted to get a look at the woman. Maybe, just maybe if she could lock eyes with her, Kara might see reason—a woman-to-woman thing. But all she saw were the lights.

At least Kara's voice had stopped Banjo from rubbing his naked skin against hers…for now.

"You see this, you little turd?"

And suddenly from the center of the spotlights, Shauna saw a woman with tar-black hair approaching the makeshift table. It was Kara Matiste.

"Do you see this?" Kara waggled what looked like a two-inch long, glass test tube with a cork in it. "What do you think you're going to do, Mr. Brilliant, when you fall off the high you're on? You'll shrivel, that's what. What are you going to do then? You think I can't get another asshole like you to play bait? You forget; you need us a lot more than we need you. There is a lot that goes on behind the scenes in this operation, and you know it. Without me, you don't get to the big man. So here's the deal—you've got about thirty minutes left on your high horse, then it's going to buck you off. Are you going to play ballsy or are you going to keep acting like an ass?"

A long pause, then that wretched, twittering laugh.

"Yeah, yeah, I—I know how we roll," Banjo said. He was jitter talking again, which meant anything—and everything—could happen now.

With her fear spiking off the charts, Shauna wiggled

and twisted, struggling to get away. She knew even if she were able to get Banjo to hear her now, there was no way he or Kara was going to let her go. She had heard too much. That left only one option on this table—she was going to be raped—and die.

"That's right, little man, I know you do," Kara said. "See this vial? Everything that's in it will belong to you, I promise—but first you've got to tell me who's the boss around here."

"You—You—You the boss!"

"That's right, and what are you gonna do?"

"What—whatever Kara say. That's—what we gonna do. Gotta get me some—get me some of that…" Banjo grunted loudly, and Shauna felt him pushing against her again.

More flesh against flesh now, and his hands were trying to spread her open.

Shauna's tears came in a flood. She could barely breathe. It didn't matter to her anymore if they saw her move and slammed her head against the table. They could cut it off as far as she was concerned. But there was no way she was going down this hellhole without fighting to her last breath.

She opened her mouth as wide as she could, shoved hard with her tongue, rubbed her mouth against the rough plywood, hoping some little splinter of wood would grab on to threads in the rag.

"No need for you to get in a hurry now," Kara said to Banjo. "Remember, we have an audience. That was part of the deal."

Then, as though rising from some black hole, Gris Gris suddenly appeared. Shauna saw him clearly, saw how excited he was to be a spectator at this event. Simone, who was draped about his neck as usual, seemed to be exceptionally calm. Kara appeared alongside Gris Gris and put a hand on his shoulder.

"Well, does he plan on getting on with this or should I make reservations for a future matinee?" Gris Gris asked.

"Drop the big talk, " Kara said. "There's no one here you need to impress. He'll be done with her soon enough, and you'll have your turn."

Then Kara walked up to the table, leaned over, and looked Shauna right in the eye. "Poor, weepy baby. You see what you get for sticking your nose in other people's business? You should have left it alone."

Shauna looked deep into the woman's eyes, hoping she could hear the question rolling over and over in her head. "Why—why?"

"Sometimes a woman just has to do what she has to do in order to survive in a man's world," Kara said. "You of all people should know that, Shauna MacDonald—Keeper of the weres." She let out a sarcastic laugh. "Keeper, you can't even keep your legs closed. You're out there whoring around with a were, tainting the breed. Then you have the nerve to go around acting like you're going to save us all? Oh, I think not."

"Now who's highbrow talking?" Gris Gris asked. "Tell your boy to go on about his business. Dip his wick and get it over with, so I can have my turn."

"My turn now—mine," Banjo said, and wiggled against Shauna again.

Kara laughed and stood up, placed the vial right in front of Shauna's face so she could see it. A fine brown powder that looked like it had glitter mixed in with it was packed inside the vial.

"You see, the mistake a lot of women make, the mistake you made, MacDonald, is thinking a woman's power is between her legs. It's not. It's right here in this vial, and I own it. Granted, it was easier for me to get the information I needed to make this happen by appreciating what power I do have between my legs. That's how I discovered this little secret. An old, horny, blabbering idiot from the council was more than happy to spill his guts for a chance to dip into my honey pot. Sadly, the council got rid of him, because they caught him stealing something or other, but that's okay. I got what I needed and didn't really have a use for him anymore. Now everything belongs to me."

"Simone is getting anxious, Kara," Gris Gris said. "Let's get this over with. I want my turn before we have to dispose of her. Too bad, too. Good-looking girl like that. Can't help it now, though. You and that stupid kid spilling your guts the way you did. Somebody needs to staple both of your fat mouths shut. Now get on with it, boy, or I'll get me a piece of you instead."

Shauna caught a glimpse of Gris Gris petting Simone. And his other hand was petting his groin.

Oh, God—God!

She knew how this would end. How it all was going

to play out. Banjo would get his turn at her while Gris Gris watched. Once Banjo was done, the fat man would take his turn. When both were done, Kara would finish her off, kill her if for no other purpose than to make sure she stayed silent—forever.

Giving one more hard thrust with her tongue, the rag suddenly popped out of Shauna's mouth, and she opened her mouth wide to scream. No matter where she was, no matter how far away this place was from anything else, she had to try.

Shauna drew in a quick, deep breath and forced it out to give the scream volume. But a scream didn't come out of her mouth. Instead, it was a loud, off-pitch howl—the sound of a wolven calling for help. It was long and loud and vibrated from her—from the very center of her. She thought of the way she growled and made other animal noises when she and Danyon made love.

Then she understood.

This howl was her call to him, an acknowledgment of the love she had for Danyon and that she knew that love to be endless, timeless. This was her soul calling out to its mate—crying out for him—

One last time. "Woooah!" Banjo yelled, and Shauna felt him back away from her. "Shut her up—shut her. Kara, make her stop. Voodoo man, put the hoodoo on her—put it on, like you do with the weres. You gotta— she sound like one—sound it. Shut her up—shut up!"

While Banjo, Kara and Gris Gris yelled at one another, Shauna forced the last bit of air out of her lungs, squeezing the last sound out of her raw vocal chords.

It wasn't much, and what little she had she was losing quickly, but it was enough to keep Banjo freaked out.

"Just hurry up, you stupid weasel," Gris Gris yelled.

"If you are so anxious for it, old man, why don't you go first?" Kara asked.

"Just do it, boy. Finish what you started. Go on, finish it up."

"I can't, can't—can't. You hear her? She sound like them—can't. Do your hoodoo—make her stop!"

"For heaven's sake, old man, just go over there and get your stuff. The boy ain't gonna do it."

"You know I can't do anything unless I watch first," Gris Gris said. "You know the drill."

"Hold up—hold up!" Banjo exclaimed. His voice two octaves higher and excited. "Got it back—I—got it back. It's all good—good to go. Looka here—rocky solid— good. Gonna get me some—get some! Rock solid, good to go! Gonna get some—gonna get some!"

Shauna tried desperately to make a sound—scream, a howl, anything. All she managed was the weakest of howls, so low she could barely make it out.

"Now, look here at what she did! I can't now—shut her up, Kara. Shut her—shut! It's no good no more—all gone. Shut up—you, shut up!"

Shauna suddenly felt a slap on the back of her thigh. She twisted, bucked, wiggled. Her voice might have been gone, but whatever energy she had left, she planned to wring it dry.

"Stop your jabber-talking," Kara shouted at Banjo. "It

drives me up a goddamn wall! You wanna stop the bitch from making noise—this is how you do it."

Shauna saw black hair, a plaid shirt—a cocked fist up in the air. Kara let out a long, low growl, and Shauna squeezed her eyes shut, waiting for the punch, praying it would be hard enough to knock her out.

A sudden crash and the sound of shattering glass pried Shauna's eyes open wide. In that moment, she caught a flash of something huge racing toward them, a second later it sprang into full view.

It was a massive, mahogany-brown wolven, teeth bared, his eyes locked on Banjo. Shauna's heart triple-timed in her chest and thundered in her ears. The wolven was Danyon, she knew it as sure as she knew her own name.

Then, as quickly as the wolven appeared he vanished, his mass flying by her, then out of sight. She heard a growl loud enough to wake the dead, and a heartbeat later came a long shrill, then the ripping and tearing of flesh.

Shauna squeezed her eyes shut against the sounds, wanting to tap into that small light in the center of her mind—her peaceful place.

But there were too many screams—too many shrill, tortured, horrific screams.

Then Kara yelling—Gris Gris shouting back—more tearing and shredding of flesh. Crashing, thudding, feet racing over concrete…silence.

It felt like hours had gone when Shauna suddenly felt hands around her ankles. She jumped, startled, and tried to scream. All that came out was a raspy whisper. Then she heard the most beautiful sound—Danyon's voice.

"Shh, it's okay now. It's me, Shauna, it's me."

The next thing she knew she was cradled in Danyon's arms. She wept as he held her close, rocking her as he would a troubled child. He kissed her forehead, her eyes, her wet cheeks.

Danyon had never known anger as he did when he saw Banjo standing behind Shauna, naked from the waist down and ready to enter her, to defile her. And the sneer on Gris Gris' face… And Kara Matiste. He had known she was odd, that there was something very different about her, but he never would have suspected this.

When he had seen them all together, he wished with his entire heart he could have been in three places at one time. But it wasn't possible, so he'd had to pick one. Banjo was the greatest threat, so he became Danyon's primary target. He made sure Banjo understood suffering, when he'd torn through his chest, his arms, his groin, making him feel every ounce of pain to the fullest before he ripped his throat out and watched him drown in his own blood.

By that time, Kara and Gris Gris were no longer in the warehouse, having scampered away like rats. But they were of little concern to him right now. They'd be found soon enough. His priority now was Shauna.

She curled into him closer, held on to him tight. "How…how did you find me?" she asked, her voice shaky and hoarse.

"It was easy," he said. "You called for me."

She lay silent for a moment, then nodded and closed her eyes.

Danyon smoothed the hair from her brow. She had indeed called to him. Like an alpha female calling for her mate. It was then that Danyon knew without any doubt that Shauna not only understood his true nature, she was part of it. She knew him. She may have been human, but she was still part of his true nature. She knew him in ways he could have only hoped for.

He tightened his arms around her, feeling such a swell in his chest and heart that there was no denying the power of the love he had for her. He couldn't ignore it any longer, Shauna was his mate—his alpha.

Chapter 21

St. Louis Cathedral was the perfect location to hold the wedding of the year.

The colossal, three-steepled basilica was a masterful confluence of Spanish Colonial and Renaissance architecture. Its high rococo-gilded altar included columns with busy entablature. Two rows of wooden columns divided the church into center and side aisles with a view of the gallery. Its massive organ towered at least fifty feet above the choir loft, and its pipes ranged from a few inches to over thirty feet in height.

It was in this aged splendor, under a massive stretch of sculptured, hand-painted ceiling that Father Antoine's voice echoed when he said, "I now pronounce you man and wife."

The cathedral erupted with cheers and applause so

loud Shauna expected the thousands of pieces of multi-colored stained glass to shatter. Even if they had, she doubted anyone would notice. Vampires, werewolves, shape-shifters, and humans; all of them laughing and cheering, so happy for the new couple.

Outside, a twelve-piece, brass band was already playing the traditional rendition of "When the Saints Go Marching In." Saxophones, trombones, tubas and trumpets, along with bass and snare drums were warming up for the second line wedding march, which would take dancing celebrants all the way down to Decatur Street.

Shauna couldn't help but tear up at the sight of so many different races with various skin colors, faiths and beliefs, all celebrating as one. It made her overwhelmingly happy.

This was the New Orleans she loved, and who loved her back—where friends, neighbors and family had enough faith in each other to put their differences aside and celebrate life—share life.

This was so different from all the turmoil they had gone through this past year, which, at this moment, seemed a thousand years ago.

It had been four months since Nicole, Simon and Teddy's death, and the nightmare Shauna had lived through in that warehouse. It had taken two of those months for Shauna to feel some semblance of normalcy and stop looking over her shoulder every time she walked down a street.

Kara had been tracked down not that long ago. She had been found hiding out in a deserted cabin out in a pine forest in Alexandria, Louisiana. August had been the one to take her to Atlanta, where she faced the were-council and magistrate, both of whom were responsible for the were packs living along the entire southern rim of North America. August had returned from that trip alone, and when he did, he looked as though he had aged a hundred years. No one asked him about Kara, and he never offered any information. Judging from his haggard face, and the haunted look in his eyes, it wasn't hard to imagine the severity of the magistrate's sentence and Kara's punishment.

Two weeks following Kara's capture, Gris Gris' body, or what was left of it, was found floating in the marsh by three local fishermen, just north of Lake Pontchatrain. The cause of death had yet to be determined, and Shauna suspected that with the handful of wolven who worked for the coroner's office and as filing administrators for the Clerk of Court, it might never be. Either that or the death would be labeled accidental. After all, considering the enormity of the man, it wasn't hard for one to imagine Gris Gris falling out of a skiff…unable to swim…

Some things in life simply had no direct answers. And some had no answers at all.

As for Banjo, Danyon had had to stand before the vampire council, which included David Dulac, and give an account of all that had transpired that day in the ware-house. After only a few hours of questioning, the matter was dismissed, and Danyon had been free to go.

As the jazz band grew louder outside, everyone gath-ered in the center aisle of the cathedral, ready to head outside and take their place in the second line. Every woman here looked so beautiful dressed in their finery and the men very handsome, especially Jagger in his black, long coat-tailed tuxedo. Amidst the tangle of suits, tuxedos, taffeta dresses, and ball gowns, Shauna caught only a glimpse of the satin, beaded chapel train before the bride was whisked away.

Shauna didn't know how weddings were celebrated in other cathedrals around the country, but old St. Louis seemed to relish the clapping, whistling and joyous chatter.

As everyone filed through the front doors of the Cathedral, Rita Quinn, August's assistant, handed each attendee a white, linen handkerchief. The handkerchiefs were a customary and necessary part of a wedding's second line, for celebrants waved them in the air as they danced their way to the reception.

So much happiness on the heels of so much pain.

It seemed like the universe had a way of balancing out the good and bad one had to experience in life. Sometimes it felt like the scales tipped too far to the left and stayed that way too long. But sooner or later, without fail, the universe shifts, and tips that scale in the other direction. Maybe the key to finding peace in life was understanding that times were not always good, but they were not always bad. And if you can learn to straddle the center of that scale as it tips first one way, then the other, life might feel much more balanced.

* * *

Trailing the procession out of the church, Shauna squinted against the brilliance of a cloudless June day. The jazz band had already started its march, the musicians bouncing, dancing and swaying as they played their instruments.

Following directly behind the band, were the happy bride and groom, both dancing and clapping, determined to celebrate this day for all it was worth. Shauna felt like her heart would burst with joy as she watched the two of them from the top step of the Cathedral—the new Mrs. Lurnell Clarice Johnson and her long awaited new husband, Tyree.

Trailing the newly married couple was Jagger DeFarge and Fiona, who looked stunning in her satin, emerald green dress. As it turned out, Tyree was in his second year of training as a detective for the NOPD's eighth precinct. Jagger had been his supervisor since day one, and the two had become close friends. Since Tyree had no biological brothers, he had asked Jagger to be his best man.

Behind the best man and his beauty were Caitlin and Ryder, both waving handkerchiefs in the air and bouncing in time with the music.

Not remembering a time when she had felt this happy, Shauna danced her way down the steps of the Cathedral and waved her handkerchief. Sunlight set the two karat diamond on the ring finger of her left hand ablaze, and sparkles of light danced to their own tune.

The stone was indeed magnificent.

But not nearly as magnificent as the precious Stone dancing beside her.

* * * * *

A Note from the Author

Writing may be a solitary job, but, for this writer anyway, it's far from lonely. I'm blessed to have wonderful people in my life, and without the help and support of some of them, this book would not have been possible. I offer my deepest appreciation and heartfelt thanks to:

Heather Graham, a dear friend and the epitome of grace and selflessness. Thank you for inviting me to share in this project.

Leslie Wainger, a phenomenal editor and a true gift from the universe. Thank you for your patience, your guidance, and for simply being the extraordinary person you are!

Tara Gavin, a sweetheart of an editor and such a joy to work with. Your enthusiasm and joie de vivre are priceless and contagious!

Sarah and Rebekah, my beautiful daughters, my greatest gifts in life. Thank you for your help and for understanding every time I have to say, "I can't, I'm on a deadline!"

New Orleans, my home, my soul. Thank you for holding me close and refusing to give up.

And to Richard Paul, the life in my life, my heart. Thank you for seeing me.

HARLEQUIN®

nocturne™

COMING NEXT MONTH

Available December 28, 2010

HARLEQUIN®

A Romance

FOR EVERY MOOD™

Spotlight on

Classic

Quintessential, modern love stories
that are romance at its finest.

See the next page
to enjoy a sneak peek from
the Harlequin Presents® series.

*Harlequin Presents® is thrilled
to introduce the first installment of
an epic tale of passion and drama by*
USA TODAY *Bestselling Author*
Penny Jordan*!*

*When buttoned-up Giselle first meets
the devastatingly handsome Saul Parenti,
the heat between them is explosive....*

"LET ME GET THIS STRAIGHT. Are you actually suggesting that I would stoop to that kind of game playing?"

Saul came out from behind his desk and walked toward her. Giselle could smell his hot male scent and it was making her dizzy, igniting a low, dull, pulsing ache that was taking over her whole body.

Giselle defended her suspicions. "You don't want me here."

"No," Saul agreed, "I don't."

And then he did what he had sworn he would not do, cursing himself beneath his breath as he reached for her, pulling her fiercely into his arms and kissing her with all the pent-up fury she had aroused in him from the moment he had first seen her.

Giselle certainly *wanted* to resist him. But the hand she raised to push him away developed a will of its own and was sliding along his bare arm beneath the sleeve of his shirt, and the body that should have been arching away from him was instead melting into him.

Beneath the pressure of his kiss he could feel and taste her gasp of undeniable response to him. He wanted to devour her, take her and drive them both until they were equally satiated—even whilst the anger within him that she should make him feel that way roared and burned its resentment of his need.

She was helpless, Giselle recognized, totally unable to withstand the storm lashing at her, able only to cling to the man who was the cause of it and pray that she would survive.

Somewhere else in the building a door banged. The sound exploded into the sensual tension that had enclosed them, driving them apart. Saul's chest was rising and falling as he fought for control; Giselle's whole body was trembling.

Without a word she turned and ran.

Find out what happens when Saul and Giselle succumb to their irresistible desire in

THE RELUCTANT SURRENDER

Available January 2011 from Harlequin Presents®

HPEXP0111

REQUEST YOUR FREE BOOKS!

2 FREE NOVELS PLUS 2 FREE GIFTS!

 HARLEQUIN®

n o c t u r n e™

Dramatic and Sensual Tales of Paranormal Romance.

YES! Please send me 2 FREE Harlequin® Nocturne™ novels and my 2 FREE gifts (gifts are worth about $10). After receiving them, if I don't wish to receive any more books, I can return the shipping statement marked "cancel." If I don't cancel, I will receive 4 brand-new novels every other month and be billed just $4.47 per book in the U.S. or $4.99 per book in Canada. That's a saving of at least 15% off the cover price! It's quite a bargain! Shipping and handling is just 50¢ per book.* I understand that accepting the 2 free books and gifts places me under no obligation to buy anything. I can always return a shipment and cancel at any time. Even if I never buy another book from Harlequin, the two free books and gifts are mine to keep forever.

238/338 HDN E9M2

Name _____ (PLEASE PRINT)

Address _____ Apt. #

City _____ State/Prov. _____ Zip/Postal Code

Signature (if under 18, a parent or guardian must sign)

Mail to the **Reader Service:**
IN U.S.A.: P.O. Box 1867, Buffalo, NY 14240-1867
IN CANADA: P.O. Box 609, Fort Erie, Ontario L2A 5X3

Not valid for current subscribers to Harlequin Nocturne books.

Want to try two free books from another line?
Call 1-800-873-8635 or visit www.ReaderService.com.

* Terms and prices subject to change without notice. Prices do not include applicable taxes. N.Y. residents add applicable sales tax. Canadian residents will be charged applicable provincial taxes and GST. Offer not valid in Quebec. This offer is limited to one order per household. All orders subject to approval. Credit or debit balances in a customer's account(s) may be offset by any other outstanding balance owed by or to the customer. Please allow 4 to 6 weeks for delivery. Offer available while quantities last.

Your Privacy: Harlequin Books is committed to protecting your privacy. Our Privacy Policy is available online at www.ReaderService.com or upon request from the Reader Service. From time to time we make our lists of customers available to reputable third parties who may have a product or service of interest to you. If you would prefer we not share your name and address, please check here. ☐

Help us get it right—We strive for accurate, respectful and relevant communications. To clarify or modify your communication preferences, visit us at www.ReaderService.com/consumerschoice.

HN10